Food and Romance Go Together Vol. 1

Sue Stewart Ade
Randi Perrin
Ryan Jo Summers
Sonja Gunter
Jody Vitek
April & Holly Marcom

Published by
Satin Romance
An Imprint of Melange Books, LLC
White Bear Lake, MN 55110
www.satinromance.com

ISBN: 978-1-68046-454-2 Print

Cover Design by Caroline Andrus

Food and Romance do go together.
These stories prove it. Thank you Sue Stewart Ade, Ryan Jo Summers,
April and Holly Marcom, Sonja Gunter, Jody Vitek and Randi Perrin,
for writing the scrumptious stories in this new anthology from Satin
Romance.

Nancy Schumacher, Satin Romance,
An Imprint of Melange Books, LLC

Food and Romance Go Together, Vol. 1

Pumpkin Blossoms by Sue Stewart Ade
Jillian yearns for love and falls for a dog and her sister's former boyfriend. But the dog bolts and the boyfriend seems to still have feelings for her sister. Can she find love with a man who can't see who she really is?

Coffee Cake Chaos by Ryan Jo Summers
Avianna Goodman needs cash. That's why she agreed to cater her ex-boyfriend's engagement party. Seeing Sawyer again confirms Avianna still isn't over him. The biggest mistake Sawyer Steele ever did was walk away from the one girl he was crazy about. Now Avianna's back in his life--and he can't have her.

Apple Pie Delight by Sonja Gunter
Lost loves reunite after forty years of deceptions. Can a Sun-Kissed Apple Pie bring Toril Swanson and Erik Sutton together again?

Peanut Butter Kisses by Jody Vitek
Beth Canton attends her ten-year class reunion to catch a glimpse of her long-time, school-girl crush, Hank McGrath, but doesn't hope or even dream of anything more. She leaves with more than a glimpse, while Hank can't get enough of her peanut butter kisses.

Boston Crème Breakdown by Randi Perrin
Kestin just wants to return to life as normal after returning home from the war, but there's no way his life will be the same again. Looking for easy money to make bills, he stumbles over an ad to teach perpetually-single Erica to cook, and can't resist answering it. He never expected to actually get the job—or to be attracted to her.

The Chocolate Queen by April & Holly Marcom
In a world sprinkled with superheroes, you never know when the person beside you is one of these few elite. When Clarissa begins to fall for a guy who harbors *a* super secret, it feels like she's not good enough. But he may just help her discover a super *sweet* secret of her own.

Pumpkin Blossoms

Sue Stewart Ade

Chapter One

Summer wasn't supposed to start out stuck in the blistering hot cab of a pickup truck, chasing a dog, no less. Well, not any dog. My dog. A Saluki, one of the oldest breeds of man's best friend. Although right now, I would disagree with the bit about man's best friend.

Summer was supposed to be romance and falling in love with the right guy. I had fallen in love—with a dog, and even my dog was not sticking around.

"There he is," I said, leaning my head out the window of Pop's pickup.

Pop wasn't my dad, although he was old enough, around sixty, and sometimes protective enough. He was my next-door neighbor and my go-to guy when I needed help. I pointed my finger at the sleek gray dog stretched out on the boulevard underneath the maple tree.

"Stop and let me out. Maybe I can sneak up on him."

Pop pulled the truck to the curb. I grabbed the leash and jumped out. I crept toward Honda, the name I'd given my Saluki. Bushy gray ears perked up, and his slim head turned toward me. His face was outlined in black and his eyes were wary. Barely breathing, I inched closer... closer... closer. As I leaned over to loop the leash around his long neck, he shot off in the opposite direction.

"Doggone it!" The dog definitely was gone.

I didn't try to run after him. My twenty-nine-year-old body would never be able to catch him. Not that I was out of shape. I was five foot five and tipped the scales at a hundred and twenty-five. With his long, stilt-like

1

legs, Honda resembled a full-grown greyhound and could run just as fast. Pop had clocked him with the truck at almost fifty miles per hour.

I slunk over to Pop's side of the pickup. "We'll never catch him. You're just going to have to shoot him."

"Me?" Pop's eyebrows shot up. Well, the few white hairs above his eyes shot up. Removing his John Deere cap, he swiped a hand over his sweaty bald head and slowly nodded.

We exchanged places, and Pop rode shotgun.

Two weeks ago, I'd been sitting at my breakfast nook, sipping my usual cup of coffee and watching a report on TV about the overcrowding in a nearby animal shelter. The camera panned several dogs that would be euthanized unless some sucker, which was not going to be me, stepped up and saved them.

The dogs were hyper, jumping around the studio and barking, except for one. He was just lying at the feet of the woman from the shelter. His head rested on his paws, and he looked dejected. When the camera zoomed in, his regal head rose. That's when his mournful dark eyes looked directly at me.

I couldn't turn away. Pain. Too much pain for one of God's gentle creatures. I wasn't planning on getting a dog. I wasn't even a dog person. Yet I couldn't ignore those eyes.

That day at school, I flitted around like one of the second graders I taught. I tried to talk myself out of going to the pound. What would I do with a dog? I'd never owned a dog. Besides, Salukis were valuable. Someone else would probably snatch him up. Yet after school he was still there, locked in a cage, waiting for me.

"He's been abused," the woman at the pound confided.

I'd underestimated what those words meant and how hard I would have to work to get Honda to trust me. When I set his bowl of food down, he wouldn't eat until I was out of sight. When I tried to pet him, he whimpered and backed away, cowering in the corner.

Today, however, I thought I'd made progress. I'd finally been able to put a leash on him and gone for a walk around the block. Only the walk turned into a jog, then a run, and when my lungs were about to be ripped out of my body, I tugged on the leash and it snapped.

Now I was trying to retrieve Honda before he trampled too many gardens or got into more doggie doo-doo.

Pop fastened his seat belt. "Ok. Move 'em out, Jilly," he said in his best Western twang.

I hadn't minded being called Jilly until third grade, when our class read *Silly Billy*. Some kid thought the book was really funny and started calling me Silly Jilly. After that I wanted to be called Jillian. But once you have a nickname it's kind of like putty. It sticks.

My sister Victoria never had that problem. No one ever called her Vicky or Tory. She was always Victoria and had breezed through school victoriously. When I came along five years later, the teachers were thrilled until they discovered I was just Jillian, an average student.

I stepped on the gas a little too hard, throwing us back against the seats. On my second try, I eased down on the pedal and carefully maneuvered the truck onto the deserted street. At the corner, I turned and headed toward the country.

We passed the city limits sign for Becks Creek, population 5,500. You won't actually find any creek meandering through our village. Maybe the lake at the edge of town used to be a creek or maybe the creek dried up, just like the town did some fifty years ago, when the coal mine shut down forcing other businesses to close, too. The town had been able to keep the hospital, although no doctors did surgeries there, and so far the school district had not been forced to consolidate like other rural Illinois communities, but I'd heard rumors.

A mile out of town, we caught up with Honda, running along the side of a cornfield. The stalks were about two feet high, so he couldn't hide in them.

Pop picked up the gun lying on the seat between us. "When you get closer, slow down so I can get a good shot."

I didn't have to let up on the gas much. Pop's truck wasn't exactly a hot rod, and I'd always believed in those speed limit signs, especially after the accident.

"Aim at his rear," I told Pop. "The vet said even a stun gun might kill him if he's hit in the wrong place."

Pop loaded the first of three tranquilizing darts the vet had given me. When we were alongside Honda, Pop stuck the gun out the window and aimed. Just as he shot, the truck hit a rut. The dart sailed over Honda's rump and landed in the cornfield.

Pop's red face made him look as if he was about to come uncorked. He spewed out a barrage of colorful words I didn't even know were in his vocabulary. Then he picked up the second tranquilizer and reloaded.

I didn't want to see my dog go down, so I kept my eyes on the road full of potholes.

A minute later Pop shouted, "Bull's eye!"

He didn't actually hit Honda in the eye. He hit him in the rear, which only slowed him down.

"Guess it's going to take all three." Pop aimed and shot again. The dart stuck just above the other one. Honda stumbled and began slowing down.

"You get out here, Pop, and I'll drive ahead. Then we'll have him sandwiched between us."

By the time we'd coaxed Honda into the truck, Pop and I were panting as hard as the dog and dripping with sweat.

~ * ~

That night I pushed open the back screen door and walked outside to check on Honda and my garden. Not much of a garden really, a few rows of tomatoes, peppers, and green beans; the rest was a pumpkin patch.

"Pumpkin blossoms taste just like morel mushrooms, maybe even better," Dad would say after eating a big mess of fried pumpkin blossoms.

On half of the patch, I grew pumpkins for school. I loved the way my students' eyes lit up when I carted in a wheelbarrow full of pumpkins in various shapes and sizes for them to decorate and take home.

Tonight, the soil looked cracked and dry, so I unsnaked the hose and dragged it to the edge of garden. I left the water running and tiptoed over to Honda chained to a stake at the corner of the house. He was lying on his side, his eyes open. "Hey, boy, how ya doing?" I said softly, trying not to startle him. I didn't want to spend another day chasing him around town.

He blinked, but didn't scoot away. I took that as a good sign and plunked onto the ground beside him. Maybe if he smelled my scent, probably peaches 'n cream from my shampoo, he'd get used to me. I put my hand on his head. His front paws twitched and his side heaved up and down.

"It's okay," I said, stroking his short gray coat. "You're home now, and safe."

I looked into his eyes. What had caused all that pain? I understood about pain. For the last five years, I'd been struggling with my own pain, not physical, emotional pain.

The day I graduated from college, I was ready to venture into the world. I had my first teaching job in a nearby town plus a boyfriend who said he loved me and was ready to settle down. My parents came to my graduation and cheered as I walked across the stage and received my diploma.

"I'm proud of you, Pumpkin," my dad said, kissing me on the forehead before we got into the car and headed to Becks Creek.

I didn't know those would be the last words I would remember my dad saying. I'm sure he said other things on the drive home, but I don't remember them or the accident.

I was in the front passenger seat and Mom, who was less than five foot two and barely a hundred pounds, had squeezed into the back. Our SUV was packed with all my college stuff—books, pillows, pictures, laundry, and even my fold-up bike.

From what others told me, a drunk driver swerved into our lane and hit the back of the driver's side. I don't remember the impact. What I remembered were the sounds. The screeching brakes, the crashing metal, the shattering windshield, the high-pitched screams—mine and Mom's—and then silence. Deadly silence.

Mom and the drunk driver died at the scene. Dad lingered for three years, but never spoke another word. He just wandered around our big old two-story house looking for Mom and his lost life.

My injuries were minimal, a few cracked ribs, lots of bruises, and a broken leg. But the emotional wounds cut deep.

"You're lucky to be alive," people said to me.

In the mere turn of the wheel, I'd lost my parents and my future. Somehow, I didn't feel lucky.

I declined the teaching job and stayed home to take care of Dad. The boyfriend tried to be supportive, but he didn't understand, and I couldn't explain why I couldn't move on, so he did.

A week after Dad died, my sister came over to help me go through our parents' things. Victoria was a planner and doer. She'd probably written it down on her infamous to-do list. Clean out parents' house. Check.

She breezed through the wooden front door ready to whip my life into shape, just as she'd done when we were kids. Around sixth grade, she stopped growing and stayed short and petite. Her hair was dark like mine, only now she had one of those wash-and-wear, soccer-mom haircuts. Even in her jeans and T-shirts, she looked cute. I was still in my lounging pants, which used to be called pajamas.

Victoria was like Mom, who usually made the plans, and I was like Dad, who usually followed them. Maybe that's why my sister was so surprised that day when I didn't jump into action.

Her eyes roamed around the house, taking in the plaid couch, the lopsided recliner, and the console TV. "You know what? I think we should just sell this place."

Victoria meant well, but her words were like darts, piercing my heart. "I don't want to sell it." I crossed my arms. "I like living here."

"Well, at least make it your own place. It feels like a mausoleum, and it's suffocating."

Victoria marched over to the recliner and grabbed the green-and-gold afghan Mom had crocheted while sitting on the couch next to Dad. Victoria wadded it up and tossed it into a big black garbage bag as if it were trash. "You need to get rid of all this stuff."

"It's not stuff." I yanked the sack away from her and pulled out the afghan. I buried my face into the soft wool, searching for the lingering smell of Mom. "It's comforting… and it's all I have."

Victoria put her arm around me. "I just want you to be happy, Sis."

"I'm happy." My nose was running and tears streamed down my cheeks. "I am," I repeated. Then we both burst out laughing.

That's the way it was with us. We could be fighting one minute and best buds the next because nothing trumped the fact that we were sisters and loved each other.

But Victoria had a great husband, two beautiful children—a boy and a girl—and a future.

I had a past.

I used to dream about marriage and kids. So far I hadn't fallen for the right guy. I'd tripped when I was engaged and that had smarted. But I wasn't willing to settle for anything except the kind of love I'd seen between my parents.

Over Christmas vacation, I'd once again been a bridesmaid. That left me the only teacher at school called "Miss." I'd just have to accept it. I'd missed out on marriage and motherhood. All my mothering would be for my second graders and now Honda.

I ruffled Honda's ears. "We're alike, you and me." The dog had bolted, not knowing where he was going, and I wasn't happy where I was but didn't know how to find what I wanted.

Victoria was right. I did need a change. Maybe I could fix up the place, just a little. But all I had was this house, my memories, and a dog.

~ * ~

The next morning, my hair was still damp from my shower as I walked up and down the pumpkin patch looking for open blossoms to pick. I hadn't bothered to tie my hair into the usual ponytail, but let it hang onto the shoulders of my ribbed tank top. My jean shorts showed more of my legs than normal, but no one was going to see me. Pop was my closest neighbor, and our back yards were separated by a line of tall boxwood trees.

I picked three blossoms, the first of the season, and put them into my basket. I turned to check on Honda stretched out on the ground. Then the leaves rustled and a boy about eight years old squeezed through the boxwoods and into my yard. In his uplifted hand was a baseball glove. The boy backed up and up—straight toward my pumpkin patch.

"Hey, stop!"

Too late. He continued backward, barreling into the garden, his high-tops flattening pumpkin hills. He did a major league leap into the air and the ball, sailing toward him, plunked into his glove.

"Caught it," he yelled as his feet sank into another hill.

A man, wearing a baseball cap and sunglasses, rushed out of the boxwoods. I hadn't seen the man for more than ten years, but I recognized his gait and wide shoulders. Pop's son, Ash, Victoria's old flame and my first serious crush.

When Victoria and Ash were in high school, I'd idolized them. They were the golden couple. He was the baseball star while she was the editor of the *Beacon*, the high school yearbook. In their senior year, they were voted prom king and queen.

After graduation, they'd gone to separate colleges. At Christmas when Victoria returned home, she broke up with Ash. According to Victoria, she'd met the love of her life. I'd been prepared to hate the guy, but when I met Reese I had to admit he was everything Victoria had said.

Ash turned in my direction and slid his sunglasses onto his hat. "Jilly? Silly Jilly Randolph?"

The basket of pumpkin blossoms slid out of my hand. My legs went limp and my head bobbed up and down. No wonder he'd called me Silly Jilly. That was exactly the way I was acting.

At thirteen I'd wanted those dark brown eyes under hooded eyebrows to turn in my direction, and now they were staring at me. More than staring. He was doing that man thing when boy meets girl. Instant appraisal. His eyes moved up my bare legs, over the curves in my ribbed top, and scanned my face.

Then he rushed forward, his arms opening. I expected a welcoming hug, but he gripped me around the waist, lifted me off the ground, and spun me around. It was what I used to beg him to do when I was little.

"Spin me around, Ash. Please, please." Then he'd twirl me until I couldn't walk straight.

I should have been screaming for him to put me down. Instead my hands tightened around his neck, and I was flying with my hair streaming behind me. My mouth opened and I laughed. No, not laughed, giggled.

When he set me down, the earth was solid beneath my sandals, yet something had shifted. I was off kilter.

His face was close to mine and his warm breath caressed my burning cheeks.

When I was a teenager, I'd mooned over Ash's senior picture. I'd imagined running my hands through his dark hair or a finger down the curve of his nose, which was little too large. I'd stared at his mouth with that one dimple on the side and dreamed about him kissing me. It was the way I felt now, wanting—no, yearning—for his lips to brush across mine.

"You've changed," he said, his voice deeper and manly.

I nodded. I no longer had braces or pimples or hairy legs.

"Jillian, that's what you like to be called, right?"

I nodded and hoped my voice didn't sound squeaky. "So you're Ashton?"

He chuckled and his mouth broke into a wide grin with that dimple on the side. "No, still Ash."

Then he was the Ash I knew. The fun-loving boy next door who'd taught me to throw a two-finger, spit curve ball, tie a sailor's knot, and fillet a fish. The boy who never seemed to mind if I tagged along.

"Hey, Dad. There's something's wrong with this dog."

We broke apart, and Ash walked over to his son, who was staring at Honda. The dog's whole body was shaking.

"I didn't do nothin' to him." The boy raised both hands palms forward. "I swear."

Ash stepped toward Honda, his hand out for the dog to sniff.

I rushed to them. "I think he's just scared. I rescued him from a kennel." I turned to Honda. "It's okay, boy." Honda cowered and backed away more.

So much for bonding. "It's going to take him a while."

Ash nodded and put his large hand on the boy's shoulder. "Jillian, this is my son, Zach." Zach's dark serious eyes matched his dad's, and he looked like an adorable little man.

"That was quite a catch you made." I stuck out my hand.

Zach's chest puffed up as he gripped my hand and shook it.

Ash looked at my pumpkin patch. "I'm afraid he did some damage. Maybe he can make it up to you by weeding."

A girl about ten wiggled through the trees. "Dad, Pop doesn't have Internet. I can't stay here all summer."

"Lily, I want you to meet an old friend."

The girl, wearing polka-dotted lounging pants, stomped over to us and stood next to her dad. She pushed her dark-rimmed glasses up on her nose and kept her head down. Her sandy brown hair was tied in a crooked ponytail. She was at that awkward, chubby girl stage that I remembered all too well.

"Lily. What a pretty name."

She mumbled something I couldn't hear. By the slumped shoulders and the arms across her chest it might have been one of Pop's colorful words.

Pop had told me his grandkids were coming for Memorial Day. He hadn't said they were staying for the summer. Pop was going to be in for a real treat.

Chapter Two

Memorial Day started the way summer was supposed to—lying on the beach with a yellow sun above and blue water ahead. An added bonus was Ash beside me in Hawaiian-print trunks that showed off his manly chest and muscular legs. Of course, Pop, Zach, and Lily were at the lake with us, but a girl could dream, and with Ash there was plenty to dream about.

Usually my holidays were spent with Victoria and her family, but they'd gone to St. Louis for the weekend because her husband was flying to Charlotte to help a friend start her own real estate business.

I reached for my spray can of sunscreen. Spraying was easier, but lotion took two to slather on. With lotion, I could have turned to Ash, batted my eyes, and asked him to rub some sunscreen on my body. Thinking about his hands on my bare skin sent chills clear down to my hot-pink polished toe nails. But what would be the point in handing him a spray can of sunscreen?

I resprayed my own legs and lay back, letting the butter-yellow sun melt into my winter-white skin. Not that I had all that much skin exposed. I wasn't wearing one of those string bikinis that Ash seemed to enjoy so much whenever a girl came jiggling by. A bronze-tanned blonde in skimpy red had jiggled by three times, and she had plenty to jiggle—in all the right places.

I'd opted for a one-piece black Speedo, practical for playing with the kids. When I'd taken off my swim cover-up, Ash had given me another one of his head-to-toe man looks. The way his mouth split open in a wide grin made me think he'd been woman deprived.

Yesterday, just being close to Ash made me act like an awkward

11

junior high girl. Today, the vibes rippling through me were different. My body wasn't going spastic, but I could feel a quiet undertow pulling me toward him, and I didn't know what to do about it.

My body seemed to be acting as if I wanted to be his woman, but I couldn't see how that was going to work. Although Ash was divorced, I lived in Illinois and he lived in Colorado and was here for a week. Not much future. But I could enjoy being with him for a few days, and hopefully take away some of the sadness in his dark blue eyes.

This morning we'd rented paddle boats, a two-seater and a four-seater. We'd raced from the pier to the buoys, about ten minutes of full-throttle pedaling. When our legs were as rubbery as squid, we'd paddled to a shaded cove, and let the boats drift.

Pop coaxed the kids into the larger boat with him, leaving me and Ash lazily floating together and catching up.

After Ash graduated from college, he had been hired by a big Colorado company that was experimenting with drone technology. According to Pop, Ash's wife always wanted a fancier car and a bigger house. Two years ago, he'd been blindsided when his wife asked for a divorce. She'd found someone who already had the fancier car and bigger house—actually several sports cars and a villa in Italy. She didn't just walk away from Ash, but from her kids, too. You had to wonder about a woman who didn't even want to see her kids.

"I'm sorry about the divorce," I said to Ash after he mentioned how hard it was.

"It was my fault, too," he admitted. "I was all wrapped up in work. I didn't spend much time at home." His blue eyes filled with pain. "It's been rough on the kids."

I wondered if the pain was for his kids or for him.

"Zach was younger and has Pop and me. Lily doesn't have a woman around, other than our nanny, Consuela, and she went back to Mexico because her sister got sick. I'm not even sure if she'll be returning."

I'd lost my mother when I was twenty-two, but Lily had been eight at the time of the divorce. It must have been heartbreaking to have her mother leave. In September, she'd be entering junior high, an age when a girl especially needed her mother. No wonder Lily acted unhappy. She was unhappy.

"I called you after the car accident," he said. "I'm sorry I couldn't come back from Colorado."

"There's nothing you could have done. Victoria wouldn't leave my side and later she helped with Dad." It meant a lot that Ash understood even after several years my parents' deaths were hard for me and probably always would be. "Sometimes I still have nightmares about the accident."

He reached over and put his hand on my arm. A bolt of electricity sizzled through me.

For lunch, we ate at the Shack. The name aptly described the ramshackle restaurant at the end of the pier, famous for its foot-long hot dogs. The snow cones were great, too. You ordered a cup of shaved ice and squirted on your own flavored syrup. With more than two dozen choices deciding was difficult.

"I remember your favorite," I said to Ash as he eyed the carousel of syrups. "Root beer with a squirt of lime."

"I'd almost forgotten." He pumped on three squirts of root beer and one lime. "M-m-m good."

I cocked my head. "My favorite was...?"

He put his finger on his chin and looked up as if he expected the answer to be written on the exposed wooden beams or corrugated tin roof. "Something purple," he said. "Because afterward you had these funny purple lips."

Maybe it would have been better if he hadn't remembered. I reached for a straw before I sampled my blackberry grape.

Zach slurped his rainbow-colored snow cone. "Dad, this is the coolest place ever."

Lily enjoyed it, too, even though when she finished, her upper lip was stained watermelon red.

I glanced over at Lily, lying between Ash and Pop. I'd discreetly made sure she ditched the mustache, but the poor girl had yet to venture into the lake. She must be suffocating in that terrycloth cover up. Zach was in the shallow water, practicing his back float. Every time he went under, the muscles in Ash's neck tensed.

I stood. "I'm going in with Zach. Why don't you stay here and relax?" I stepped around to Lily. "Want to come with me and cool off?"

She scowled. "I'm not getting into that lake. There's fish."

13

"We could dunk your brother."

Her blue eyes lit up and she looked over at her dad. He lifted those hooded eyebrows and merely shrugged.

Zach wasn't too happy about being dunked, but Lily squealed in delight. A few minutes later, Ash came splashing into the water.

"We guys have to stick together," he said right before he dunked me.

~ * ~

When we returned from the lake, Ash grilled hamburgers. Pop wasn't much on cooking, not even grilling. We scarfed most of them down, and at dusk the kids were fascinated by lightning bugs. They'd never seen them in Denver, so they zigzagged around the yard catching and putting them into a glass jar with slits in the lid.

I was too wiped out to join them, so I collapsed onto the lounge chair next to Ash, content to listen to him and Pop.

"How can I make it up to you for dumping the kids here all summer?" Ash asked Pop.

Pop cleared his throat. "I like spending time with my grandkids." He wasn't able to hide the hurt in his voice. "They're the ones who don't seem too happy."

"Lily thinks she's old enough to watch Zach, but I don't think leaving them alone all day is such a hot idea. Zach will be fine here, just sign him up for baseball. But I don't know what to do about Lily."

"Well, I have an idea about how you could help out." Pop pointed to the side of the house where the gray paint was peeling. "This place needs a little sprucing up. Maybe this week we could get a start on painting it."

Pop and Ash continued to discuss painting the house, so I forced myself out of the comfy chair to check on Honda tied near the boxwood trees. I'd brought him with me, hoping he might get used to a few more people. As I stepped off the patio, the middle section of trees shook, and Victoria, along with her two kids, ducked out from underneath the branches.

When she spotted me, she waved. "Hey, sis, I thought you might be here. The kids want to see your new dog. I told them—" She stopped in midsentence and squinted at Ash. Then she squealed and sprinted across the yard.

"Ash! Ash!"

He stood up just in time to catch Victoria before she plowed into him. He wrapped his arms around her, giving her that hug I'd expected yesterday. The way their bodies were glued together seemed more than a nice-to-see-you-again hug.

My heart flattened. I wanted to be the one Ash was holding in his arms. What was wrong with me? Victoria was a happily married woman. At least I thought she was happily married. Still, she'd dated Ash for a whole year. Maybe some of her old feelings had flared up, the way mine had. I couldn't blame her. Ash was a great guy, inside and out. His sleeveless tee showed off his big biceps—the biceps my sister was holding onto.

Victoria was petite and probably weighed about a hundred pounds with her clothes on. Her short, sporty haircut emphasized her big eyes, outlined in black and surrounded by long curled lashes. Whenever I tried to put on mascara, I looked like a raccoon with big black rings around my eyes. I hadn't even bothered with makeup after being at the lake all day. As usual, though, Victoria's luscious-looking strawberry lips were flawless.

"Aunt Jilly! Aunt Jilly!" My nephew and niece bombarded me. Braden, nine, let me hug him, and Misty, six, covered my face with sweet kisses.

They were great kids, and when Victoria introduced them to Ash, her voice filled with pride. Then my sister plopped onto my lounge chair and pulled Ash down next to her. "Tell me everything," she said.

I wasn't exactly jealous. I just didn't like seeing them together. Even after all this time, they looked like the golden couple.

"Come on, kids. Pop said we could feed Honda some extra burgers." I walked over to the picnic table, stacked up the used paper plates, and handed Misty a cupful of plastic silverware. "Braden, can you get the other cups?"

Braden grabbed the empty ones. "Why did you name your dog after a car?"

"He's fast like a Honda motorcycle," I explained.

We went inside, and when we returned, the back yard was dark. I couldn't see Ash and Victoria, but their laughter punctuated the night air, and I imagined them huddled together.

I led the kids over to Honda, who backed away. "Stay here. I'll feed him first." I stepped forward with my arm outstretched, giving him a whiff of the hamburger patty in my hand. He inched forward, snatched the burger out of my fingers, and swallowed it in one gulp.

I gripped his collar. "Okay, Braden. Hold out your hamburger and walk over to us."

When Braden was close, Honda swiped the burger from him and gobbled it whole. Then Misty followed.

Next I held up the palm of my hand the hamburger had been in and moved it under Honda's nose. He started licking my hand. Braden and Misty held out their hands, and Honda licked them, too.

A burst of laughter made me glance over my shoulder. Someone had turned on the yellow porch light. Victoria and Ash were still sitting together on the patio. Just because I was attracted to Ash didn't mean things had changed for him. Maybe the attraction was just as one-sided as it had always been. My just-eaten hamburger lumped in my stomach.

I turned back to Honda, surprised he was letting the kids pet him. I sighed. At least I was making progress with my dog. However, he wasn't the best friend I'd hoped to have eating out of the palm of my hand.

~ * ~

The next morning, I picked pumpkin blossoms in the garden, carefully selecting only the male blossoms. The females had bulbous ends and would produce pumpkins. Voices from Pop's back yard made me straighten up. Ash's words drifted my way. "Let's get started."

Maybe the house project was underway. I told myself not to check it out unless I wanted to get talked into helping, which I didn't, but curiosity won.

I moseyed over to Pop's, and Ash greeted me with that cute smile, the one with the single dimple. "Morning," he said in a slow Western drawl that reminded me of Pop.

Strange words tumbled out of my mouth. "Do you need some help?"

Ash thrust a putty knife into my hand and led me around to the front. I didn't mind scraping paint. But after an hour, sweat rolled down my back, and my underarm deodorant had gone on strike. Getting sweaty wasn't the best way to entice Ash to get closer to me. However, I was committed. Pop always helped me when I needed it, so spending my first week of summer vacation painting his house instead of lying on the beach with my friends wouldn't be too bad, especially if I could be around Ash and his kids.

Wednesday, it rained, and we stayed indoors playing a marathon game of Monopoly. When Lily won, she pumped her fist into the air and beamed. A wide smile spread across her face transforming her. It was dimpled, like her dad's, only she was fortunate to have a matching pair. Her sandy-brown hair fanned out across her shoulders, and when the blue eyes behind her glasses sparkled, I could see the pretty woman she would become.

At the end of the week, Pop stood on the front sidewalk, rocking on his heels and beaming at the gray house trimmed with white. "I remember when my Molly and me bought this place." He looked at Lily and Zach sitting on the front porch swing. "It's good to have kids here again."

Ash stood a few feet from the side of the house taking pictures with his phone. He'd already snapped some of the back and now walked toward us.

"Why are you taking pictures?" I gazed up at the peeling paint on the two dormers at the top. "We still have the second story to paint."

"Don't worry about that," Ash said, aiming his phone at the front of the house. "I'll finish when I return Fourth of July." He leaned closer and whispered sotto voce, "Can I come over tonight before I leave?"

I nodded and wanted to pump my fist into the air, too. Finally, some alone time.

~ * ~

That night was the first time Ash had been in my house since we were teenagers.

"Not much has changed," he said when he walked into the kitchen.

He was right. The butcher-block table still had benches along the sides and seats on the end. The floor was the same brick linoleum, just a little more worn. Even the printed, red-apple curtains above the sink were the same, except now they were faded.

I crossed my arms over my chest. "I'm getting ready to redecorate."

At least I was thinking about it.

His eyebrows shot up. "Really? I kind of like seeing the place the way it used to be."

I was glad he understood. Even as kids we'd seemed to think alike. "I just finished making some sweet tea. Want some?"

We sat on benches across from each other at the kitchen table. In the center was Mom's big red apple cookie jar.

Ash took a sip of tea and said, "I came over to talk to you about Lily."

I lowered my head so he wouldn't see my smile disappear. If I wasn't going to get romance, I might as well eat chocolate, so I lifted the lid on the cookie jar and pulled out two oatmeal-chocolate-chip cookies. I handed one to Ash.

"Thanks." He put it on the table. "I was hoping you'd be able to help Lily. She has trouble reading. Last year she barely passed and was supposed to take summer school. Pop checked, and it's not offered here. I thought maybe you could tutor her."

I nibbled on my cookie. Usually I tutored in the summer, but last year had drained me. To save money, the school board combined the two sections of second grade into one. Instead of fifteen students, my classroom was packed with twenty-five second graders. Half of them needed special attention in either math or reading. I tried, but it was impossible to help all of them. I needed the summer away from teaching to rejuvenate.

"I'll pay you, of course," Ash added when I didn't answer.

So now this had become a business deal. I wiped my face with a napkin. "You might have noticed I'm not exactly Lily's favorite person."

"No one seems to be Lily's favorite right now."

"What does she think about the idea?"

He picked up his cookie and ate it. "I had to bribe her. I told her if she worked hard and made some progress by the Fourth, I'd increase the data on her phone."

"And if she doesn't?"

"Then the phone goes home with me."

"I would definitely not be her favorite person then."

He reached over and put his hand on mine. "I think you'd be good for Lily in a lot of ways."

I didn't pull my hand away. Until tonight, Pop or Zach or Lily had been around. Now it was just the two of us, alone. The vibes were spinning out of control. I wanted him to tell me he thought I'd be good for him, too.

"I got your number from Pop," Ash said. "I'd like to call you."

With his eyes studying me, I couldn't get my mouth to work, but my head bobbed up and down. Too quickly his hand slipped away, and he cleared his throat.

"I'll need to check on Lily. Find out how she's doing."

So calling me was also about Lily. Nothing personal. All week I'd hoped he felt a connection, too, and was thinking about us. Now there was no us. To Ash I was still Victoria's little sister Jilly.

"I have another favor," Ash said as he rose.

About Lily, I assumed.

"My flight from St. Louis leaves at seven a.m. The kids don't want to get up at four, and Pop doesn't want to leave them alone. He suggested you might watch the kids…or drive me to the airport."

Stay with the kids or take Ash to the airport. This time my mouth worked fine. "I'll take you."

~ * ~

On the two-hour ride to the airport, Ash and I talked about our jobs. He explained how most people thought drones were for the military, and I told him about how my teacher friends and I had started an annual coat drive when we saw children coming to school without a coat.

At the airport, I parked my Tucson in the fifteen-minute unloading zone and popped the trunk. Ash pulled out his suitcase, and I stood next to the car, stretching. I wasn't looking forward to getting into the car to drive two hours back to Becks Creek.

Ash wheeled his suitcase around to the driver's side and stopped in front of me. "Thanks," he said. "For everything."

He leaned toward me. Finally, I was going to get that hug. His strong arms engulfed me, and I inhaled his manly scent. Being in his arms felt good, and I wasn't anxious to pull away. He put his finger under my chin and lifted my face. His lips pressed against mine. Ash was kissing me, and I was kissing him back.

The kiss was nothing like I thought it would feel back in those junior

19

high days when I'd kissed his picture on my pillow. It wasn't one of those awkward first kisses. His lips were smooth and soft. They melted into mine. The longer we kissed the softer they felt.

Then without saying a word, he backed away and reached for his suitcase. With easy graceful strides, he walked toward the airport.

I stood there, stunned. What had that been about? I couldn't just get back into the car and drive away, not after a meteorite had hit my world.

"Ash. Hey Ash."

He stopped and turned back. "Oh, right. I forgot something."

He took two long strides, pulled me back into his arms, and kissed me again. "To be continued on the Fourth of July."

I practically floated home.

Chapter Three

Three days later, Lily brought me crashing to earth. She didn't show up for her first tutoring session. I'd spent an entire day hunting for a diagnostic test that would be grade appropriate. I phoned one of my friends who taught fifth grade to ask about strategies to use with older students. She also suggested checking out high interest/low level reading books from the library. Then she'd ask about the cute guy at the beach on Memorial Day.

Victoria was my confidant, but because it was Ash, it felt weird, so I gave my friend the scoop, although I didn't know what the scoop was because I had no idea what Ash wanted "to be continued."

Plus tutoring his daughter was never going to work if I had to drag Lily over here. I didn't call or go next door. The next step would be up to her.

In the afternoon, Victoria and the kids showed up. We sat outside on the back stoop while Braden and Misty threw a ball to Honda. They wanted him to chase it. He chose to stare at it rolling by.

"Seeing Ash sure brings back the old days," Victoria said.

Her comment surprised me. I was the nostalgic one. She was the one who kept telling me I couldn't live in the past.

Victoria gave me a sideways glance. "His wife must have been crazy to dump him and their kids. Too bad he lives so far away."

I shrugged. Victoria already knew I wanted a husband and family. If she suspected I was even mildly interested, she'd go on an all-out campaign.

Her sigh seemed wistful. "I used to think I was in love. Remember how you mooned over his picture and followed us around?"

"I was only thirteen!"

She elbowed me. "Old feelings don't always go away."

That's exactly what I was worried about. Seeing Ash with my sister made me wonder about their old feelings for each other, especially after what happened my senior year of high school.

The prom had been my first formal date. The guy who asked me was a champion wrestler. All of my friends thought he was a hunk, but the date had flopped. He'd driven me home early and hadn't bothered to walk me to the door. He'd just dumped me at the curb and said, "I thought you'd be like your sister."

Maybe Ash still had feelings for Victoria and thought I'd be like her. I needed a man who wanted me, not my sister. I changed the subject. "I haven't seen Reese lately. Everything okay?"

My sister's big eyes widened. "He didn't tell you about our little tiff, did he?"

I shook my head. "What tiff?"

"Oh, about him flying to North Carolina to help an old friend, an old female friend."

Maybe Victoria's marriage wasn't as solid as I thought.

~ * ~

The following morning Lily knocked on the back door. She lowered her head and mumbled, "Pop said I had to apologize."

I waited for the apology.

She pushed her glasses up on the bridge of her nose and lifted her head. I guessed that was the apology. Taking a deep breath, I opened the door and pointed to the basket on the counter.

"Put your phone in that empty wicker basket when you come in."

Lily reached into the front pocket of her jean shorts and pulled out her cell phone. "I'll just turn it off."

My voice took on a teacher tone. "You'll need to focus on what we're doing, so the phone goes in the basket."

Lily shuffled to the counter and deposited the phone.

We sat at the kitchen table on benches across from each other. "Why do you think you're having trouble reading?"

Lily glared. "Isn't that your job?"

Obviously, she was not going to make this easy. "It'll work better if I know where you need help."

Lily scrunched up her mouth. "Can you show me how to make the words quit jumping around on the page?"

I'd heard other students say they saw words in that way. I pulled out the folder of materials. "First, you'll have to take this reading test."

"I've been tested lots of times."

"I don't have those tests." But I was relieved the school was aware of her problem.

Lily chewed on her pencil and worked on the test for the entire hour. "I'm done," she said and walked toward the basket to retrieve her phone.

"Whoa. You didn't make up the time you missed yesterday."

She glanced over at me. "I said I was sorry." At least in her mind she had.

"I was thinking maybe you could help me do some cooking."

"Consuela doesn't let me cook."

"Well, you're going to be here all summer, and I think Pop would be pretty happy if you helped him out."

"He probably won't let me cook either."

I laughed. "Don't worry. Pop doesn't like to cook." I tossed her an apron. "If you help fry these pumpkin blossoms, you can take them home for lunch."

Lily looked down at the blossoms. "Those are flowers."

"Yes, and Pop loves them."

She rolled her eyes in a whatever kind of way, but followed me to the sink where I showed her how to wash the blossoms and remove the green stems. "You can eat pumpkin blossoms raw. Most people around here like them fried."

I plugged in the electric skillet and asked Lily to fill it half full of vegetable oil. "While the grease is heating, we'll make the cracker-crumb coating and egg mixture."

I opened the refrigerator and handed Lily an egg. "Use the glass bowl on the counter."

I reached for the milk. *Whack.* I turned expecting to see egg splattered all over my kitchen. Instead, Lily had cracked the egg and plopped it into the bowl. No mess.

"Nice job."

Her hunched shoulders straightened with pride. "I've watched Consuela and lots of cooking shows."

Handing her a measuring cup, I showed her how to whisk a fourth-cup of milk with the egg. Then I demonstrated crushing the sleeve of crackers with a rolling pin. Lily smiled as she ran it back and forth over the crackers until they were fine crumbs.

"Now dip the pumpkin blossoms in the egg mixture, roll them in the cracker crumbs, and carefully put them in the skillet so the grease won't splatter."

When Lily bit into her first crunchy blossom, her eyes lit up. "No wonder Pop likes these. They're great."

We fried three dozen blossoms, and Lily didn't complain when I asked her to help clean up the kitchen.

"Am I done?" Lily gazed around the kitchen now back in shape.

I handed her a blank notecard. "Write down the recipe so next time you'll know how to fry them."

"It was easy. I can remember."

"Yes, but if you like, we can cook again, and some of the recipes will be more complicated."

"Can I print instead of writing it?"

"Sure."

Lily printed the recipe and held it out to me.

I waved it away. "I wanted you to write it or print it so you could read it, not me. I'll get you a recipe box for them."

When I gave her the platter of fried pumpkin blossoms, she hurried out the screen door. A few minutes later she rushed back. "I forgot my phone." She grabbed the phone out of the basket. "Next time after tutoring, can we cook again?"

I nodded and grinned, glad Lily didn't realize cooking was part of the lesson.

~ * ~

Lily's test confirmed what I suspected. Her reading problem was neurological. She had dyslexia. Reading would never be easy. However, I could help her with some reading strategies and aids, such as a colored transparency to put over the words so they would stand still on the page.

When I told Lily she had dyslexia, she didn't act surprised. "You won't tell Dad, will you?"

"He's going to call and check on your progress."

"Please, please, don't tell him. I don't want him to know I'm dumb."

I was at the kitchen table sitting next to Lily on the bench. "Dyslexia doesn't mean you're dumb."

"Yes, it does. The school wanted to put me in a special reading class, but Mom wouldn't let them. She said it was for dumbos."

"Oh, Lily, I don't think you're a dumbo and neither will your dad." I put my arm around her shoulder and gave her a reassuring squeeze. "Do you know who Walt Disney and Steven Spielberg are?"

"Sure. I've watched their movies."

"What about Benjamin Franklin and John F. Kennedy?"

"We studied them in history."

"They all had dyslexia."

"Really?" She still didn't want her dad to know.

"Okay, I won't tell him," I said.

Lily sighed with relief.

"You're going to tell him."

The next night, Ash called. "Have you talked to Lily?"

"Yes. She said she has dyslexia, but she also told me you said she wasn't dumb."

"Did she say anything else?"

His voice was soft, and I strained to hear his answer. "That she's known about it for two years." Regret sounded in his voice.

"You're a good father, Ash. Don't beat yourself up about what your wife didn't tell you."

I explained some techniques that might help Lily read, such as using yellow paper to write with instead of white and tracing the letters on sandpaper so she could feel them. "I asked Lily to teach me some text abbreviations so she realizes she's not dumb."

"She knows plenty of those."

"When my friends message me, I end up calling them to explain."

"I could text you so you'd have some practice."

"I like your calls."

"You'll like my messages, too. Just don't show them to Lily because they might be FYOE."

"I don't even know what that means."

"For your eyes only."

I liked the sound of that.

~ * ~

Summer settled into a pattern. Three mornings a week Lily trudged over and stumbled through her reading, frustrated by basic sight words that she knew on one page and did not on the next. I gave her simple techniques to use like thinking of a picture. For example, in the word "look" I drew two eyes in the *o 's*.

When Lily was cooking, her beautiful smile appeared. I bought colored recipe cards so they would be easier for her to read and she saved them in the recipe box I gave her.

Some afternoons I took the kids to the lake to give Pop a break. Then my friends or Victoria would be there. We soaked up the sun and read paperbacks, romance was my favorite, while the kids splashed or swam in the water.

At night, we cheered at Zach's ball games, swung on Pop's front porch, or rode our bikes to the park. Pop had fixed up Ash's old twenty-four inch Zephyr for Zach, and I'd given Lily my sister's vintage bicycle with a striped banana seat and a white basket on the front.

The paint samples and decorating books that Victoria had dropped off were still piled on the counter. I'd browse through them, idly flipping the pages, but couldn't decide on a specific color or style. I wasn't in a hurry. I had the whole summer.

Then July, which had seemed so far away, finally came and so did Ash. Two days before the Fourth of July, he knocked on my back screen door.

When I opened it, he reached in and grabbed my hand. "Come over to Pop's. I want you to see this." His face was flushed with excitement, and he looked the way he had as a boy when he wanted to show off some new toy he'd invented.

He led me through the boxwood trees and across Pop's yard. We stopped along the side of the house near a large paint tray filled with gray paint. On the ground next to it was what looked like a toy helicopter with four propellers.

"What's that?"

"A drone," he said, "with some additions." Extending from the front was a long wooden dowel rod and attached to it was a paint roller. "Watch this."

He turned on the radio-controlled drone and the propellers began to whirl. The drone rose and hovered over the large paint tray. Then the roller dipped into the gray paint and flew over our heads. I shaded my eyes with my hand, and my mouth dropped open. The paint roller touched the siding on the house under the peak and then started moving slowly back and forth, leaving a large swath of gray paint. The drone was actually painting the second story of the house.

"Ash, that's awesome!"

He rocked back and forth on his heels. "I still have to hand-paint the trim."

"Is this what your company's been working on?"

"Actually, the company fills military orders. I explained the idea, but they weren't interested, so I've worked on it during my own time and now I'm in the process of patenting it. I've tested it by spray painting warehouses and water towers, but this is the first house. If I covered the windows, spray painting would work, too, but I wanted to experiment with a roller."

Pop walked out of the front door, followed by Lily and Zach. "What's that buzzing?" Pop looked up and saw the drone with the attached roller painting his house. "Well, I'll be." He slapped Ash on the back. "Heck of an idea, son."

Goggle-eyed, the five of us stood on the ground as the drone moved back and forth, painting the house.

~ * ~

On Sunday morning, we went to church, crowding into the pew with Victoria's family. Afterwards we ate at Pizza Station, ordering three family-size pizzas. Still, not a single slice was left for Honda.

In the afternoon, Ash trimmed the windows on the second floor, and I made sure he stayed hydrated with water and lemonade. Watching him work without his shirt made me gulp lots of ice water, too.

When he climbed down the ladder for the last time, he handed me his empty glass. "I was hoping maybe you and I could do something tonight, alone."

Exactly what I'd been hoping. Ash would be here for five days, and then he was flying back to Colorado. So far, we hadn't had any alone time.

He suggested a romantic comedy at the downtown theater, the same theater we'd gone to as kids. As we drove through town, he gawked at the boarded up windows on empty buildings.

"I never realized how many businesses have closed."

"Lots of people around here can't find jobs. If Becks Creek's schools ever consolidate, I might not have a job either."

"I hope they don't have to consolidate. A town loses its identity without its school."

Inside the theater, we settled into the back row with a big tub of popcorn between us. When the lights dimmed and the previews started, Ash leaned closer and slid his arm around my shoulders, giving me a light squeeze.

"This is good," he said when he reached in for his first handful of popcorn.

I hoped he meant being with me. The smell of buttery popcorn mixed with Ash's manly scent and made me feel giddy. The movie was funny and I laughed in the right places, but I was distracted by Ash.

I yearned for a man who looked at me the way Dad looked at Mom. Ash was looking, but I couldn't tell what his eyes were saying. Did he want a summer fling or something permanent?

I'd been burned when my fiancé dumped me, but Ash's divorce must have scorched him. For the past three years, I'd been drifting. Ash seemed to tether me, and I wanted more than a temporary anchor.

After the movie, we drove back to Pop's and pulled into the driveway. "I'll see you home."

A full moon lit the yard, and a myriad of white twinkling stars dotted the canvas of the night sky. Hand-in-hand we walked around to the back of house. Honda rose and barked, but when he saw us he didn't tuck himself away. Finally, a little progress.

As I turned to thank Ash at the door, his arms circled my waist, and he drew me toward him. He leaned down and kissed me. His lips were soft and warm, the way I remembered, plus a little salty from the popcorn. Then he tightened his arms on my back and pressed me against his hard body. The kiss changed and became more passionate. He parted my lips, exploring. Tentatively, I ran my tongue over his teeth. Ripples of pleasure shivered through me. I trembled.

"You're shivering. If you're cold, we could go inside."

"No. I'm fine." My body was generating enough heat to warm my house on a cold winter's day. If I invited him inside, we'd do more than kiss, but I needed to know where we were headed. I didn't want to drift any more. Ash had always been my friend, but now I wanted more than friendship. So much more.

Chapter Four

Fourth of July was a beautiful summer day with an ocean-blue sky and a cool breeze. In my head were Ash's words "to be continued on the Fourth of July," and for weeks I'd been looking forward to a fire-cracker holiday.

The fun and relaxation would start in the afternoon at the lake with Victoria and her family. The finale would be the fireworks over the water.

In the morning, we gathered supplies and packed coolers. I made potato salad and helped Lily bake brownies, Victoria ordered a platter of cheeses and cold cuts, and Pop supplied the chips and drinks.

At the lake, we found a picnic table in the pavilion and a spot on the beach near the horseshoe pits to watch the fireworks. Victoria suggested renting canoes. I thought lying on the beach would be more relaxing, but no one objected, and Pop offered to watch the food while he organized the horseshoe tournament. I was hoping Ash would be my partner for the tournament.

Canoeing was anything but relaxing. Victoria, Reese, and the kids settled into one canoe. Ash, Zach, Lily, and I climbed into another. Lily and Zach had never paddled a canoe, so we spent most of the time going in the wrong direction or flipping upside down and flailing in the water.

"You look like a wet puppy," Victoria said, laughing at my mop of tangled hair and soaked shorts and top.

If I'd been a dog, I would have shaken my wet hair all over her immaculate white T-shirt and very short shorts.

The horseshoe competition was a doubles tournament with single elimination. We drew playing cards for partners. Reese was my partner; Victoria got Ash.

"No switching," warned Pop, who must have read my devious mind.

I should have been happy. Reese was an expert and last year's champion. We easily won the first round, but so did Ash and Victoria.

Right before the second round, Reese's phone began playing that happy song. He checked the screen. "It's a client."

I knew what was about to happen even before he hung up. "Sorry, Jillian, gotta go. When house fever strikes, you have to catch the wave."

Victoria never seemed to mind when her husband was called away from family events, but I was not happy. Now I didn't have a partner. Most of the people crowding around the pits had already been paired up. I spotted Lily lounging in a chair, listening to music on her headphones.

"Hey Lily, help me out. I need a partner."

She shook her head. "I'm not very good."

"Come on," I coaxed. "We'll make a great team."

And we did. Luckily, I threw a few ringers and Lily made one, too. We high-fived our victory.

Ash congratulated us, too. "So, my girls are winners." Lily blushed at her dad's praise, and I liked being called Ash's girl. However, as Victoria and Ash knocked off their next opponent, I didn't feel like Ash's girl. Victoria celebrated in Ash's arms, which is where I wanted to be. I thought a polite handshake would have sufficed.

In the third round Lily and I lost. "It's okay." I put my arm around her. "Last year I lost in the first round."

I was disappointed, too. I'd wanted to compete against Ash and Victoria. Of course, they made it into the championship. Lily enthusiastically cheered for her dad. I was a little less enthusiastic. If Ash's partner had been any other woman, maybe I wouldn't have minded. But it was my sister, and they had a history.

My gut clenched. Together they seemed like royalty, the prom king and queen again. I didn't want to be the court jester.

The game went back and forth until Ash's leaner tied it up at eighteen points. His opponent didn't score. Ash had one throw left. He aimed the shoe and pitched. It sailed through the air and clanked against the stake. A ringer! Lily and I jumped up and ran toward him.

Victoria reached him first and threw her arms around his neck. "We always were a good team."

I stepped back and let Lily charge ahead. Ash picked her up and swung her around. Pop enthusiastically pumped Ash's hand.

Finally, when most of the crowd drifted away, I approached him. "Nice throwing," I mumbled.

"When are we going to eat?" Zach asked. "I'm starved."

I turned to Victoria. "What time will Reese be back?"

"I'll text him." Within minutes she had an answer. "He said go ahead and eat. He's writing up an offer."

At least Ash sat next to me at the picnic table, but Victoria planted herself across from us. I pushed my food around on the plate. Ash, however, wolfed down his food and piled on seconds.

Lily, who was on the other side of me, leaned over. "Hey, Dad. What do you think of my brownies?"

He reached for a third one and gave her a thumbs up.

On the way back from canoeing, Ash had whispered that Consuela wouldn't be returning from Mexico. "I haven't told Lily yet."

"Were they close?"

"Not really, but at least she was a woman in my daughter's life."

I glanced over at Lily beside me. She deserved more than a paid nanny who was just a woman in her life.

We gathered up the leftovers and tidied our spot.

"The volleyball court's empty," Victoria said. "Let's go play."

The kids jumped up and ran toward the court. Zach turned back. "Dad, come on. I want to be on your team."

"Hurry up, Jillian," Lily called.

Ash looked over at me, and I shrugged. Fourth of July definitely wasn't turning out the way I'd hoped. I didn't really want to play volleyball. All day we'd gone from one activity to another. I wanted to relax and talk to Ash.

We'd had little time together, and he hadn't given me any long romantic looks or even held my hand. I told myself it was because of Zach and Lily. Yet I wondered if it was because of Victoria. Maybe being around her again had rekindled some of his old feelings.

At dusk, we spread out the blankets to watch the fireworks over the water. Zach and Braden stretched out with Victoria while Lily and Misty crowded in with Ash and me. While we waited, Lily entertained Misty by fixing her hair into cute little pigtails.

When the fireworks finally began, we *oohed* and *aahed* at the patriotic colors cascading through the sky and reflecting in the water. Sitting under the inky night sky made me feel small and insignificant. I yearned for Ash to lean over and whisper something sweet in my ear or place his hand over mine. But Lily was sitting by her dad and I knew she needed time with him. So even though we were on the same blanket, the distance between us seemed vast.

The fireworks ended with the ground display of the American flag. When the red, white, and blue embers had burned out, I rose to gather up the blanket, but Misty had crawled into Lily's lap and had fallen asleep.

"I'll take her." Ash reached down and scooped up my niece, who snuggled against him. He turned to Victoria. "I'll carry her to your car. Where are you parked?"

"Oh no. Reese took it. Could you give us a ride?"

"Sure. Zach and Lily can go in Pop's truck."

Ash gently laid Misty across the backseat of his car, and Braden stretched out beside her. Victoria slid into the front seat, and I started to follow.

"Lily, Zach, come on," Pop called from the truck.

Zach ran toward the truck, but Lily didn't budge. "Jillian's going with you. That's not fair. Why can't I go, too?"

"We don't have room, Lily."

She hunched her shoulders and hung her head as she stayed firmly planted next to me. Lily had been rejected by her mother. I didn't want her to feel as if I was coming between her and her dad.

"I'll ride with Pop," I said.

Ash frowned. "You don't need to do that."

"It's fine." Of course it wasn't fine. I wanted to be sitting in the car next to Ash.

Lily, however, seemed overjoyed. She grabbed my hand, pulling me toward Pop's truck

"I thought you wanted to go with your dad."

"No, I wanted to ride with you."

I hadn't expected that and wasn't sure how to react. For now, all I could do was climb into the truck with Pop and Lily and pull Zach onto my lap.

Ash walked to the truck and leaned into the open window. "I'll be over when I get back."

All day I had seen Ash and Victoria together. Now they were piling into the car and driving away like a family. "I'm tired, and it's late." Before he could say anything to change my mind, I rolled up the window and Pop drove off.

Once I was home, I regretted telling Ash I was too tired to see him. Maybe without Victoria around, I'd be able to think more clearly. Instead of going up to bed, I sat on the porch waiting for Ash. Victoria's house was only five minutes away so he'd be back soon. Fifteen, twenty, forty minutes passed. After an hour, I trudged inside.

I couldn't sleep. I kept thinking about Ash. However, it wasn't just Ash. I was concerned about Zach and Lily, too. At the end of the summer, Lily would return to Colorado and I would be another woman saying good-bye to her.

Even if Ash wanted something more than a summer fling, I couldn't spend all my holidays like today. I didn't want to feel as if Ash had settled for me because he couldn't have Victoria. Hot tears wet my cheeks. I might as well end it now before we became more involved.

~ * ~

The next morning Lily came over for her tutoring and afterward I showed her how to make spaghetti. She planned to take it to Pop's for lunch, and I was supposed to go, too. I handed Lily the steaming bowl of pasta.

"Tell your family I need to catch up on things here, so I'm not coming over."

Lily's smile faded. "I could help you later. That way you can still have lunch with us."

I opened the door for her. "Thanks, but I need to do it myself."

Five minutes later Ash called. "Why aren't you coming?"

"I told Lily to tell you I was busy."

"She said that. What time will you be finished?"

I hesitated. "It's going to take the rest of the day."

"Oh." Ash paused so long I thought he might have disconnected.

"Will I see you tomorrow?"

Reluctantly, I clung to my decision. "Probably not."

"It's my last day, Jillian."

"I know."

In the background, Zach yelled, "Hurry up, Dad. I want to eat."

"You better go, Ash."

After I hung up, I thought I would feel better. I wandered around the house, usually a place of peace and solace. Today it felt empty, like my heart.

On the mantel were family pictures—Mom and Dad on their wedding day and school pictures of Victoria and me. My parents' marriage was based on love and respect. It was the foundation of our home and what I wanted in my life.

I couldn't deny the way I felt about Ash. I loved him, but I wasn't willing to settle for being second best. I didn't want to hurt him or his family. Eventually Ash would see how different I was from Victoria. Then we would all be hurt.

I picked up the afghan from the couch and wrapped it around me. Logically it was better to end it now. Logic, however, couldn't stop the ache cutting through me.

~ * ~

That evening I was surprised by a knock on the back door. Ash. I thought he would get on the plane and fly back to Colorado. Years later when we saw each other again, we might think about this summer and the possibility of what could have been.

"May I come in?"

On the phone telling him I didn't want to see him had been hard. Now he was here and when he stepped into the kitchen, his presence filled the room. I forced myself to take a step back.

He jammed his hands into the pockets of his khaki shorts. "Do you have any more of that sweet tea?"

"No. I'd have to make some."

He cleared his throat. "I'm not in any hurry."

So he wasn't going to make this easy. I turned my back to him, filling the teakettle and putting it on the stove.

"We've always had a special friendship, haven't we, Jillian?"

I nodded, not sure I could trust my voice.

"I thought maybe we were becoming more than friends." He moved closer and brushed his hand over my shoulders.

I shivered and closed my eyes, yearning to lean into him. Instead I kept my back ramrod straight and didn't answer.

"Now you seem to be avoiding me." His voice filled with heart-felt emotion. "I hope we're good enough friends for you to tell me why."

He'd let down the barriers and was being honest. I owed him honesty, too. Taking a deep breath, I turned and faced him, but I couldn't meet his eyes.

"I'm not my sister, Ash."

His forehead furrowed, and he frowned. "I know. She's this short little dynamo who's wound up all the time."

I crossed my arms. "I'm nothing like Victoria."

"I'm glad."

"I don't want you thinking...whoa." Now I frowned. "What did you say?"

He shuffled his feet and hesitated. "I came over to talk about you and me. I'm not sure why we're talking about Victoria. She's your sister so I don't want to hurt you by saying anything negative."

"But you dated Victoria, and she broke up with you."

"Thank goodness. She was driving me crazy with all her lists and plans."

My head popped up. "Really?"

He raked his fingers through his dark hair and began to pace. "She did the same thing yesterday. We rented canoes, played horseshoes, and then to top it off we had to play volleyball." He turned to me, his eyes filled with longing. "I wanted to lie on the beach, enjoy the day and relax… with you."

"But last night you took Victoria home and… you stayed a long time."

"Is that what this is about? Reese was there and he was interested in my drones."

"Oh. So you don't still have lingering feelings for my sister?"

He broke out in a wide grin and moved closer. "You've always been the interesting sister. The one who takes time to enjoy life." He reached out, encircled my waist, and drew me against his chest. Heat radiated from his body. "Besides, your sister is a terrible kisser."

My mouth dropped open. "She is?"

"I always felt that if she didn't have the kiss written on her to-do list, it wasn't supposed to happen, and when we did kiss she acted like she wanted to get it over with so I wouldn't smudge her lipstick."

I couldn't help it. I giggled. Ash knew exactly what Victoria was like, and he didn't want her. He thought I was the special one.

"At the airport, I had to work up the nerve to kiss you because I didn't want to ruin our friendship. It felt so natural and warm, just like you. When I came back for another kiss, I wanted to miss my plane and keep on kissing you—forever."

The enormity of the word made it stick in my throat. "For...forever?"

"Look, Jillian, I can't make promises. I have more to think about than me and how I feel. There's Lily and Zach, and we live in different states."

His piercing blue eyes searched mine. "I'm doing all the talking here. I hope I'm not being a complete fool."

"No, I'm the one who's been Silly Jilly." I reached up, put my hands around his neck, and drew his lips to mine.

The teakettle on the stove began to whistle, adding more heat to the already steamy kitchen. The tea would have plenty of time to steep.

Chapter Five

A week after Ash returned to Colorado, Victoria phoned me. "I have big news." The way she emphasized "big" sounded ominous.

I didn't want to be outdone. "I have big news, too."

"I'll be right over," Victoria said.

The back door opened and Lily shuffled inside. "I knocked but..." She stopped when she saw me standing in the kitchen, talking on my cell.

"Lily's here for tutoring. I'll call you later." I hung up and slipped my cell into my lounge pants.

"Was that Dad on the phone?"

"No. My sister."

So far Ash had phoned and texted every day. This morning his text was "BG TOU <3." I knew "thinking of you" and the sideway heart for love, but I had to look up BG "big grin."

Lily gave me a sideways glance. "I think Dad likes you."

Heat rushed to my face. "Did he say that?"

"No, but he gets this dopey grin on his face when you're around."

That made me smile. I wondered how to text "dopey grin."

Lily slid onto the bench across from me. "So do you like him?"

I didn't know how much Ash had told Lily and Zach, but I thought he should be the one talking to them about us, not me. "You know your dad and I used to play together. We sat at this very table eating cookies and drinking Kool-Aid."

"I'm not talking about the Stone Age. I mean now."

"Stone Age?" I opened my mouth, pretending to be offended, which wasn't hard to do.

Lily was determined to get an answer. "So, are you Dad's girlfriend?"

I squirmed. "How would you feel about it if I was?"

Lily looked down at the table as if studying a hard question. Finally, she shrugged. "I guess it would be okay."

That wasn't exactly the gold seal of approval I'd hoped for. Lily's mother had walked away from their family. For Lily to accept another woman into her heart was not going to be easy.

I wanted to be the woman she accepted. I wanted to give her the kind of unconditional love my parents had given me. I wanted her to feel loved and know love didn't have to hurt. So I would have preferred "awesome" or "cool," but "okay" was a start.

~ * ~

That afternoon, after the kids went over to Pop's, Victoria and I settled on the couch. "I'll tell you my news first. Just be prepared. It's bad." She emphasized "bad" and didn't look at me. "The president of Becks Creek's school board appointed Reese to chair a committee on consolidating with Bunker Hill."

My hands flew to my mouth. I'd been prepared for bad. But consolidation knocked out my propellers. "Would...would Becks Creek keep their grade school?"

"According to Reese, those are the decisions the committee will have to consider, but I don't want my kids bused to another town."

I slumped against the couch. "I don't want to lose my job."

Victoria's lips formed a big red *O*. "Why would you lose your job?"

"It takes five years to be tenured. I've taught only three. So I would be one of the first to be pink-slipped."

"That's not fair. You're a great teacher."

A big lump lodged in my throat.

"Remember they're only studying the possibility," Victoria said. "Maybe some company will come in and revitalize Becks Creek."

"I don't see that happening any time soon."

"Let's talk about your big news." Victoria's bright red lips curved into a smile. "I hope it's about Ash."

She was trying to cheer me up and thinking about Ash did make me happy. "Why would my news be about Ash?"

"Because of the way he was looking at you on the Fourth of July and because you were glowering at me."

"I was glowering because you were flirting."

"In case you haven't noticed, Ash is a hottie."

"What I noticed was you flirting with him."

"I did it for you. I wanted to see if he was interested in women or one particular woman."

I frowned. Victoria had this weird sense of doing things for me that I didn't always appreciate.

"So are you serious?"

I sighed. "He's the one."

Victoria threw her arms around me. "I'm glad for you." She pulled back. "I hope his kissing has improved. He's a terrible kisser."

I picked up a pillow and playfully hit her. She squealed and grabbed the other pillow. Suddenly the years slipped away, and we were on the floor, having a pillow fight and giggling.

Then Victoria jumped to her feet. "What am I going to do when you move away?"

I stopped laughing. "Move?"

"If he's the one, you'll want to be together."

The pachyderm I'd been pushing away was now planted in the center of my living room. I couldn't imagine living anywhere else. I'd have to give up everything—my family, my friends, this house, and my job (if I had one.) However, Victoria was right. I loved Ash, and I wanted to be with him. I hadn't realized falling in love would mean his happiness was more important to me than my own.

I reached for Mom's afghan. "Ash hasn't asked me to move."

"But you know he will."

Even as I nodded, I wondered why Ash hadn't already mentioned it. Maybe he knew how hard moving would be for me and was giving me time to accept it.

"Ash is a great guy, Jillian. Don't keep holding onto the past. Mom and Dad wouldn't want you clinging to this house and their memories. They'd want you to be happy, just like I do."

After Victoria left, I went outside to check on Honda. Behind me, the screen door slapped, and Honda wobbled up. He rose as if to move away from me. I heaved a heavy sigh. I thought he was done with being spooked. Then his tail swung back and forth, and he took a step toward me.

He'd never greeted me or wagged his tail when he saw me. My heart melted. "Here, Honda. Here, boy."

Slowly he loped over and nuzzled my hand. I leaned down and threw my arms around his neck. Honda trusted me. He could have stayed in the past, but he'd been brave enough to take a chance and move forward. I needed to be brave, to trust in love and move forward, too.

Since the accident, I'd been trying to rebuild my old life. But it would never be the same. Even if I stayed in Becks Creek and lived in this house forever, Mom and Dad were not coming back. Their memories weren't stored in this house. They were stored in my heart.

~ * ~

Texting and talking to Ash on the phone weren't enough. Some days I ached to see him so much I thought I wouldn't be able to take another breath. The highlight of my day was curling up in bed with my phone, telling him about Zach scoring a run or Lily's progress in reading.

"She really likes the whisper phone Pop made."

"Whisper phone. That sounds sexy."

I laughed. "It's pieces of PVC pipe that you read into and then hear the sound of the words in your own ear."

"I'll never get her off the phone now."

"At least this phone is helping her read," I said. "Remember the summer you made those walkie talkies and we were spies?"

"Yeah, you insisted on being 007, so I had to be 0007."

"I never told you, but I used to sleep with my walkie talkie under my pillow."

"So now do you sleep with your phone under your pillow?"

I didn't want to admit it. "A girl needs to have some secrets."

Our conversations always included one question. "When will you be coming back?"

Ash never gave me an exact date. "Work is unpredictable. I'm hoping by the middle of August."

On the calendar, I circled August 15. Yet I knew as soon as Ash arrived, I'd be counting the days until he left. Only this time Lily and Zach would be going, too, and I probably wouldn't see them until Thanksgiving.

I waited for Ash to ask me about moving. When he didn't, I took a tiny step forward. I checked on the Internet for states that had reciprocity with Illinois for a teaching license. Scanning the list, I saw Colorado. Joy and dread shot through me.

All the teaching positions were probably filled for the coming school year, but I clicked on the website for Denver school districts and found two positions posted. The one for second grade was at Cherry Creek. I wasn't sure I wanted to apply, but if Becks Creek consolidated, eventually I would need to find another job, so why not start the process now?

Ten days later, I had my resume, transcripts, and recommendations. I still hadn't talked to Ash. Maybe he was waiting for me bring up the move.

That night as I anxiously awaited Ash's call, I practically danced around the house. I couldn't remember the last time I'd felt this hopeful about my future. By eleven the euphoria evaporated. I hadn't heard from Ash, and when I phoned him, it went straight to his voice mail. I reread Ash's text from that morning. "SOT H AM <3." Lily had been teaching me, so I knew "short on time" and Ash had ended with "hugs, all my love."

I was too wired to sleep, so I flipped on the late night show. A special news report interrupted the program. Scenes from a burning airplane that had crashed in Atlanta filled the screen.

I didn't expect Ash for another week, but maybe he'd flown home to surprise me? Was that why he was short on time? Usually he flew straight from Denver to St. Louis. What if he'd booked a flight with a stopover in Georgia?

I knew all too well how easily life could change. One minute you're flying through the air and the next your airplane is in cinders on the tarmac.

I called Ash again and got his voice mail. This time I left a message. I couldn't sleep. I was too worried, so I stretched out on the sofa listening to the drone of the TV.

I must have dozed off because the sunlight streaming in through the living room window woke me from my nightmare about the accident. I groped for my phone under the pillow. No messages.

I dragged myself into the kitchen and drank my morning coffee, trying to steady my nerves. Where was Ash? Why hadn't I heard from him?

I picked up my basket and walked out to the garden. As I was plucking the pumpkin blossoms, Honda barked and the boxwood trees rustled. I turned. Striding toward me was Ash. My heart surged. I dropped the basket and rushed to him. He caught me in his arms, twirled me around, spinning my whole world just as he always had done.

"You're shaking," he said when my feet hit the ground again.

I reached up and pushed a wayward lock of hair off his forehead. "I was so worried. This plane in Georgia... Why didn't you tell me you were coming?"

"I texted you. 'H AM.' Home this a.m."

"Oh, I guess I need a few more lessons from Lily." I grabbed Ash's hand. "I have a surprise."

"You do?" He gave me that dopey grin Lily had described.

I picked up my basket of blossoms and led him into the house. On the computer, I pulled up the teaching application for Colorado. "All I need to do is hit 'send.'"

He chuckled and pulled me into his arms. "At least you didn't cut your beautiful hair."

I frowned.

"Maybe you'd better sit down for my news." We sat on the couch. "The company I work for in Colorado was bought out."

My stomach lurched. "You lost your job?"

"Yes, but they offered a very lucrative severance package, enough for me to start my own business."

"What kind of business?"

"Building drones like the one I used to paint Pop's house. I wanted to tell you earlier, but I needed to talk to the kids first, to see how they felt about living here."

"You want to start your company in Becks Creek?"

"The Midwest is centrally located, and over the Fourth of July I talked to Reese about some vacant buildings." Then he took a deep breath. "There's this certain girl here I want to marry."

"Oh, Ash." I threw my arms around his neck.

"Money will be tight, so I wouldn't be able to afford a house right away."

"I have a house."

I glanced around, and my old life had faded, replaced by a new life with Ash and the kids and Honda. I could hear laughter and joy filling the house once again. My eyes paused at the family pictures on the mantel.

My dad seemed to be winking at me. "See, Pumpkin, I always knew you would blossom."

THE END

About the author

Sue Stewart Ade lives in her hometown of Pana, Illinois, with her husband, Larry. They have two children, Missy and Nelson, and four grandchildren. Sue has taught creative writing in high school and college. Her short stories have been published in anthologies and have won awards at Indiana University, Midwest Writers, and Central Indiana Writers. *Friends Forever* was a finalist in the Pacific Northwest Literary Contest.

Sue wrote her first novel in fifth grade to share with her girlfriends at slumber parties. She enjoys sharing her writing with friends and family.

Author Contacts

Website: http://sueade.com/
Facebook: https://www.facebook.com/SueStewartAde/
Twitter: Sue Ade @sueade890

Pumpkin Blossoms

Ingredients:
- 2 dozen pumpkin blossoms
- 1 sleeve of crushed crackers
- 1 egg
- ¼ cup of milk
- Vegetable oil for frying

Clean and stem pumpkin blossoms. Heat oil to 350 degrees. Whisk egg and milk together. Roll blossoms in egg mixture and crackers. Fry in pan until brown on one side and turn, 1 to 2 minutes.

(A quicker way is to buy coating mix, such as Fry Magic, and follow the package directions for vegetables.)

Drop me a line at sueade890@aol.com and tell me how they turned out.

Boston Crème Breakdown

Randi Perrin

Kestin walked in the door and threw his keys on the table before he immediately stumbled for the bathroom. So much for walking around the block.

His soon-to-be ex-roommate, Jack, came out of his room with two boxes. Kestin nearly slammed into him, knocking the boxes off balance.

"Whoa, what's wrong?"

"Nothing," Kestin said. "I just tried to walk too far and my leg is talking to me." He took a step and a jolt of pain almost knocked him to the floor. "No, it's damn near cursing at me."

"Don't let me stop you, man." Jack slid out of his way. "Let me load this stuff in the truck and then we'll have one last beer before I'm out of your hair."

Kestin nodded and hobbled his way to the bathroom. He sat down on the toilet and removed the artificial limb before he leaned back and enjoyed the sweet freedom that came with its absence. His stump looked a bit swollen, which explained the pain. He washed the socket of his prosthetic and then he washed his stump, the warm water soothed as it coated his skin. He had one area that didn't play well with his prosthetic, and he flipped off the small circle of inflamed, raw tissue.

He hoisted himself up using the crutch next to the sink and stared at himself in the mirror. His face still looked young, but his brown eyes appeared tired and worn, like he had seen it all and, in his twenty-nine years, he definitely had.

Jack met him at the doorway to the bathroom and handed him a beer.

"Cheers, man," he said, clinking his brown bottle to the one he'd just handed Kestin.

"Cheers." He tried to smile, but it was thin and tight, and he was pretty sure Jack could see right through him.

"Dude, I'm just following orders—getting shipped to the great state of Kentucky. Bourbon, fast horses, and faster women. I can't wait." Using Jack and his crutch for balance, Kestin slowly made his way to the living room.

"Just don't marry one of them," Kestin said with a sigh as he collapsed into the recliner. "Wait, why is the recliner still here?"

Jack smiled. "It's yours now. You need it more than I do. Plus, look at this place, you need something."

Kestin looked around the barren room—a dingy old couch that was far too difficult for him to get on and off of since his amputation, a coffee table, the recliner, a reading lamp, and an empty entertainment center. It hadn't always been empty, it used to be home to a 46-inch flat-screen TV before his ex-wife cleaned the house of just about everything right before he came home horribly mangled and damaged from the war.

"No, I don't need to take your recliner. I can get one of my own," he lied.

He didn't have the money. Hell, he wasn't sure how long he was going to be able to make rent or much of anything without Jack. He had been Kestin's saving grace, moving in to split the bills and help as he adjusted to life without his leg or his wife. Jack was the best friend he'd ever had.

"If I take it, it will end up on the side of the road somewhere."

Kestin took a long pull of his beer. "Well, since you put it that way, I can't deny this thing a good home where it will be loved."

"Exactly." Jack polished off his beer and rose. "I'm going to miss you, man."

"Don't be a stranger," Kestin said, though something told him that once Jack walked out that door he'd never see him again. Such was the way Kestin's life went. No one stuck around.

"I won't, I promise." Jack pulled him up from the recliner and gave him a man hug. "The lady next door will take care of you. I made her promise."

Kestin rolled his eyes. Mrs. Sanchez was crazy as a loon, but she was sweet enough and had been very supportive since his return home from overseas. She assured him that she hated that "hussy ex-wife of his," and had stepped in to help when Jack wasn't able to drive him to doctor's appointments and to the store.

"I'll text you when I get to Kentucky, okay? Maybe we'll get you out there one of these days."

"Don't count on that. The car ride to the grocery store has sent me into panic attacks, I don't know that I can handle one longer than ten minutes."

"Well, work on that with your therapist so you can come and see me, okay, man?"

"Sure thing," he said with a heavy layer of sarcasm.

Jack pulled his key out of his pocket and set it on the table. "It gets better man, I promise. You just have to let it."

Kestin looked at him with a wary eye. "I'll keep that in mind."

With that, Jack stepped out the door and out of his life. One more down. First his wife, then his leg, now his best friend. How much more could a man handle before he lost it?

He finished his beer and left the empty on the coffee table before he hobbled to his room and took off his dog tags. He laid them reverently across the top of the dresser. Not that he needed them anymore, but after nearly ten years of wearing them, it was a hard habit to break. He just didn't feel like he was complete without the metal against his skin. He had made so many damn adjustments in the past few months, he wasn't ready to give that one up yet. He ran a finger over the embossed metal before he sank down onto the bed. Sleep was a welcome respite from the pain, even if it was punctuated by haunting nightmares.

He glanced down at his leg and laughed. He hadn't signed up for this.

Ten years ago, when he enlisted, he signed up to be a fighter, a warrior. Now he was knocking on the door of thirty with fewer limbs than he started with, and on his rare trips outside the walls of his house, strangers stopped him to tell him he was a hero. He didn't feel like a hero.

No, he came home permanently disfigured. Despite his vehement refusal, he was handed a medical discharge, a Purple Heart, and told to run as far away from the Army as possible. As far and as fast as a below-the-knee amputee could run, anyway.

He pulled out his computer and checked his email. He was hoping for a bite on the giant grill he'd posted on the online buying and selling site. The grill had been the first purchase he and Marie made together when they got married. Now, it sat out in his backyard, a constant reminder of his failure at marriage, life, everything. The lack of unread messages in his inbox told him no one was interested in the last physical reminder of his marriage gone south either.

He clicked the help wanted ads. Now that Jack was gone, he needed to find something to help make rent because the disability checks just weren't going to cut it. That, however, was going to be difficult as hell given the fact he couldn't even walk around the block.

There wasn't much in the help wanted ads, but still he continued to scroll through the list until one caught his attention:

Teach me to cook, please?
My mom always told me the way to a man's heart is through his stomach, and I foolishly dismissed her, fully convinced there were other, more effective ways.

As is always the case, Mom was right because, well, let's just say I've never held a man's heart for very long.

I'm getting older and clearly my ways are not endearing me to anyone—or my cat.

I'll stop rambling, the point is I just need someone to teach me to cook something. A few somethings. Some staple dinner meals, maybe one fabulous meal, and a go-to dessert that people will beg me to make at their potlucks.

I will pay for these lessons, I'm really not asking you to teach a stranger to cook for nothing. We'll discuss payment later, I'm not posting money details online. That's even crazier than posting online that I want to learn how to cook to land a man, don't you think?

I want real recipes. I want real background. If you're going to email me, you should include a bio, a resume, and the recipes you think will work well.

He laughed. That poor woman, she was going to get the craziest responses. He closed his computer and turned off the light, resting his head on the pillow.

Unfortunately, sleep didn't come. Instead, his mind kept turning over the words he read. He really felt sorry for that woman. Sighing, he turned on the light and opened his computer. The ad was still open on his screen, so he clicked the link to send an email.

Date: Wed, 20 April 2016 10:24 PM
From: "B. Kestin" <Kestin83@gmail.com>
To: 234vdjrtbemydir@onlinewantads.com
Subject: Cooking Lessons

Hello Miss—well, I don't know what your name is, actually. Let me start over.

Hello.

My name is Kestin, and I wanted to respond to your ad.

Regarding your request for a resume, I don't have one. I dropped out of college halfway through and joined the Army. Truth be told, though, I've actually cooked my entire life. My mom taught me everything she knew.

I hope that's background enough.

Regarding what I would teach you to cook. Being a man, I am familiar with what we like. Well, what most of us like. I don't know about all those hippy-dippy vegan guys out there, but for a normal man, we like steak, we like burgers, simple foods, really. Maybe an Italian dish, too. Everyone likes Italian, right?

For dessert, I think a simple cake will do it. Once you master how to make a simple yellow cake, you can easily transform it into other things. My favorite of those being a Boston Crème Pie, which is yellow cake with a layer of vanilla pastry cream between layers and topped with chocolate ganache.

I wish you luck in your endeavor.

Kestin

~ * ~

When Kestin woke the following morning, he was stiff and sore. The idea of not putting on the prosthesis seemed fantastic. He didn't have anywhere to go or anyone to impress.

He grabbed his laptop and hobbled to the living room so he could sit in the recliner while he checked emails and watched *Top Gun*. Those Navy boys always made him laugh.

Outside, a car backfired and his hands instantly rose to his head. He crouched down in his chair, his breath coming in rapid-fire bursts. When he regained his bearings and looked around, he realized he was in his living room, and not in the desert. He was in a recliner, not a Humvee. Hell, he wasn't even in uniform. He took a deep breath and waited for his heart rate to return to normal.

Maybe watching some military movie, even if it was those Navy flyboys, isn't the best idea right now.

He opened the computer and checked his email to find one unread message from an unfamiliar email address. Figuring it was spam, he almost hit delete. Then he noticed it was a reply to the message he sent the night before. Damn, she was quick.

Date: Thur, 21 April 2016 02:12 AM
From: "Erica Willis" <ewillis5-0@mail.com>
To: "B. Kestin" <Kestin83@gmail.com>
Subject: RE: Cooking Lessons

Hi Kestin,

I'm Erica. Whoops, I probably shouldn't have given you my real name, huh? Too late, it's not like you don't already know I'm single, have a cat, and can't cook, so how much worse can it really get for me, right?

I'm intrigued by your proposal. I admit, you're offering me much more than I expected.

Your background isn't exactly what I pictured when I put the ad out, but that's okay. I mean, I put an ad on a free want ad site, I don't know what I actually had in mind. I just sent up a prayer that I wasn't going to attract killers or woman-beaters. You're not either one of those, are you? (Who am I kidding, not like you'd actually tell me if you were.) I doubt you are though, because you're the most polite of all the responses I've received.

What I didn't put in the ad was that I'm doing this at the request of my mother. My mother died a few months ago, and left me some money, with some of it earmarked for me to get cooking lessons. I looked into some of the classes, but they didn't fit my schedule or, you know, I just didn't really want to take them. I do better one-on-one, and obviously, that costs a lot more at some cooking school than my mom left me.

I really ramble a lot when I type, don't I?

Anyway, Kestin, I like your style and what you're offering me. You give me details about when you can get started, how many lessons it will be, and I'll start cleaning the house. Apartment, really, but I'll have to clean it regardless of what it's called. For your trouble, I'll pay you $200.

I look forward to hearing from you. Unless you're a killer or a woman-beater, and then let's pretend this email never happened, okay?

Erica

~ * ~

Date: Fri, 22 April 2016 10:01 AM
From: "B. Kestin" <Kestin83@gmail.com>
To: "Erica Willis" <ewillis5-0@mail.com>
Subject: RE: RE: Cooking Lessons

Hi Erica, nice to meet you.

First of all, let me assure you that I'm not a killer or a woman-beater.

I'm honored that you want to learn from me, but I've never taught anyone before, so you'll have to bear with me.

(This is your chance to back out now and find a quality, experienced teacher for your mother's money.)

Would you like to start Sunday?

It might be easier for you to come to my house because I have all the tools necessary. Eventually you'll need to buy them yourself, but it seems kind of silly to make you go out and buy everything when I already have it. I mean, what if you end up not liking a quality steak on the grill? It seems pointless for me to make you buy a grill, meat thermometer, tongs, and a grill brush, don't you think? I can email you directions.

In the meantime, why not scour the internet and find something you want to learn how to cook, and we'll see about that as well. Might as well learn something you want to learn and not just what you think a man wants. Don't ever live your life for a man. Live it for you.

Kestin

~ * ~

Date: Fri, 22 April 2016 11:08 PM
From: "Erica Willis" <ewillis5-0@mail.com>
To: "B. Kestin" <Kestin83@gmail.com>
Subject: RE: RE: RE: Cooking Lessons

Hi Kestin,

You're so very sweet. It makes me feel a little bit safer about coming over to a stranger's house. Just a bit, mind you, because so many things can go horribly awry. I'm really starting to think this is a bad idea. A horrible idea.

Maybe we should just forget the whole thing.
Erica

~ * ~

Date: Sat, 23 April 2016 9:19 AM
From: "B. Kestin" <Kestin83@gmail.com>
To: "Erica Willis" <ewillis5-0@mail.com>

Subject: RE: RE: RE: RE: Cooking Lessons

Erica,

I understand your apprehension. I admit I share a bit of it myself. If you want to bail, that's totally fine. It's your choice if you want to let your mother down and not fulfill her dying wish for you to learn how to cook.

Let me see if I can make you feel a little bit better about me.

I'm 29 years old and an amputee. Even with my prosthesis, I can't run very fast, so let's face it, even if I did want to chase you around with a butcher knife (which I assure you I absolutely do not), it would be incredibly easy for you to outrun me.

I'm still learning how to walk on this prosthetic, so you'll have the upper hand all the way around. So there you have it. I certainly hope you can trust me. I'm kind of looking forward to seeing if I can translate the knowledge I have into effective cooking lessons.

I've attached directions to my place. Why don't you come over at 1700? We'll cook dinner together, and it will be your first lesson. If you're allergic to something, let me know, because I'd really hate for you to trust me and then have you go into anaphylactic shock and then I'd have to rush you to the emergency room, and as I've already mentioned, running and rushing aren't really my strengths anymore.

Kestin

~ * ~

Date: Sun, 24 April 2016 8:17 AM
From: "Erica Willis" <ewillis5-0@mail.com>
To: "B. Kestin" <Kestin83@gmail.com>
Subject: RE: RE: RE: RE: RE: Cooking Lessons

Kestin,

Thank you for talking about yourself. That makes me

feel a little better. It makes you seem a bit more real, as opposed to some faceless person on the internet. Oh, God, no, you better not be catfishing me. I will be checking for a prosthetic immediately upon arrival, and if not I will run. (Then again, if you don't have an artificial limb, then you'll likely catch me. Oh, I don't know that I planned this very well.)

I appreciate the offer for dinner, but I don't want to put you out more than I already have. Since you asked, I am not allergic to anything. That I know of, anyway.

My mother made the most fantastic cheesecake, ever. I remember the cookbook she always used, and I pulled it out of the collection she left me and marked the page. It was so deliciously rich and velvety smooth. If you could teach me that, I'd, well, I don't know what I'd do, but I'd be so grateful and I'm sure my mother would beam down from Heaven. (If, you know, that's what you believe about where she is. I mean, I think that's where she is, but I don't want to push my beliefs onto you.)

By the way, what is 1700?

E-

~ * ~

Date: Sun, 24 April 2016 11:37 AM
From: "B. Kestin" <Kestin83@gmail.com>
To: "Erica Willis" <ewillis5-0@mail.com>
Subject: RE: RE: RE: RE: RE: RE: Cooking Lessons

Erica,

To answer your question, 1700 is five o'clock. I'm sorry, I don't always remember that not everyone uses the twenty-four hour clock. I'm Army, remember? I'll try to remember to talk civilian.

Cheesecake, I can do cheesecake. Bring the cookbook, but I have a pretty good recipe of my own.

I look forward to meeting you later.
K-

~ * ~

After Kestin slammed his laptop closed, he stretched and curled his lips in a tiny smile. He'd tried to picture Erica since they started emailing, and his mind always landed on a short redhead with a face full of freckles and frizzy hair, and constantly in a frazzled state. He imagined she carried a purse the size of his Army-green duffle bag, so she would have anything and everything she might need for any occasion—a book, makeup, tissues, pepper spray, feminine needs, aspirin, cough drops, a screwdriver, and a gun. With her spastic nature, could she hold a gun steady? She'd probably carry one anyway.

He wasn't exactly sure why he wasted so much time trying to picture her. He'd never been right when he'd done it in the past, and honestly, what did it matter? This was a job, who cared if she had frizzy red hair and a gun she couldn't shoot? The gun in her purse could be an issue, but he also knew he could disarm her faster than she could pull that trigger providing he didn't have to run across the room to do it.

Using a crutch, he pulled himself out of the recliner and hobbled to the bathroom where he took a shower and put on his prosthetic. The small spot that the prosthetic rubbed raw was getting better, though it wasn't quite perfect yet. Still, progress was progress.

Back in the bedroom, he dressed, making sure to wear a pair of cargo shorts. She said she was going to check for his leg upon arrival, so it made sense to make it visible. Besides, it was 72 degrees out, so why not? Although no longer on active duty, he still wore a buzz cut. His therapist said it was because he couldn't let his active duty days go, much like still wearing his dog tags. Kestin contended it was just because it required no upkeep save for the trim every few weeks. He didn't need a brush, gel, hair spray, or have to worry about it falling in his eyes. The fact his therapist couldn't see that baffled him. He slid his dog tags over his head and tucked them under the collar of his Go Army, Beat Navy t-shirt.

His phone trilled in his cargo shorts pocket, so he pulled it out. Caller ID informed him it was his sister Aubrey.

"Yo, what up little sis?"

"What's up, homeslice? How's it hanging?"

"Short, shriveled, and to the left, same as usual."

"You are so gross, I mean, legit, didn't need to know that about you." He laughed out loud at her horror. "So, what's going on?"

"Nothing, have a woman coming over for dinner."

"Oh, a woman, do tell."

"Not much to tell, she had a rather pathetic ad online begging someone, anyone, to teach her how to cook. Me, being the gracious person I am and possessing all the cooking talent in this family, made her an offer she couldn't refuse." He wandered to the kitchen as he spoke, trying not to let the pain show in his voice.

"Is she pretty?"

"I don't know, online, remember?"

"She could be some scary 800-pound man."

"Or she could be this really skittish, apprehensive crazy cat lady like she portrayed herself. Sheesh, you watch way too many crime shows." He opened the fridge and stared inside. "Dammit, Aubrey, I have nothing for us to drink. What do I get? Do I get Coke? Do I get beer?"

"Seriously, did Marie screw you up that bad, that you don't even remember what the elusive woman drinks?"

He slammed the fridge shut and ground his teeth together. "We both know Marie's not the reason I'm confused as hell these days."

"Relax," she said, stifling the laughter in her voice. "Get Mrs. Sanchez to pick up a case of beer for you. Maybe a six-pack of Coke, too. Oh, and Kool-Aid, you definitely want her to drink the Kool-Aid."

"You could have stopped at Coke, thanks," he muttered.

"Seriously, Beau—"

"Do. Not. Call. Me. That."

"Seriously, bro, come home. You don't have to live alone with nothing but your bad memories to keep you company." Her voice dropped to a whisper. "I know you can't afford that place without Jack."

Kestin raked his hand across his face. "How do you know that?"

"A little birdie told me. A little birdie who wanted to make sure you were taken care of."

"I'm going to kick Jack in his nuts next time I see him," Kestin growled.

"Screw your pride. You need help and I'm willing to give it to you. Please come home."

The idea had merit. It wasn't like he had any better options at his disposal.

"Aub, I love you, but you do realize what you're signing yourself up for, right?" He hated to be a burden, though Fate had a way of blowing that all to hell.

"Yes, I do." She sounded like she wanted to add something more but she stopped herself.

He held his hands up in surrender, not that she could see the action. "Fine, Aubrey, fine. I'll call my landlord this week."

The sound of heels on linoleum floated through the phone, and he knew she was in her kitchen. She usually called him when she stood in the room, confused about what the various appliances did. He was quite surprised a stupid question about food hadn't come up at all, then again, his dumb question about drinks may have filled their quota for that conversation.

"Let me get with James and I'll let you know when we can come get your stuff."

He looked around the living room and sighed. "What's worth keeping will likely fit in the bed of the truck. It shouldn't be hard."

"Oh, then you can drive your damn self," she said with a laugh.

His breath quickened at the thought. "Aubrey, that's not even funny."

"You're right, it's not. I'm sorry." She paused a moment. "Now, go annoy your neighbor to get you some beer. I'll be in touch."

He shook his head as he ended the call. He opened his door and walked out onto the porch, pleased to see Mrs. Sanchez filling the birdfeeder. At least he didn't have to go far to find her.

"Buenos días," he called as he waved. She replaced the lid on the bird feeder and walked over to him.

"Buenos días, what can I do for you today? Do we need to go to the store?"

"Yes, if you do not mind. I'm low on groceries, and I have company tonight."

The old woman raised an eyebrow. "It's good to see you socializing again. I was starting to worry."

"It's not like that. She just wants me to teach her how to cook."

"You'll do wonderfully. I love it when you cook for me. It's been far too long, you know," she said with a nudge and a wink.

He wasn't sure if the nudge was pointing out it had been far too long since he had been with a woman or made her dinner. Hell, both were true.

"I will be more than happy to drop you off at the store while I run some other errands. Just give me twenty minutes."

She scurried off his porch and into her house.

At the grocery store, he loaded his cart with some charcoal, ground beef, hamburger buns, potatoes, tomatoes, and lettuce. He grabbed a twelve pack of Miller then he thought better of it and picked up Miller Lite instead. He rolled his eyes, light beer was god-awful, but most women he knew drank it. Not that he knew too many women these days. Once he became a washed-up Army Ranger with a fake limb, they ran like the wind.

~ * ~

The clock over the stove told him it was a little after three. He had two hours to kill, and he wasn't exactly sure what to do. He stared at the contents of his tiny pantry and was surprised to see a can of cherry pie filling. He didn't remember ever buying it, but he was happy to see it there. He could make a pie and that way they'd have dessert. Perfect.

He turned the oven on and then hauled out his food processor, which must have escaped Marie's wrath because it was hidden at the bottom of the pantry. A few minutes later, what started as disparate flour, sugar, butter, cinnamon, and water had formed into a large, cohesive dough ball, which he took out of the food processor and cut in half. Pie crust had such a bad reputation, but it was so easy, he didn't understand everyone's fear.

He put half of the dough into the fridge while he rolled out the other half and shaped it to fit the pie plate. He sobbed a tiny bit as he dumped the contents of the can onto his pie dough—his mother would kill him if she knew he was using canned filling instead of fresh, but it wasn't cherry season just yet, so he used what he had. He rolled out the second half of the dough and then covered the pie. His knife hovered over the top, debating what design to cut in it. He ultimately decided on a simple flower, and then he painted the top with melted butter and sugar.

It might have canned filling, but at least it was pretty.

He put the pie into the oven, and cleaned up the mess in the kitchen. Forty-five minutes later, the pie looked good, though it needed just a bit longer. He leaned against the oven while he waited on the timer to count down another five minutes. It was right at four-thirty, so he had a half hour before Erica arrived.

A ring broke through constant tick of the clock above his head. He bent down to check the oven again, even though he was pretty sure five minutes hadn't passed yet. While he had the oven door open, the sound tore through his place again.

Oh, the doorbell. He hadn't heard that in a long time.

He walked to the door and slowly turned the knob. He was greeted by a brunette, about five-foot-seven, roughly his age, with captivating jade green eyes. Her long hair was in a French braid that fell over her left shoulder. She had a small leather purse over her shoulder and a bottle of wine in each hand. His eyes drifted across her body, which he had to admit wasn't half bad. She wasn't model thin, though he'd never understood anorexic-looking models anyway. She had a decent chest, and legs that simply wouldn't quit, even if they were encased in extremely tight, dark blue jeans. Skinny jeans, if he remembered the random stuff he read in the magazines piled up in his doctor's offices post amputation. She stepped through the door, and he closed it behind her.

"Umm, Erica?" She nodded. "You're early."

His oven timer dinged and he jumped. He returned to the kitchen to turn off the timer and pull the pie out of the oven. She trailed along behind him.

"Did you make that?" she said.

"Yes."

"From scratch?"

"Most of it, yes."

"That's amazing." He turned to her and she smiled broadly. "So, yeah, I know I'm early. I hope that's not a problem. I left super-early in case I got lost, but as it turned out your directions were incredibly thorough and I definitely didn't get lost. I actually sat in my car in your driveway for the past ten minutes, but then I thought that seemed almost stalker-like, so I figured I'd take a chance that you wouldn't freak out that I was early."

63

He really couldn't take his eyes off her mouth as the words spilled from her lips. They were a rosy red color, plump, and alluring. In a word—perfect.

He shook his head in an attempt to tame his thoughts. No matter how perfect her cupid-bow lips were, he had to teach her how to cook and be on his way with her money. This was a business deal. Nothing more, nothing less.

"It's fine."

"Well, I am happy to see you weren't lying about the artificial leg," she said with a grin. She handed him the bottles of wine. "Here, I brought wine. I didn't know what you drank, or what was for dinner, so I picked up a bottle of red and a bottle of rosé. I guess I probably should have picked up white so every scenario was covered, but I only have two hands, so two bottles of wine it is."

"Red will work well. We're having beef."

She smiled. "Awesome, I love it when things work out."

"I also bought Miller Lite if you'd like a beer while we wait."

She turned up her nose. "Is light all you've got? Because light beer blows."

He couldn't resist the smile. Sure, he just spent some of what precious little money he had on that twelve-pack, but this woman drank real beer. He could appreciate that.

"I don't, sorry. It's not my normal beer either, for whatever it's worth."

"You wasted your money on light beer for me, that's so sweet and sad all at the same time." She ran her hand across his bicep and he tensed.

He wasn't used to this, nor did he know what to make of it. Was she flirting? Being friendly? Was this her normal thing? To talk and touch too much?

"It's okay. Now, are you ready to get started on cooking lessons?"

"Sure thing, what's for dinner? Beef, obviously."

"Burgers and oven fries."

She rubbed her belly and made an *mmmmm* noise that was so adorable his lips involuntarily twitched upward into a smile.

"First, let's get started on cutting up potatoes for oven fries."

He handed her a cutting board, a knife, and a potato. He grabbed his own, and they stood next to each other at the counter. His hand made quick work of the potato and she watched, seemingly hypnotized by the motion of the knife on his board.

"I… I don't think I can do that."

"Yes, you can, I'll help. Just relax." He moved behind her and placed his hand over hers and helped her make slow and deliberate cuts, while also avoiding her fingers. "The hand holding the potato, curve your fingers under, you don't want the knife to accidentally take fingertips with it." She grimaced and pulled her fingers in.

With the potatoes cut, he lined a baking sheet with foil and spread the potatoes across the sheet then coated them in olive oil. Reaching into the spice cabinet, he pulled down salt, pepper, and rosemary, which he sprinkled on the potatoes before tossing them into the oven.

Wiping his hands on his shorts, he opened the fridge and pulled out a nauseating beer. He popped the can open, and took a swig before he held it up to her, in a silent question. She nodded so he pulled another one out and tossed it to her, which she caught. Impressive.

"All right, let's take this horrendous beer out back and get the grill going."

She trailed behind him like a puppy dog as they went outside to his postage-stamp sized backyard. The grill took up most of it, to be honest. As he turned on the gas, he chuckled.

"What's so funny?"

"I was actually on that buying and selling website because I was trying to sell my grill when I stumbled on your ad. Guess it's a good thing no one wanted it."

"Guess so," she said as she took a drink of beer, making a face.

"Okay, grill's warming up, let's go get the burgers ready."

Once again, he traipsed to the kitchen and pulled the meat out of the fridge. He dumped the hamburger into a bowl. "Some people will tell you to put an egg in burger mixture, others breadcrumbs, to keep them moist. I haven't found that either really works, and I prefer not to mar my burgers with that stuff, so we'll just spice them up."

He dumped salt, pepper, garlic powder, and onion powder on top of the ground meat. She looked at the contents of the bowl and then back at him.

"Now what?"

"Now you put those pretty little hands in that bowl and mix it up." He motioned at her perfectly-manicured fingers that were painted blood red.

"You want me to put my hands in raw ground up cow?"

"You wanted to learn how to cook for a man, right? This is nothing compared to gutting a fish. I wasn't planning on that, but you keep this up and I just might. Now, massage those spices into the meat." His Army voice came out, he didn't mean it to, but it did, and she looked scared as she dropped her hands into the meat.

She squeezed the meat through her fingers, a cringe plastered on her face. When she had sufficiently mixed everything together she looked at him hopefully as she moved to the sink.

"Nope, not so fast."

He used his hand to score four quarters in the meat. He pulled out one of the quarters and dropped it into her hand. "Now we form the patties." He reached for another quarter and quickly formed a round disc of meat. She tried, but hers kept falling apart. He took it from her hand and made another burger. Her face was a mix of discouragement and frustration.

"Don't feel bad, it takes practice to learn how to make burgers that don't fall apart."

He formed a couple more patties and placed them on a plate. He washed his hands and walked back out to the grill, Erica following along behind.

Fifteen minutes later he placed a handful of good looking burgers on the table.

"Can I set the table?" she said. "I need to do something, and setting the table is something I know how to do. It was my job growing up. My brothers had to take out the trash every night after dinner, and I had to set the table. Mom was big on it, and I always got yelled at when I put the knife on the wrong side of the plate, so I learned how to do it right really quickly."

He handed her some plates and silverware with a smile. "I promise I won't yell if the knives are wrong," he said, making sure there were no remnants of the Army voice in his words.

Returning to the kitchen, he pulled out buns, lettuce, a tomato, and condiments. Then he removed the oven fries and turned off the oven.

He pulled the bottle of red wine out of the refrigerator, but was dismayed when he checked the cabinet and found no wine glasses. He sighed and pulled out two regular glasses, and then he rummaged around in the drawer to find a corkscrew. Once again, he came up short, but he knew he had one in his Swiss Army knife. He pulled the knife out of his pocket and placed it on the table next to the wine and two perfectly-set places.

"We can eat now," he called to Erica, who had disappeared into his living room.

She returned to him, her eyes wide. "You lied to me."

He cocked his head to the side, confused.

"You said you weren't a killer, but you are. You're a Ranger."

"I was a Ranger, yes," he said, dropping his head.

"Have you killed anyone?"

He closed his eyes and was immediately taken back to his first kill. It was the first of many, but the first was the only one that haunted him from time to time. The man came up behind him in the dark, his footfalls silent until he tripped, which is what made Kestin turn around. He made eye contact with the man before he fired his weapon. As it turns out, the guy was there to set a bomb and Kestin's kill saved the entire unit. Even so, taking his first human life was a little hard for him to handle, despite the fact this stranger was on a mission to take more than just one. Perspiration formed on his forehead and he wiped it away.

He nodded and refused to look at her.

She stepped closer and placed her arm around his shoulder. "It's not easy for you, is it?" He shook his head. "It's okay, I trust you."

"I've done nothing to earn your trust." He stiffened. "In fact, I withheld information that may have altered your decision."

"No, you withheld information that you didn't think was relevant to the job I was asking you to do, I can't really hold that against you. I mean, I could, but that wouldn't be the least bit fair, now would it?"

She sat down, as if she was proving her point that she wasn't running scared. She looked at the glasses next to the wine bottle and laughed.

"Sorry," he mumbled as he sat down. "My ex apparently took off with my wine glasses and my corkscrew, along with my dignity."

Erica reached out and placed a hand atop his. "You're still plenty dignified."

He gave her a shy smile as he screwed the Swiss Army knife into the cork. They ate in silence, with only the sounds of her fork and knife on the plate to fill the void in conversation—not that he understood why she needed a fork and knife for burgers and fries. He wasn't sure if she'd ever gone that long without speaking.

When she finished her burger, she pushed her plate back. "That was amazing. I don't know that I'll be able to recreate this, but it definitely was good."

"You just have to practice," he said, not looking at her.

"Can I ask a question?"

"Can't promise I'll answer it." It was a lie, there was something about her that made him want to spill every secret he ever had and he'd only known her an hour.

"Fair enough." She motioned to his leg. "How did it happen?"

He sighed, he hadn't told this story to anyone outside of Aubrey. "I was in Afghanistan, it was my second tour there. I was driving the Humvee, and an IED sent us flying. I should have seen it, I should have dodged it, a lot of should-have-beens." He paused and took a deep breath. "There were four of us. All of us came home—two of us in coffins, the other two broken beyond repair. We were lucky. At least that's what they tell me anyway."

"You are definitely not broken," she whispered as she reached out and touched his hand. Shivers of excitement ran up his arm at her touch. "I'm sorry I didn't trust you."

"It's okay, I've given you no reason to."

"But I do now."

"Again, I've given you no reason to."

"You opened up to me, I can tell it's not easy for you. That's enough."

He rolled his eyes. "You sound like my shrink."

"Well, I am one, so, that might explain that."

He jerked his hand back. He hated shrinks. His shrink made him feel like complete crap for refusing to get behind the wheel again, and even worse for being suicidal after he returned home from war without a leg to find his wife had left him.

"You've had a bad experience with therapists. It's written all over your face." She softened her gaze. "I'm not here as a therapist, I'm here as a student. Remember? I promise all the Freud mumbo-jumbo stays in my office and out of my personal life. I mean, not really, sometimes he comes up when people ask me a question, but I'll be honest, I think he was a little off on most everything, but there was some merit to some of his stuff. However, I've never had penis envy and my brother never had a thing for my mom. That I know of, anyway."

His face cracked into a tiny smile. "You always keep talking, don't you?"

"Yes, often to my detriment. Which is why I'm thirty-two, single, and begging some stranger to teach me how to cook so I could impress a man someday."

He looked up and right into her green eyes. He could get lost in those eyes. They were gorgeous. That wasn't why she was here, he reminded himself.

"Would you like pie?" he said.

"I thought you'd never ask."

~ * ~

Date: Mon, 25 April 2016 01:12 AM
From: "Erica Willis" <ewillis5-0@mail.com>
To: "B. Kestin" <Kestin83@gmail.com>
Subject: Thank You

Kestin,

I just wanted to thank you for my lesson tonight, and the fantastic meal. I don't know that I've had a meal that good in a very long time, maybe ever.

Also, thank you for sending me home with pie, but, in the interest of honesty, I have already eaten it all. I was watching an episode of "Hoarders" on the DVR. It's work research, I swear—okay, well, I can usually diagnose their problem before the producers of the show reveal it, so I consider it great practice. Anyway, I was hungry while I watched and I ended up eating it all. (My cat, Belle, licked the plate clean, so she clearly approves of your cooking.)

I'm not really that much of a food hoarder, but it was so good. I'm not a runner, but if I was, I'd totally run it off tomorrow.

I can't wait for our next lesson.
Erica

~ * ~

Date: Tues, 26 April 2016 11:45 PM
From: "B. Kestin" <Kestin83@gmail.com>
To: "Erica Willis" <ewillis5-0@mail.com>
Subject: You're Welcome

Erica,
You're very welcome for dinner, and for the pie. If we're being honest, I ate another piece after you left as well. I can teach you how to make pie crust, it's not as hard as you might think, and then you will have something to share with your cat.

Why don't you come over Friday night at six? We'll make pizza.
K-

~ * ~

Date: Wed, 27 April 2016 7:30 AM
From: "Erica Willis" <ewillis5-0@mail.com>
To: "B. Kestin" <Kestin83@gmail.com>
Subject: RE: You're Welcome

Kestin,
Ohh, pizza. I do love pizza. It's probably one of my favorite foods, ever. Well, aside from that pie you made, that was pretty amazing too.

Of course, I'm sure everything you make is amazing.
Friday at six works for me.
Erica

~ * ~

Kestin almost wished his hair was longer so he could do something with it. Almost. It was dinner on a Friday night and felt like a date. Except it wasn't. It was a job. He paid extra close attention when he shaved though. If he couldn't fancy up his hair, at least he could get a good shave to improve his haggard appearance.

Fifteen minutes before six, the doorbell rang. He was starting to think she didn't know what the meaning of the word "late" or hell, even "on time."

He opened the door and was pleased to see her with a twelve-pack of Miller in her hand. Ahh, real beer.

With a smile and a side-step away from the door, he let her enter. She walked into the kitchen and put the beer in the fridge as if she owned the place. For some reason, Kestin was oddly okay with that.

She turned to him with her hands on her hips. "Please tell me you still have pie. I've been craving that pie all week."

Regret consumed him as he shook his head. "No, sorry. After you left Sunday and I ate some more, I realized I couldn't be trusted with it, so I gave the rest to my neighbor."

She snapped her fingers in disappointment. "Oh well, guess I don't need dessert anyway."

What the hell kind of nonsense is she talking?

"It's not a matter of need, it's want. If you want dessert, I'm sure I can whip something up, though no promises on how good it is. It might have dehydrated things that used to resemble fruit that I pilfered from MREs."

Her laughter filled the room and his heart beat double-time at the sound. "MREs? You mean those awful things you have to eat in the field with a shelf life of, like the end of time, right?"

"Not quite that long, but yes. They are god-awful. Anyone military who says they like them is a liar." He took several steps through his galley kitchen and peered into the pantry. Flour and sugar, both pretty full bags. Okay, so he could do pie or cake or cookies. That was a step in the right direction. He pulled them out and set them on the counter.

Next up, the fridge where he found four eggs. Better than no eggs. Plenty of butter. He could work with this.

"Hey, Erica, there's a cookbook on the top shelf of the pantry, can you pull it out for me, please?"

"Of course." She breezed behind him, her hand grazing the small of his back in the process. He started to pull ingredients out of the fridge—milk, eggs, butter—and set them on the counter next to the flour.

Then he pulled out baking powder, cornstarch, and vanilla extract, followed by a big bowl and two round cake pans.

"Oh, goody, cake," she said when she saw the cake pans. "You told me you were going to teach me how to do that."

He gave her a smile to make it look like he did it on purpose, the truth was that he had completely forgotten about teaching her cake. He forgot a lot when he was around her.

Taking the book from her hands, he opened to the page marked with the ribbon bookmark. He should have the recipe memorized by now, he'd made it so many times over the years, but he always pulled it out just to make sure he got the measurements correct.

He rummaged around in a drawer and produced a small handheld mixer.

"Well, that's a bit disappointing," she said, looking at the tool in his hand.

"You have no idea," he muttered. "There was a time I had a nice one. Although Marie left most everything in the kitchen alone, it seems the mixer and my wine glasses didn't escape her path of destruction out of here. She didn't have a clue what it was used for, but she knew how much it cost, so I bet that's why she took it." He paused a moment. "Or the fact she knew it would piss me the hell off."

Erica rested her hand on his arm. "Stop. Don't let her live in your head anymore. Whatever she took, she took. It's stuff, it can be replaced."

Her words echoed through his mind. Sure, his sister and Jack both had said similar over the past few months, but the words just didn't seem to make sense until they fell from Erica's lips. Her hand was still on his arm, and she looked at him with an expectant smile.

"Uh, okay, so I don't have measuring cups, but I do have a scale, so we're going to measure everything out by weight, okay? It's a bit more time consuming but it's also more accurate."

"Whatever you say, you're the teacher here." She winked. "I'll blindly follow whatever you tell me to do."

Twenty minutes later they had the cake batter ready. He handed her a pan and a stick of butter, and she looked at him with her head tilted to the side. She really was adorable when she had no clue what was going on.

"We're going to flour the pans." She continued to look at him like he was speaking Greek, so he took the butter out of her hand and picked up his own pan. "Just watch."

He ran the stick of butter around the inside of the pan, making sure the slimy sheen of butter covered every interior surface. He dug his hand into the bag of flour and dropped some in the pan. He tilted the pan, tapping and rotating ever so slightly to spread the flour around. When the pan was completely coated, he dumped the excess in the sink and held it up.

"Voilà," he said, his southern accent butchering the foreign word.

She picked up the butter and coated her pan, a triumphant smile on her face when she was done. She hesitated, so he pointed to the bag of flour. She reached in and emerged with a large handful and dumped it into the pan.

"Whoa, little much," Kestin said with a laugh. "But it's okay."

She tapped the pan and twirled it around with jerky, imprecise movements that reminded him of when he tried and failed at labyrinth puzzles with his sister. It didn't take too long before Erica failed to contain the flour and it flew everywhere.

His gaze dropped to the white dust on the floor, on her pretty blue shirt, and all over the front of his jeans.

"I'm so sorry," she said. She set the pan down on the counter with a dejected sigh. "I'm hopeless."

"You are not hopeless." He stepped to the pantry and pulled out the broom. "No harm, no foul. I'm not looking to impress anyone right now, I don't care if I have flour on me."

Hurt flashed across her face before it was replaced with a playful smile. She stepped forward and placed her flour covered hand on his chest, leaving a white handprint on his black t-shirt.

It was the closest he'd been to her, hell, to any woman since before he left for Afghanistan. Worst of all, he didn't know what to do about it.

Part of him told him to kiss her.

Part of him told him to push her away.

Part of him wanted to run in the bedroom and hide.

His heart raced beneath her touch. When she put her other hand on his chest, he thought it might damn near explode.

She was right there, with the most adorable smile he'd ever seen. He took a deep breath. She closed her eyes and stood on her tiptoes.

What was she doing?

He couldn't do this. This was wrong.

He grabbed both of her wrists, nudged her away, and reached for the broom. As he swept up the flour, she disappeared out of the kitchen and he swore he heard crying in the other room.

~ * ~

Date: Sat, 30 April 2016 3:45 AM
From: "B. Kestin" <Kestin83@gmail.com>
To: "Erica Willis" <ewillis5-0@mail.com>
Subject: I'm sorry—please don't hate me
Erica,

I have been unable to sleep all night, because I know I hurt you tonight and I'm sorry. I don't ever want to hurt anyone—least of all you.

Will you please allow me the opportunity to make it up to you on Friday night? Does Italian sound good? Chicken parmesan and cannolis?

K-

~ * ~

Date: Sat, 30 April 2016 4:30 PM
From: "Erica Willis" <ewillis5-0@mail.com>
To: "B. Kestin" <Kestin83@gmail.com>
Subject: RE: I'm sorry—please don't hate me

Kestin,

First of all, I don't hate you. You didn't hurt me, I hurt myself.

I would love to come over on Friday for dinner. I've never had a cannoli before.

Should I bring white wine this time?
Erica

~ * ~

Date: Sun, 1 May 2016 7:31 AM
From: "B. Kestin" <Kestin83@gmail.com>
To: "Erica Willis" <ewillis5-0@mail.com>
Subject: RE: RE: I'm sorry—please don't hate me

Erica,
No, we can do just fine with the wine we have. It may
not be the perfect match, but there's no need for you to buy
more.
I'll see you at six. I can't wait.
K-

~ * ~

Kestin was more than a little excited. He spent Thursday night making cannoli shells and frying them, so they'd be ready. He fell asleep on the couch covered from head to toe in flour and grease, his prosthesis still attached.

The car down the street backfired, which pulled Kestin from his slumber Friday morning. He rolled off the couch, his heart pounding. By the time he realized where he was, he was covered in perspiration and pain tore through his leg; he knew it was going to be a bad day. Sleeping in the prosthesis was never a good thing, his stump needed time to breathe, and seeing as how he had to go grocery shopping, going without it wasn't going to be an option.

He removed the prosthetic long enough to rinse the socket and take a shower. He made sure to dry his stump thoroughly before he put the leg back on, but it was tight, still slightly swollen. He took some ibuprofen and prayed for the best.

He and Mrs. Sanchez went shopping, and not only did he pick up all the ingredients for dinner and some real beer, as promised, but also some wine glasses, a real corkscrew, and taper candles for his table. The old woman looked at him with a knowing smile and suggested he pick up some flowers, too. How did she know he needed to make amends? Was his ineptitude with women that obvious?

He made it through the store just fine, but by the time he got home, his leg was screaming for relief. Unfortunately, he had a cooking lesson to get through, and whereas he was pretty sure Erica would understand if he called to cancel, he really wanted to see her. The promise of seeing her again is what got him through the day. He took a couple more ibuprofen, chased them with a beer, and pulled out all the ingredients for dinner. They were going to start with cannoli cream because it had to chill.

At quarter to six, the doorbell broke the silence of his house, and ripped his mind from constant focus of pain. He grabbed the flowers off the table and opened the door to find her standing there, shoulders tense and a loaf of garlic bread in her hand.

"My mom told me to never go somewhere empty-handed, and since you said I didn't need to buy wine, I needed to do something. I hope you haven't made garlic bread from scratch, because then I'll feel really dumb for going to the bakery to get this."

He laughed quietly as he closed the door behind her. "Actually, that's perfect because I forgot to buy some." He glanced down at the red roses in his hand and held them up. "Here, these are for you."

Her shoulders dropped and a large grin formed on her lips as she put her nose into one of the buds.

Everything seemed to be okay between them again so he let out a small sigh of relief before he walked to the kitchen. When he turned around, she had a look of concern on her face.

"You're not walking right, is everything okay?"

"I have a fake leg, I will never walk right again."

"No, you're having a much harder time than you did last week."

He sighed. She was perceptive, he'd give her that.

"I fell asleep in it last night, so I didn't give it time to rest. It's been bothering me all day, but the ibuprofen I took should kick in soon and I'll be okay."

"No, no, no. None of that," she said, nudging him into a chair. "I'm here for cooking lessons, so, you tell me what to do, and I'll do it. Trial by fire."

He grimaced at her words. Since coming home from the desert, that wasn't a phrase he particularly cared for. If only people knew what a real trial by fire was.

"Okay," he agreed, but only because he knew if he didn't, she'd go on some long-winded story about how she had to do something like this when she was seven and it changed her life forever. Not that he'd really mind if she talked—on the contrary—but he was hungry.

~ * ~

Three hours later, he had successfully talked her through cannoli cream and chicken parmesan. Then he cringed through the pain while he helped clean the kitchen.

Once the dishes were done, he collapsed onto the recliner. He couldn't see because of the jeans he wore, but he could tell his stump was swollen. He needed to take the leg off, but that would involve kicking her out, and that was the last thing he wanted to do.

She sat down on the couch and twirled the stem of a brand-new wine glass between her fingers. "You know, you can go take it off, I won't mind. If you want me to leave, I will. I get that you're tired and in pain."

"I am, but I don't want you to leave." *Ever.*

"Well, go take care of you, and I'll wait, okay?"

He slowly stood and limped to the bedroom where he grabbed a pair of shorts before he hobbled into the bathroom. Twenty minutes later he returned to the living room. He had some ointment and a wrap to cover the open wound from where his prosthetic rubbed him wrong for too long.

"I'm sorry," he whispered. "I should have cleaned the wound in the bathroom. I just usually use the light there." He motioned to the reading lamp behind his recliner before he turned to go back down the hall.

"No, don't worry about it. I've seen worse, I guarantee it. In fact, I bet you I can clean that up better than you can." She put her hand out and led him back to the chair.

"You don't have to do that," he said as he landed in the recliner.

She set her empty wine glass on the coffee table and knelt in front of him. "Shhh. Just let me do something for you. This entire relationship has been about me taking. Let me give something." She took the medicated ointment, gauze, and wrap out of his hand and leaned back so she was sitting on her heels.

Moving quickly, she slathered the ointment on his stump, then blew lightly to alleviate any sting. Oh, God, those lips. Within seconds it was wrapped, and she was right, she did a better job than he ever could.

"That's amazing."

From her spot on the floor, she beamed. "What I didn't tell you was that Daddy also lost a leg. Mama couldn't handle the sight of blood, so I was the one who had the job of helping him. That's why I'm a head doctor, not a real doctor."

"How did it happen?" His voice was practically a whisper. He loved having her hands on him. His stump was the most personal, private place he had on his body these days, and she just dove in headfirst.

"Gangrene. He was diabetic and stupid and refused to go to the doctor for as long as he could. In the end, it was too late to save it. Let me tell you, that tiny little wound you've got there is nothing, absolutely nothing, compared to gangrene."

"You're a good daughter. A good person."

"You're a good person, despite the fact you're convinced otherwise."

"How do you know that?"

She sat up a bit straighter. "Your reserved nature, the way you close yourself off at the mention of things, the PTSD. All of it culminates together in the fact you don't think you're worth much, and I'm here to tell you that you are."

"Did you just go all therapist on me?"

She shook her head and stood. "No. I went all woman who is madly attracted to you."

The words swirled in his head and her lips dropped down to his. They were soft and warm, and everything he imagined they would be. What he didn't expect was how insistent they were, how strong, how much they wanted to be on his.

He tugged her down so she sat on his lap and pulled her close as if he was squeezing out all the air between them. Her hands found their way behind his head and her fingers lightly traced the lines of his neck while her tongue caressed his. His mind was everywhere at once, and he wasn't sure if he should stop or take her right then and there in his recliner.

She finally pulled her head back with a slight chuckle. "Wow, and I thought it was just me."

"Definitely not just you. I've wanted to do that the moment you walked in the door and started rambling about wine a couple weeks ago."

"Well, now that you have me here, what are you going to do with me?"

His hand wandered beneath the hem of her shirt and touched bare skin with a feather light touch and she squirmed.

"Ticklish?" he said as his hand stilled.

"Very much so," she whispered. "But that doesn't mean you need to stop."

~ * ~

For the first time since he returned from Afghanistan horribly damaged, he was starting to feel like the damage wasn't beyond repair. Erica certainly didn't think so.

She started coming over every night for dinner, and it didn't take long before she could handle some things without his constant supervision, including wielding a knife correctly. That made him proud. He had taught her everything he promised, except the cheesecake. Part of him hated to do it, because once he did, she would have no use for him anymore, and she might give him the money and run.

He didn't even want the money anymore. Hell, because they used it so often, he'd even taken down the ad to sell the grill. He loved the fact it was no longer marred by shame and rejection, but rather a symbol of the hope that she gave him. She seemed to fill a void he didn't even think he wanted filled after Marie left him.

One Monday afternoon, just before he expected Erica to arrive, motion out the front curtains, one of the few things Marie actually left in the house, caught Kestin's attention. He smiled when he saw his diminutive landlady pounding a For Rent sign into the parched Georgia clay. He picked up his phone and dialed his sister.

"Hey Aubs, what's your favorite scary movie?"

"The one where my brother tells me he hasn't done a damn thing I asked him to do."

Kestin bit back laughter. "Never seen it."

"It's a doozy, I'm not sure you could handle it, though."

"Well, I just called to tell you that my landlord is outside struggling to put a sign in the yard now. I've started packing up a few things, too. So you can take your holier-than-thou attitude and shove it up your behind." He kicked a stack of boxes in front of him.

She burst out laughing. "Well, fiddle-dee-dee, he can do what is asked of him."

"Yeah, I just have to finish this job I've got going here, I still have to teach Erica to make cheesecake, it's the one thing she wanted me to teach her."

"You're sweet on her, aren't you?"

"No, yes, maybe, I don't know. She's a damn fine kisser though, let me tell you."

"Oh, dude, I don't want to know. I really don't. And way to mix business with pleasure you dirty bum."

He laughed. She had a point, much as he hated to admit it. "She and I should finish up in this week."

"Okay then. James is home this weekend, so we'll be there on Saturday. Can you teach her cream puffs or wedding cakes or whatever the hell it is you do and get packed by then?" He looked around his house. There wasn't too much left to pack.

"Aye, aye captain." He looked at the clock and gasped. "Speaking of her, she's supposed to be here in fifteen minutes, which means—" The doorbell interrupted his words. "She's here right now. Always early, that girl is."

"Have fun tonight. See you Saturday."

He slammed the phone down on the counter as he went to the door and answered it. Erica was standing on the porch and the red that rimmed her eyes told him something was amiss.

"What's wrong?"

She narrowed her eyes at him and took a deep breath. "Would you mind telling me what's going on with the For Rent sign?"

"I should think that's obvious, the landlady needs a new tenant."

"But why?" She stepped inside and slammed the door closed behind her.

He took her hands in his as he led her to the table. He plucked a rose from the vase on the table. He'd been stealing roses out of Mrs. Sanchez's yard to keep on hand now that Erica was coming over regularly. He ran the soft petals across the skin of her face. He dropped his lips to her forehead.

"Erica, sweetheart, I have something to tell you."

"Obviously," she said as she took the rose from his hand and placed it on the table. She turned on her therapist gaze and stared at him until he had to look away.

He sighed. "This weekend I'll be moving to Savannah to live with my sister."

Erica stared at him blankly.

"She's been begging me to move out since it happened," he said motioning to his leg. "I always told her no because I had a roommate, but he just got stationed elsewhere, and the fact is, I can't afford this place on just my disability. It's for the best."

The look she gave him chilled him to the bone. She placed her hands in her lap and stared at them. "I see."

"You see?"

"Why couldn't you tell me sooner?"

"I blame you for that, actually," he said with a laugh. "Every time I wanted to tell you, somehow or another you distracted me. Your lips, your skin, your smile, everything about you has a way of distracting me and I just forgot."

"You just forgot?"

"I enjoyed being with you so much, every thought except how to please you flew out of my mind. You should take that as the utmost compliment."

"A compliment?" She crossed her arms in front of her and glared.

"Seriously, what is up with the role reversal? Since when are you the one who doesn't talk?"

"Since you had to go and ruin my life. I thought we had something, you and me. Turns out it only was me because you could just up and walk away from it."

"It's not easy for me," Kestin said throwing his hands in the air. "The fact is I need help. I can't drive, I can't work. There's not a whole lot I can do these days."

The chair flew back as she stood. She yanked her purse off the table and stormed out of the house.

~ * ~

Date: Mon, 16 May 2016 6:45 PM
From: "B. Kestin" <Kestin83@gmail.com>
To: "Erica Willis" <ewillis5-0@mail.com>
Subject: I'm sorry, again

Erica,

I'm sorry. I'm sorry. I'm sorry. I'm sorry. I cannot say I'm sorry enough times. It seems I'm always apologizing for something.

That definitely did not go how I planned it. I can only plead ignorance.

I hope you don't hate me. I understand I hurt you, and I can never take that back. I hope all the good times we had in my kitchen can far outweigh that one bad one in your mind. God knows they do for me.

Erica, you're what I think of when I go to sleep every night, and you're the first thought that runs through my mind every morning. If you think that will change when I'm in a different ZIP code, you're sadly mistaken. I don't know that I can ever think of anything else, nor do I even want that. You give my life so much more purpose.

With you, I don't think about the fact I'm broken and can't run. Hell, when I'm with you, I feel like I could fly.

My sister will be here on Saturday I will pull out of this driveway for the last time. I really hope I get to see you again before I leave.

K-

~ * ~

Date: Sat, 21 May 2016 9:14 AM
From: "B. Kestin" <Kestin83@gmail.com>

To: "Erica Willis" <ewillis5-0@mail.com>
Subject: I guess this is goodbye

Erica-

My sweet, sweet Erica, I'm so sorry I hurt you. Far deeper than I ever intended, apparently. Your silence for the past few days tells me I shouldn't even type this email, but since I'm getting ready to disconnect the Wi-Fi, I wanted to use my last opportunity to tell you that I'm sorry for hurting you.

You will still be in my thoughts all the time. I don't know that I'll ever be able to shake you, nor do I want to. You give me purpose, more than the Army ever did.

K-

~ * ~

Kestin closed his laptop and disconnected the router. He tossed the computer and all the cables into a box, and then he loaded it into the backseat of his truck.

He walked back into the house and took one last look around.

There was the counter where they tossed flour everywhere while he taught her to make pie crust.

There was the crystal vase full of flowers he'd kept on his table for the past few weeks. He had placed it on the counter as a gift for the next tenants—along with the grill in the backyard. He didn't want to drag those physical reminders of his memories across the state with him. Those that clouded his thoughts were more than enough.

He fingered the switch before he turned the lights off one last time as he left the house.

The door slammed shut behind him. He walked out as James slammed the tailgate shut and checked the bungee cords holding his life's possessions in the bed of the truck. Peals of laughter floated to his ears—Aubrey's and Erica's, and his heart skipped a beat. *What is she doing here?*

He walked around the truck and eyed the two laughing females with a raised eyebrow. Erica shot him a tiny smile.

"I'm going to go see if James needs any help before he leaves," Aubrey said, making a quick getaway.

Erica held up a round cake covered in chocolate icing. "It's Boston Crème Pie, your favorite."

"You remembered."

"Of course I remembered," she whispered. "I will never, ever forget anything about you." She held the cake up to him and he glanced down. In shaky, red icing, the words "I love you" were written on the cake. "It's not pretty, but it was my first time."

"It's gorgeous," he whispered taking the cake from her and setting it on the hood of the truck. "But you're way more gorgeous." He pulled her tightly against him and kissed her like it was their first time all over again.

"Ignoring you has been the hardest thing I've ever done, and I was bound and determined to do it forever. I read your emails over and over again. I finally realized I was so hurt because I loved you and I couldn't let you walk away without telling you that."

"I love you, too," he whispered. "I never thought I'd get a chance to tell you."

"Now that you are hopelessly in love with me, will you tell me something?"

"Anything."

"What's the B. stand for? I've wanted to ask forever, but…"

"Okay, well, anything but that."

"I can always ask your sister."

"She won't tell you, not if she knows what's good for her."

She giggled. "Come on, what's the harm? I'm out of your life after this."

"You are most certainly not out of my life, and you're a fool if you think you are. We'll find a way to make this work." He kissed her lips one more time, languidly, lingering, putting off the inevitable. "For now, my love, I must go. I will text you when I get to Savannah."

~ * ~

The ride to Savannah was four-and-a-half-hours, but it felt like an eternity. The entire time, Kestin struggled to keep it together. He didn't want his sister to see what a big wuss he had become. Hell, he used to be part of one of the most elite military forces on the planet, and now just riding down the interstate sent his heart racing, his eyes darting all around, looking for a perceived threat that wasn't there.

When he couldn't handle it any longer, he wrestled the orange pill bottle free from his rucksack. He swallowed the tiny white pill without water, leaned back into the seat, and closed his eyes. His concentration centered on slowing the erratic song his heart beat out against his will.

A hand rested on his arm. "Kes, it's okay. Just breathe."

His hand grasped hers, and he immediately regretted it because it was sweaty and gross. He retracted his hand and wiped it on his jeans.

"Take a couple deep breaths, and then talk to me," Aubrey said calmly. Her voice was settling, it brought him back to where he was. "You're not there anymore and you don't ever have to go back."

He took a deep breath. "Thank you. I know it seems crazy."

Silence. He opened his eyes a slit and looked at his sister who shook her head. "Not crazy at all, big brother. But, remember, we can't do everything by ourselves. Sometimes you just need a hand to hold, and that's why I'm here."

She meant well, he knew she did. He loved the fact he was going to stay with her, because they'd always been close. The truth of the matter was, though, her hand wasn't the one he wanted to hold. He took a quick glance at the cake on the backseat. Regret filled his heart, and he turned back. He slumped down in his seat until the seatbelt sliced across his throat.

"Tell me about it."

"No."

"How can I help if I don't know what demon you're fighting?"

He looked down at his leg and then back at his sister. "You know very well what demon I'm fighting. You're driving my truck, for God's sake."

"Tell me about something else, then. Tell me about tanks."

Kestin snorted. "Hell on Earth."

"But they're so cool. They take no prisoners as they cross terrain, charging forward on their mission. That's how I always pictured you. You were my tank." She paused. "Are my tank."

"You had it right the first time," he said with an exasperated sigh as he glanced out the window. The mileage sign told him that Savannah was still a couple hours away. "I'm nothing like I was."

"You are still my big brother, and always will be. Nothing else matters."

He took a breath. "I'm nothing like the big brother who shipped out."

"You're better. Look what you've overcome. You're stronger than I could ever be." A laugh escaped his throat before he could stop it and she glared at him. "I mean it."

He exhaled deeply. "A tank is the one of the most awful place to be." He studied her face as she stared out the windshield, debating whether he should continue. "You're stuffed into this thing like sardines, rolling through foreign territory completely blind. You have no idea what's out there, plotting your demise. The smell of sweat and fear grips you, clings to you, and clouds your thoughts. You're locked and loaded, but your mind is thinking about anything else, everything else. Every time I got in a tank, I was convinced it was my last ride."

She turned to him and gave a tiny smile. "But it wasn't. You're in the truck with me."

The brake lights of the car in front of them lit up, but Aubrey continued forward. Kestin slammed his hands into the dashboard to brace himself, breathing hard. "If you don't pay attention, this will be my last damn ride. Pay attention, woman."

Aubrey slammed the brakes and the grill of his precious Dodge Ram stopped mere inches before it ate the trunk of a bright red Honda Accord. "I had plenty of room," she lied.

He rolled his eyes before he leaned back and closed them again. His dreams weren't really a pleasant place to be, but neither was the truck. "Wake me up in Savannah. If we live long enough to make it there."

~ * ~

Date: Sun, 22 May 2016 6:23 AM
From: "B. Kestin" <Kestin83@gmail.com>
To: "Erica Willis" <ewillis5-0@mail.com>
Subject: Hello from Savannah

My dearest Erica,

I made it to Savannah in one piece, though, admittedly, there was a point there where I thought Aubrey was set on taking us both out, along with the driver of an Accord.

Your Boston Crème Pie was delicious. Even Aubrey and James thought so. I have a hard time believing you couldn't do anything in the kitchen before you met me because you picked up everything so quickly. I am so proud.

I miss you. I cooked dinner for Aubs, and even though I knew it wasn't my kitchen, I still longed to see you walk through that door with a bottle of wine. (Or two.) It will take me more time to adjust to not seeing you than it will to actually being here.

Love,

K-

P.S. Beau. The B stands for Beau. I'm fully convinced my parents hated me from birth.

~ * ~

Date: Mon, 23 May 2016 9:18 PM
From: "Erica Willis" <ewillis5-0@mail.com>
To: "B. Kestin" <Kestin83@gmail.com>
Subject: Missing you

Kestin,

My love, my sweet, thank you for trusting me with the secret that is your name. I promise I will never call you that. Though, I find it hilarious my cat is Belle and you are—well, I said I wouldn't say it.

I have to admit, it's been hard for me not going over to your place for dinner. I was craving burgers yesterday so I made some on the new George Foreman grill I bought and they turned out okay. They weren't as good as yours, but, well, I'm pretty sure nothing I can make will compare to anything you can. Belle approved, though, and she ate one, quite voraciously, in fact.

I'm glad you like the Boston Crème Pie. It took me a couple different tries to get it. I won't say get it right, because I don't know if I did, but I tried and that's the important part. My neighbors got to eat all the rejects and they were happy with them as well. See, and you doubted yourself as a teacher.

I hope you didn't have too much anxiety on the drive. You try to hide it, but I know it's still there, and it's okay. It's really okay, no matter what your military-appointed-shrink tried to tell you.

For me, I've spent the past couple nights cooking and then eating my feelings. When I finished eating my feelings, I'd wash them down with some wine. So, take that for what you will. You've got me cooking, so that's good, but on the flip side, I'm going to wind up fat and alcoholic in my newfound loneliness, so that's not so good. Maybe I need to sit down and have a therapy session with myself.

I have a peach pie in the oven. I saw some pink peaches at the store today and couldn't resist, they are my favorite. Have you ever had the pink peaches? Of course you have, you live in Georgia. What kind of silly question was that?

Sdgljh3e4

Sorry, Belle just walked across my keyboard, she clearly wants some attention, and maybe some peach pie.

I miss you more each and every day. I love you.

E-

~ * ~

Date: Tues, 24 May 2016 11:21 PM
From: "B. Kestin" <Kestin83@gmail.com>
To: "Erica Willis" <ewillis5-0@mail.com>
Subject: Missing you more

Erica,

I'm sorry I have been quiet—I just am at a loss for what to say. Normally words flow so easily when it comes to you. You're like Aubs in that respect. She's the only other person in the world I will actually talk to like that, even if I don't particularly care for what she's got me talking about.

I met my new therapist today. He's a prick and makes me feel crazy. He's definitely not as pretty as the therapist I left sobbing in my front yard.

I meet my other new doctor later this week. I probably won't like him either. I don't like doctors.

Come to think of it, there's not much I do like these days. Save for you.

Love,

K-

~ * ~

Date: Wed, 25 May 2016 9:37 AM
From: "Erica Willis" <ewillis5-0@mail.com>
To: "B. Kestin" <Kestin83@gmail.com>
Subject: Call me

Kestin,

Seriously, if you need to talk to someone who doesn't make you feel crazy, you can always call me. In fact, I'd prefer it. There are questionable therapists out there. I'm not saying those who have been assigned to you are. It's not my place to judge them. However, I know not everyone understands just how important their job is. As long as it's not during office hours, you can always call me. If it's the middle of the night, I will wake up for you. I promise. Your mental health is important to me. Everything about you is important to me.

I will always be here for you.

Because that's what you do when you love someone, right?

I love you.

E-

~ * ~

Date: Mon, 30 May 2016 10:11 PM
From: "Erica Willis" <ewillis5-0@mail.com>
To: "B. Kestin" <Kestin83@gmail.com>
Subject: Happy Memorial Day

K-

Are you okay? I haven't heard from you in almost a week.

It's Memorial Day, I'm sure it's a hard day for you. I wish I could be there to make it easier. Maybe I should make plans to visit Savannah this weekend. What do you think?

Please, please get in touch with me and let me know you're okay.

Love,

E-

~ * ~

Date: Fri, 03 June 2016 7:19 PM
From: "Erica Willis" <ewillis5-0@mail.com>
To: "B. Kestin" <Kestin83@gmail.com>
Subject: Now I'm really worried

K-

Okay, you're not answering my emails, my calls, my texts. Internet searches aren't bringing up anything for your sister, so I can't call her. I don't know another way to get in touch with you. I'm scared.

Please let me know you're okay.

Someone's at my door. I have to go. Call me. Please.

E-

~ * ~

Kestin took a deep breath and knocked on the door again. What was taking her so long? Damn, he felt foolish.

The sound of the chain being unlatched made him smile before the door cracked open.

When she opened the door completely, she flew through the doorway and wrapped her arms around him, knocking him off-balance. He grabbed the doorframe to steady himself. She rested her head just above his frantically beating heart.

"Oh, my God, Kestin, you had me so worried. I've been emailing, calling, texting, and nothing. I thought something happened to you."

"A lot happened, but the important part is that I'm home."

She pulled her head back and looked at him quizzically. "Home?"

"Home is where your heart is, right?" She nodded. "You have my heart. So clearly home is with you."

She wiped a tear from her eye and hugged him again. Then she pulled away abruptly. "How did you get here?"

"I drove."

Erica's green eyes grew wide. "You? You drove? You drove to—"

He dropped his lips to hers, silencing her barrage of questions. He pulled her against him, tightly, until he could feel her breath.

She abruptly pulled away. "Does your sister know where you are?"

He nodded. "She strongly advised me not to do the drive, but she knows."

"Text her right now and let her know you're safe and not in a ditch somewhere." Kestin chuckled at the authoritative tone as he pulled his phone out of his pocket and typed out a quick text.

He tossed his phone onto the couch. "There, all done, now where was I?" He pulled her close again. She fit so perfectly in his arms, against his chest.

Erica led him to the couch and sat down. "I can't believe you actually drove across the state for me. That must have been so incredibly hard."

A breath he didn't know he was holding escaped through his pursed lips. "I don't even want to admit how much Xanex it took, but I knew I had to be back on this side of the state. Aubs is great, but she's not where I want to be."

Erica's fingers traced the faded tattoo on his arm. "Where do you want to be?"

He dropped a soft kiss on her temple. "Wherever you are is where I *need* to be."

THE END

About the Author

Randi has spent her entire life writing in one form or another. In fact, if she wasn't writing, she'd likely go completely and utterly insane. Her husband has learned to recognize when the voices are talking in her head and she needs some quality time with an empty Word file (the key to a successful marriage with a writer).

She lives with her husband, daughter, and four-legged children (all of which think they are people, too).

A pop culture junkie, she has been known to have entire conversations in movie quotes and/or song lyrics.

She is the author of the Earthbound Angels paranormal romance series, which includes *Virtue of Death* and *Promises of Virtue*. She is also the author of the m/m novella *Wreck You,* and her short story "Just What I Need" was included in *Unintentional: North American Edition*, a friends-to-lovers anthology.

Author Contacts

Social Media links:
Facebook: www.facebook.com/randiperrinwrites
Twitter: www.twitter.com/RandiPerrin
Website: www.randiperrin.com
Pinterest: www.pinterest.com/RandiPerrin
Amazon: amazon.com/author/randiperrin
Goodreads: www.goodreads.com/RandiPerrin
Instagram: www.instagram.com/randiperrinwrites
Blog: randiperrin.wordpress.com

Boston Crème Pie

Cake Ingredients
- 1/2 cup shortening
- 1/2 cup butter
- 2 cups white sugar
- 4 eggs
- 2 teaspoons vanilla extract
- 2 1/2 cups all-purpose flour
- 1/4 cup cornstarch
- 1 1/2 teaspoons baking powder
- 1/2 teaspoon baking soda
- 1 teaspoon salt
- 1 3/4 cups milk

Pastry Cream Ingredients
- 2 cups milk (anything will work but nonfat)
- 1/2 vanilla bean, split lengthwise, seeds scraped out
- 4 egg yolks
- 1/2 cup granulated sugar
- 3 tablespoons cornstarch
- 1 tablespoon unsalted butter

Ganache Topping Ingredients
- 8 ounces semi-sweet chocolate
- 2/3 cup heavy cream
- 1 tablespoon unsalted butter

Cake
Preheat oven to 350 degrees F (175 degrees C).
Grease and flour two eight-inch cake pans.
Cream together butter, shortening and sugar.
Beat in eggs and vanilla.
Sift together flour, cornstarch, baking powder, baking soda, and salt.

Alternate adding milk and sifted flour mixture to the eggs. Mix well. Pour batter into prepared pans.

Bake for 20-25 minutes, or until cake tests done. Cool.

Pastry Cream:

Heat the milk and vanilla bean over medium heat until they begin to boil. Remove from heat and set aside for 10 to 15 minutes.

In a bowl, whisk the egg yolks and granulated sugar until light and fluffy.

Add the cornstarch and whisk vigorously until no lumps remain.

Whisk in 1/4 cup of the hot milk mixture until incorporated. Whisk in the remaining hot milk mixture, reserving the empty saucepan.

Pour the mixture through a strainer back into the saucepan.

Whisking constantly, cook mixture over medium-high heat, until it thickens.

Remove pan from the heat and stir in butter.

Cover with plastic wrap, pressing the plastic against the surface to prevent a skin from forming. Chill at least two hours or until ready to serve. NOTE: You can make the custard up to a day in advance.

Ganache:

Heat cream to a boil.

Pour heated cream over chocolate, stirring until melted completely.

Add butter and stir until melted.

Assembly:

Level cakes.

Place pastry cream on top of one cake and spread evenly.

Top with other cake.

Pour ganache on the top and over the sides of the cake.

Store in the refrigerator.

Coffee Cake Chaos

Ryan Jo Summers

Chapter One

Avianna's aunt and uncle desperately needed a new roof. That was the only reason she considered such an insane and difficult challenge. From the moment the ad fell into her hands, through all the reasons she tried to talk herself out of it, and ultimately to the firm resolution, she knew this was the answer they'd all sought.

She was going to bid for and win the catering event of the year. The income, combined with what everyone had already contributed, would pay for the new roof. She was going to cater Sawyer Steele's engagement celebration. Even if it meant she had to cry behind every closed door to do it.

As teens, she and Sawyer had dated. Avianna clutched the ad and notes tight, closed her eyes, and remembered those carefree days. Besides being the only child to the elite and wealthy Steele dynasty, Sawyer also possessed a wicked sense of humor. Back when he wore his dark hair long enough to infuriate his mother's sense of propriety, he could attract the attention of any female under the age of thirty. Yet he only wanted Avianna's.

Youth and time were their friends. They stole whatever time they could, always thinking they had the rest of their lives. It was Avianna's own personal Cinderella story, slowly unfolding each day of her life with

Sawyer.

Then his father became ill suddenly. He was not expected to live long. His mother stoutly forbade him further association with common girls. He was to settle down and be groomed to eventually take the reins of the Steele business. He cried as he broke the news to Avianna that day. Then he walked out of her life and back to his destiny.

She grew up to open a catering business. It lacked the power and resources of the Steele's, but it was her name on the sign and checkbook. Much of the money had come through her parents and aunt and uncle.

She looked at the ad's specifics and blinked, forcing herself to put distance between them back then and the situation facing her now. His mother needed someone to cater her son's engagement party, a complete planning package for two hundred guests in just a few short weeks. Her son would formally announce what everyone already knew. He was going to marry Miss Joselyn Oakley and take over as president and CEO of Steele Financial.

Avianna felt physically ill. Knowing Elizabeth Steele, she'd encourage the caterers to compete for the honor. The woman must get some twisted pleasure from subjecting others to positions beneath her. No matter. Avianna didn't care to compete. She intended to win the contract. Sawyer would marry his fiancée and she would get money for the roof her uncle and aunt needed. Afterwards her broken heart would heal a second time.

~ * ~

"Sawyer, is that you?"

He paused, hand on the bannister. He wondered how that particular tone could still make him feel like a ten-year-old trying to sneak in with soiled feet.

"Yes, Mother." So much for going upstairs now. "You called?" He entered the library where his mother sat at her secretary desk studying papers. Despite the warmth of the day a fire snapped and roared in the fireplace. She waved him closer.

"Come look at these bids. We've received five so far. I just met with another one this morning."

She shoved a fistful of papers into his hand and he dutifully shuffled through them. Could he possibly pretend to stumble and fling the whole stack into the flames?

"I really do wish you would be here to interview these people instead of leaving it all to me."

Sawyer inhaled and set the papers down. "Mother, you know you enjoy every moment of this. Besides, you're the one who wants this silly party. I've no need to celebrate an event I don't want and that's no surprise to anyone."

Elizabeth gasped, her hand going to her chest. "How can you say that you do not wish to become president?"

"I was referring to Joselyn, which you know very well." He wagged a finger in her direction. "I truly ought to end the engagement, saving both of us untold grief. It would make you either find some random soul to become president and CEO of your late husband's empire or allow me my birthright without any of your strings."

"Sawyer!" Her hand went to her chest again.

"Please don't act so surprised. This is not a new conversation between us. In fact, it's gotten to be quite old. You tend to ignore or forget each time. Yet what completely baffles me is why you insist I marry a woman I don't love."

Elizabeth straightened in her chair. "Joselyn Oakley is from a fine family. She has good qualities you lack. With her help, you can pilot Steele Financial to the next generation."

"Even if we don't love one another?"

"What use is love? Your father and I married without the benefit of love. Look where things are because of our union."

"I need only to look in the mirror for that."

"Don't be smart." She waved her hand at him. "In time, you and Joselyn may come to enjoy one another. Or not. Either way, you're responsible for providing future heirs. For heaven's sake, be intelligent and have more than just one. Joselyn will be able to help with that as well."

"Mother, we haven't even dated beyond once or twice."

She flicked her hand at him again. "That's your fault. She has always been attracted to you. No matter, she has all the qualities one needs to be a successful mate. Once you two are married, you can get to know one another."

Sawyer bit back a sigh. Children were the only part of his mother's plan that appealed to him. He wanted to fill the house with lots of happy, playful children. He'd always enjoyed large families and wanted one of his own. Except, the prospect sounded more pleasing when shared with someone he loved.

"Now, stop your sulking about foolish matters and help me." Elizabeth shoved another stack of papers at him. "We need to get interviews scheduled, I want samples from each one and I want you involved."

Swallowing back more retorts, knowing they would fall on deaf ears anyway, he scanned the list of interested caterers. A name stood out, tugging at his memory. *Avianna's Tasteful Affairs.* He pulled the paperwork from the stack.

"I'll do this one. I'll set it up immediately. Personally."

~ * ~

"Avianna, I thought you were busy today with that big interview."

"I am, Mama. I meet the Steeles in an hour. I just stopped in to see if Dad and Dale have those figures for the roof yet."

Her mother pulled a note from under the magnet on the fridge and handed it over. Avianna scanned it, frowning. It wasn't what she'd hoped to see.

"According to this, with everything that's been combined, we're still a thousand short."

Wow. She took a deep breath. Roofs were expensive. She had hoped they were less than this quote. She handed the note back.

"Okay, that's what I needed to know. See you later. Wish me luck." She hugged her mom and went to the car. Driving toward the Steele mansion, her mental wheels turned in rhythm with the car.

If she did this job for cost, not taking anything for herself, would she make enough to cover the expenses, make up the needed thousand, and still be able to win the bid? She'd have to keep costs way down and still not skimp the quality upon which she'd built her reputation. She'd really have to watch her pennies.

Nearing the Steele mansion, her hands tightened around the wheel. This was not her first time here. Once, Sawyer had her come over for a swim in their pool. The elegance of the place took her breath away then. How would it look now that she was older?

She reached the long Steele drive and slowed down, suddenly self-conscious. Passing along the tree-lined drive, doubts and memories rose like ethereal shadows. Her car wasn't new, but it looked nice and her mechanic cousin kept it running for her. Some of the other caterers in town had company vans. She wasn't there just yet. The roof came first. In the meantime, she borrowed her sister's minivan when she needed more space. With two hundred guests, she would need it.

Her first visit had been in July when she came to swim. It was hot and Sawyer thought it a good plan. His folks were out of town. They'd swam, played, and splashed, laughing and kissing beneath the watchful eyes of the servants. Sawyer taught her how to cannonball off the high dive and how to kiss underwater.

Later, they slipped up to his room, certain they'd escaped the servants' monitoring.

The house spilled into view and she paused, taking it in once more. Three vaulted stories covered in verandas, porches, and patios, all covered by an impressive roof.

Stately trees and manicured lawns, landscaped gardens, and flower beds anchored the mansion. There was a lot of catering potential. Elizabeth wanted an outside event, which might mean a tent.

After parking, she stared for a moment at the house and marshaled her courage. Fingers gripped around her portfolio, she approached the twin wooden front doors at the end of the winding brick walk. Steeling her nerves, she inhaled deeply, swept her hair into place, and knocked.

A portly housemaid swung the door open, her mouth pursed into a silent inquiry. Avianna broke into a smile, shoulders straight.

"Hello. I'm with Avianna's Tasteful Affairs Catering. I have an appointment with Mrs. Steele."

"One moment." The maid ushered her into the tiled foyer and motioned for her to wait. Feeling like a dog commanded to stay, she waited, spinning around to study the area. It probably looked the same, but she didn't remember. It spoke of elegance and wealth. Sawyer was lucky to have grown up surrounded by such lavishness. She might not have had things growing up like he did, but she always had the love of her family.

"Avianna."

She whirled at the soft purr of her name, her breath escaping. "Sawyer?"

His long hair was now neatly clipped, but still dark with a little wave she remembered. The impetuous grin he always wore was replaced with seriousness about his firm mouth and darkening his storm gray eyes. The boy of her memory was gone. Here stood the man he'd become. An electric thrill shot through her.

He nodded, looking almost relieved as he stretched out a hand. Touching, warmth shifted from him, spreading quickly through her.

"It's nice to see you again," he said. "Come on in." Cupping her elbow, he guided her along the hall to a narrow archway. Squeezing through, the room opened into a spacious, sunny solarium. He led her to an upholstered chair and released his hold.

Folding into the chair, Avianna realized how quickly she missed his touch. How much she had missed it. He slid into the chair opposite her and quietly studied her a moment, his hand resting against his chin.

"So you're a caterer now?"

"I am. A fairly successful one. A well respected one."

He smiled, reminding her of the Sawyer from their youth. Her heart skipped at the simple sight of his dimpled smile. Not as carefree as he used to be, his smile could still melt ice.

"And you're getting married. Congratulations." Forcing the words out, she knew she didn't sound very complimentary but it seemed appropriate. His smile immediately faded and a heaviness filled his face.

"Thanks. Okay, so would you like to see the preliminary plans?"

When she got this job, she wondered how she was going to balance a professional air while every muscle in her heart was constricting. She congratulated him because it was expected, but instead of making him pleased, he actually looked unhappy.

"Sure," she said slowly, struggling to understand why.

He rose and stretched a hand to her. She stepped into his hold like the years between them never happened. Their eyes met and held, as Avianna held her breath. She knew she'd never be able to stand by and watch him announce his engagement to some other woman. The pounding in her heart did not lie. She still desired Sawyer.

Chapter Two

He'd hoped it was the same Avianna he dreamed about. How many women could there be with that name? Considering how she was always cooking or baking up some great dish, he really wasn't surprised she'd turned to catering.

Seeing the girl of his youth matured into a self-assured business woman, he could hardly control his racing thoughts. As much as he once liked her long blond waves, the shorter shoulder length look fit her well. He found it just about impossible to not kiss her when she rose from the chair and took his hand. At a quick glance of her naked left ring finger, raw desire sliced through him in ways he'd always fantasized.

Swallowing, he led her outside, determined to be nothing but professional.

Once free of the doorway, she hugged her notebook to her chest and studied the lawns. Her gaze lingered on the pool before swinging back to him. The heavy look in her blue eyes assured him she remembered that day as well as he did. Seldom could he go swimming and not relive it all.

She cleared her throat. "So where did you plan on holding this?"

"Probably the pavilion. Where else can we put that many people?"

She nodded and headed over to the covered pavilion. He liked how she still twirled around as she studied something.

"We could do one tent. Use that for the food. Then we could set up the tables in here. What sort of decorations do you want?"

He shrugged, not having a clue. "What would you suggest?"

She drew back, startled by the question. Surely she was asked for her opinion before?

"Well, we could go with hearts I suppose," she finally responded. "Symbolic. Use lots of reds or pinks, mixed with white. We don't want it to look like a Valentine's event. What are your colors going to be?"

"My colors?"

She swallowed. "Your wedding colors?"

Again, he gave a shrug. Darned if he knew or cared.

"Okay, what sort of menu did you want?"

"What kinds are there?"

She grinned, probably thinking he was a hapless male. "We could do heavy hors d' oeuvres'. Or we could do light fare like soup, salads and sandwiches. We could go all out and offer a banquet of a couple meats, a couple of sides and some vegetables plus dessert. There are other options too, of course, but those are just something to consider."

"The whole banquet sounds good." If he had to endure this, he might as well eat a good meal.

She flipped her book open and made some notes. "Alcohol or dry?"

"Alcohol." He fully intended to get heavily intoxicated to survive this insanity. "With a side of carrots on a stick."

"I'm sorry?"

He waved his words away. "Nothing. Just an inside conversation between my mother and me. Regular alcohol will be fine."

She made more notes. "Sawyer, don't take this the wrong way, but it would help me if you were more decisive in what you want."

He grinned, amused at her bold statement. "Why is that?"

She hesitated, looking toward the house before turning back to him. She nibbled her lip a moment. "I really need this account."

He paused at how she emphasized the word really. "You sound a little desperate." A hint of concern worried him. The Avianna he remembered was never anxious.

"I am."

Sympathy—and fear—knifed through him. "Are you okay?"

"I'm fine." Again, she turned her gaze back to the house. She stared at the ground. "My aunt and uncle need a new roof on their house."

He analyzed her muttered words and then it clicked. He remembered how her big family was always helping each other. It was one of the many things he enjoyed about hanging around Avianna and the Goodmans. So her take from this job, if she got it, would go to her aunt and uncle. Admirable but unfair.

"Why don't they just go to a bank?" he asked. "They could get a loan."

Her harsh laugh was accompanied by angry eyes, momentarily surprising him. "They have. Several of them. They've been turned down because they had too much so they gave most of it away to me, my siblings, and cousins. Then they were turned down because they don't have enough." She drew a breath. "It's impossible to win!"

Yes, it was one of his personal pet peeves with the financial world. One he hoped to somehow correct once he presided over Steele Financial. If Joselyn didn't interfere with his plans. "I'm sorry I can't be more helpful," he said. "I'm sorry about your aunt and uncle. I remember them being good people." He'd enjoyed her large, fun-loving, helpful family. He pulled her close, hands on her shoulders. "If it were up to me, I'd never bother with any of this, but I don't have a choice. Sometimes it's not only banks that are unfair."

Now he could see how his selfish desire to see her again had hurt her. No doubt his mother had exacting ideas that would help Avianna plan better and bargain better. He had only wanted to see her again.

He rested his forehead against hers, feeling her uneven breath on his chest. If she didn't have to hold that notebook, would she wrap her arms around him like she once did?

"I can help you with one thing," he said, pulling away. "She'll want a taste sample from you. I have a recommendation."

"What?"

He smiled, warming at the memory. "You used to make this really great cake with cinnamon crumbles on top. I loved that."

"Streusel coffee cake? At an event like this?" She looked skeptical.

"Well, yeah. Maybe you could doctor it up a little. Just enough to impress my mother."

She turned the idea around, still not looking very sure of it. "I'll think about it. Thanks for the tip, but I probably should be getting back now."

Regretfully, he stepped away. "Hey, if I find out anything that would be a help, can I contact you? Share my intel?"

"That would be nice, thank you."

"Can I have your number?"

She withdrew a card from her notebook and handed it over. He'd hoped for something more personal, but this would do. In a sense, he felt he owed her.

"Before you leave, would you like a tour of the house?"

She paused, turning back, her face twisted into a question. "For what purpose?"

He faltered. "Ideas? To see the kitchen? To consider what you might have to work with." To stay with him just a little longer.

"Okay, sure." She nodded and pulled the notebook to her chest. He rushed to take her elbow before she changed her mind. He caught a whiff of her pretty flower perfume and that old desire raced through him like lightning bolts as he inhaled lavender and lilac, laced with cinnamon.

She remained silent as he escorted her inside the mansion. How did she see the large, empty rooms? To him, they were mostly hollow shells. He tried not to be too obvious in his study of her as she considered the kitchen, making more notes in her book. He swallowed back a groan as he vividly remembered her fingers pushing a pen now back when they massaged up and down his back or arm. She had a touch that could steal a man's breath away.

"It would be easy to bring some items in through the back door," she said, pen moving over the paper. "Keep hot stuff warmed in here, and take it out through the solarium. Do most the prep before arrival and finish the garnishes in here. Yes, this could work. If your mother is all right with me using her kitchen."

"We'll be sure that it is."

"So what about the rest of this place? It's so huge. Don't you want to use any of it?"

He shrugged. "All the living spaces are down here. Upstairs are the bedrooms. Mother uses one for her paints and sculptures now. And the nursery is on the third floor, sadly not used since I was about two or three."

"There must be a foot of dust up there by now."

"Probably." He exhaled. "This house needs to hear the happy laughter and feel the touch of many children. Like back in my great-grand parents' day. Before single heirs became the norm."

She set her notebook aside and stepped close enough for him to breathe in her delicious scent, pouring desire over him like honey. "Why do you suppose that changed?"

He considered the question. He'd heard stories of how, generations ago, love and laughter rang through these walls. When his ancestors ignored convention, and selected their own spouses. More children were the result of a loving union. That is what he wanted to experience. With Avianna. He envied her large, helpful, and loving family. He did not want what his parents and grandparents had.

He gave a short mirthless laugh, meeting her blue eyes. "Perhaps back then, they knew how to marry for love."

Chapter Three

Avianna studied the list in front of her. The menu wasn't coming together as smoothly as usual. Well, normally, the host provided her a clear picture of their vision. Hawaiian, Mediterranean, tailgate, whatever it was, and she could piece together a menu and plan to fit. Now, she had pretty much nothing to work with. Just her knowledge of Sawyer's tastes. At least from when he was younger. How had his culinary tastes changed as he matured?

He still remembered her streusel coffee cake fondly enough. Lowering the pen, she smiled at how his face looked almost blissful as he suggested coffee cake for such a romantic event. Coffee cake? It could be chaos if she did. What had he been thinking?

Doubtlessly he wished there was some way he could avoid the bother. So what had he meant? The catered meal? Her stomach clenched. Did he prefer the simplicity of whisking his fiancée off to be married without the fanfare? It would fit into the impulsive nature she remembered. She sensed a strong undercurrent of tension between him and his mother. Was she forcing him through the formalities and he was resentful? That would not surprise her. Sawyer and his mother used to tend to chafe each other. Apparently, they still did.

What bothered her more was wondering how she was going to watch from the sidelines as he wined and dined this woman he intended to marry. She could picture him laughing at everything she said. He'd put his arm around her. They might share food. Oh, and they would kiss.

She would be standing there, wishing it was her. Remembering when it was her.

She blew out a breath and shoved her bangs out of the way. She had to present a winning proposal. Elizabeth phoned earlier and offered her a tasting appointment with proposal at four o' clock tomorrow, if she wanted it. She'd offered no hint of her thoughts. It was a dry, take it or leave it offer. Typical Elizabeth Steele. Heart skipping a beat, Avianna grabbed it.

Now she stared at the chaos of her notes, thinking they looked as tangled as her feelings for Sawyer. She'd thought by now, after the time that passed, she'd be over him.

Nope.

Okay. She squared her shoulders, pushed her bangs away again, and gripped the pen. Food. She'd get this together yet.

First, she'd go with a generic, non-specific theme, preferring to melt the flavors of the foods together in natural pairings. Sawyer loved bacon. At least he once did. So how about candied bacon lollipops as appetizers? It was a start. For time and cost, it was a win.

Braided celebration bread would look pretty on the table. She could bookmark it with the soup and salad. Ginger pumpkin soup? No. Sausage kale soup had sautéed onions and bacon, so that would pair with the appetizer. Add in Greek salad to marry the flavors.

Okay, so far so good. She made notes, drawing arrows to the paired ingredients. Next, the main course. She could do a baked mushroom chicken Marsala. Or Argentinian grilled skirt steak. Both would work well. And a side? Grilled vegetable ratatouille or truffle mushroom risotto cakes? They both paired well, but which one, the poultry or beef?

She could offer them both and let Elizabeth decide. Either choice would keep her flavors flowing like a river. That just left dessert.

Streusel coffee cake. She smiled. Right.

~ * ~

For the second time in two days, Avianna traveled the long driveway to the Steele house. Would Sawyer be around this time? She tried to practice her pitch and how to present her ideas to Elizabeth. She had a list of questions and a few taste samples. She already knew some of the competing caterers and figured there was no room for error. She snapped on the radio for a moment to quiet her jumbled thoughts.

The song finished and went to a commercial. She left the car, carrying her goodies. The same maid met her at the door and bid her to wait in the foyer. Feeling a light sweat rolling between her shoulder blades, she gazed around for a distraction. A bouquet of fresh flowers caught her eye and she moved to the round table. She gently fingered the peony and freesia blooms and lowered her nose to breathe in the sweet scent, inhaling.

"You made quite an impression on my son."

Jerking upright, heat fanning her cheeks, she came face to face with Elizabeth Steele. She was as ramrod and uncompromising as Avianna remembered. Stepping away from the table, she sucked in an unsteady breath, turning the words around. Did Elizabeth know she once dated her son? It didn't seem like she did. Perhaps Sawyer never mentioned her name.

"That's nice to hear. How are you today?" She offered her hand.

Elizabeth lightly patted her fingertips and turned away. "This way, please."

Elizabeth led Avianna to the library and motioned her to a wooden table and pair of upholstered chairs. It resembled a small meeting room in a bank, with shelves of books ringing the room and dominated by a sizzling fire. More cold beads of sweat trailed down her back.

Seated, she waited for Elizabeth to settle herself and then, smiling, opened her portfolio. "Your son was unclear as to a few of the details, so I took the liberty of working up a generalized theme. I hope you don't mind."

Elizabeth sniffed. "If you were uncertain, why did you not think to phone me for the details?"

Yes, that would have been smart had she not been so wrapped in thoughts and fantasies of Sawyer. "I suppose that would have been the prudent choice. However, at the time, I didn't wish to bother you. You must be so busy with these additional tasks."

It was hard to say if that appeased Elizabeth or not, so Avianna plowed ahead, hoping for the best. She handed over a couple pages, explaining each.

"I think the steak would be a finer option, over the chicken," Elizabeth said.

Avianna made some quick notes, nodding in agreement. "Do you prefer grilled vegetables or risotto cakes?"

Elizabeth placed her painted fingernail over the risotto option. Avianna placed a check beside it.

"I must ask if you have adequate staff and facilities for a crowd of two hundred."

"Yes, of course. My staff and I are accustomed to catering large groups. It won't be a problem."

Again, she sniffed. "My son indicated you might wish the use of the kitchen."

Avianna stiffened and worked to keep her smile. "Only if it were not an imposition to you. It could assist us in the final garnishments. If you prefer not to allow access, it won't be a problem." What had Sawyer done now?

"I had the impression of all sorts of people haphazardly gallivanting about."

"Mrs. Steele, I can assure you my staff is professional and discreet. There would be no haphazard gallivanting." There would be a lot of lugging, toting, carrying, and walking, but absolutely no gallivanting. Honestly!

"I suppose it doesn't matter either way. Proceed."

So what did that mean? Could she use the kitchen? Or that her interest in using it just cost her the job? She'd wring Sawyer's neck. She moved down the menu, finally reaching the dessert. Her heart skipped a few beats as she brought up her transport case. "I have some samples for you. Here is the candied bacon lollipop appetizer."

Elizabeth took the skewer and nibbled thoughtfully, setting it aside half finished. "Nice."

"Thank you. This is a portion of the sausage and kale soup."

Elizabeth took the cup and spoon and sipped twice, then setting it aside. "Nice."

"I'm glad you like it." She drew an uneven breath. "This is the maple glazed streusel coffee cake." Heart stalling, she watched as Elizabeth chewed slowly through the one-inch square sample.

"Nice." She set the napkin aside. "Thank you for coming back. I have a number of other caterers to meet with today. I will be in touch." Rising, she stood, waiting for Avianna.

Stunned by the abrupt dismissal, Avianna gathered her items and rose, mustering a polite smile.

"I appreciate your time and look forward to hearing from you. Good day, Mrs. Steele. I can see myself out." She gripped her case and portfolio, lower lip quivering as she approached the door. Only when she reached the main road did she let the tears fall.

She'd no doubt lost the job. How was she going to get a roof for her aunt and uncle now?

Wiping at the tears as they blurred her vision, she also realized she wouldn't have to stand by and watch Sawyer flirt and kiss another woman, ultimately proposing to her while her own heart slowly shattered to pieces.

Chapter Four

"You are the only person I know of who binges on the Food Network when you're depressed," Paula said as she took another bite of her chocolate cream silk pie.

"Who said I was depressed? These shows give me tons of inspiration and suggestions." Avianna and her sister sat side by side on the sofa, eating their way through an entire pie she'd baked, and, yes, probably binging on the Food Network. So what? "'Secrets of a Closet Caterer'" just so happens to be my favorite foodie show, Paula. I found this particular pie recipe on "'Quick Twists on Old Picks.'"

"So what are we celebrating then?"

"Huh?"

Paula grinned and finished the last bite of pie slice. "If you're not depressed and we're not commiserating, then it must be you're excited and we're celebrating." She licked her fingers.

Interesting theory. They could commiserate she didn't get the catering job and had no idea how many smaller jobs she'd have to work to earn the money for the roof. They could celebrate because now she didn't have to stand by and watch Sawyer pledge his heart to another. Or commiserate because now she'd never see Sawyer again. This brief tryst with the past was just a painful tease—to remind her they could never be. She could never compete with Elizabeth Steele's idea of a perfect mate for her son and the Steele dynasty.

She finished the pie slice and reached for her milk. "We're not celebrating or commiserating, Paula. We're simply hanging out, sharing a new pie recipe, and gaining inspiration."

"Umm hum."

A knock at the door saved Avianna from having to reply.

"Expecting company?"

"Just you. I'll be right back. Probably a salesman or someone who's lost." A moment later she swung the door open and gasped. "Sawyer!"

"Avianna. You seem surprised to see me."

She frowned at his amused chuckle. "I am. How did you find where I live?"

"It hasn't been easy. First I called the number on your card and kept getting a recording. Since I know you left your apartment at Sugar Tree Street a few years ago, I went to your parents' house. Once I got them to remember me, they happily gave me directions here."

Okay, she'd left her phone on silence, so all calls went to voicemail. Maybe she was a touch depressed. She shifted her feet, keenly aware how handsome he looked when he was pleased.

"How do you know when I left Sugar Tree Street?"

He blushed. "I have a confession. When we first ended our relationship, I drove over there a few times. It was too painful to go see you again so I'd sit in the car for a few minutes and then drive away. One day, I came over and you had moved out. I decided then to just cut that tie and let you go."

She paused, thinking his words through. Why hadn't he just come to her door then? Because he couldn't. "Well, you went to a lot of work just to come see me now. Is there something special you wanted that couldn't be left on a phone message?"

He looked like she had just slapped him and she immediately regretted her choice of words. It wasn't meant the way it sounded. The shock of his confession warred with the knowledge he was soon to marry another woman, knifing her in two.

"Actually, yes there is," he said. "Is this a good time?"

"It's fine, come in." She stepped back, motioning him inside. "I'm just visiting with my sister."

He followed her and suddenly she was acutely aware of how his presence filled the room. He smelled spicy and she breathed deep, taking in the saffron, nutmeg, and citrus that surrounded him like a cloak. It was a good cologne on him.

Paula stood to meet them as they entered the living room. Avianna made introductions.

"Oh, wow, I remember you now," Paula gushed. "You used to come by the house a lot when you and Avianna were dating. I thought you two were such a cute couple."

He smiled. "Yes, I remember you too. No more pigtails?"

Paula's long braids had given way to a pixie cut two years ago. She gave her spikes an imaginary fluff. "No. This suits me now. So much quicker without all that combing and twisting." She gave him a fast inspection. "Besides, I'm not the only one who had a haircut and clothing upgrade."

Sawyer grinned, highlighting his dimples. Avianna's pulse leaped at the sight. She'd always been a sucker for his dimples.

"Yes, it seems the only one time hasn't touched is Avianna. I swear she still looks seventeen to me."

"Maybe. Well, looks like I'll be going now. Sawyer, nice to see you again. Don't be such a stranger. Avianna, thanks for the pie. Toodles."

"Woodles." She gave her sister a wave as she headed for the door. Once the door closed, silence hung heavy.

"Toodles and woodles?" He raised a questioning brow.

She shrugged and turned off the television. "Just something we say when we part—a sister thing."

He nodded and glanced around. "Nice place. A little bigger than the old Sugar Tree Street apartment."

"Thank you. Care to sit?"

He lowered himself to Paula's vacant spot. Avianna offered him chocolate pie and tea, but he politely declined. She folded one leg under her butt and quietly waited, but he seemed in no hurry to speak. He rubbed his hands up and down the legs of his jeans, making her think he was nervous.

"You went to a lot of trouble to find me. Is there something particular you wanted?"

"Yes, I'd like to speak to you about the party."

Apprehension stole over her. He made a special visit just for that? Was it to break the bad news for his mother? She hadn't heard back from Elizabeth so she was right to conclude she didn't have the contract. Wordlessly she nodded, her hands now clasped tight together.

He folded his hands and leaned forward, bringing a fresh breath of his cologne. "I wanted to know your thoughts about it."

"My thoughts?" she echoed, taken aback. She had plenty.

The mere thought of him embracing another woman tied her into knots. Just sitting here, so close to him now, made her heart flutter like a butterfly and her pulse race. She didn't know whether to clap or cry because she didn't win Elizabeth's favor and the job. The thought of not seeing him again was about to crush her. Did he want to hear those thoughts?

"Well, I think such an important event in your life deserves special attention." There, that sounded better. "I'm sure whoever is selected will give it that attention. You deserve to have a wonderful time. However, I'm curious why you said you didn't want to bother?"

He gave a mirthless laugh. "It's complicated to explain. Tell me, if someone was proposing to you, as a woman, how would you want it done?"

Was he comparing her to his fiancée? Something in her stomach recoiled, making her nauseous. "I suppose I'd enjoy the attention of a catered event."

Sawyer leaned back, chin resting on his upturned palm. "Go on."

How many times had she dreamed of the day when Sawyer would propose to her? How many ways had her youthful imagination played them through?

"We could have music and dancing and he could propose between incredible romantic songs." She laughed. "Oh, do you remember how we loved 'No Mountain High Enough?' That was such a great song."

His eyes crinkled and he gave a deep chuckle. "I fondly recall you were partial to 'My Love.'"

"When you serenaded me." Sudden heat spread over Avianna, both at the tender memory and his soft, dreamy expression. Her throat went dry. "Do you still sing?"

"Not much. Maybe in the shower on occasion. Okay, what else?"

A look of purpose replaced his wistful look, cooling her down just as fast. "I don't know. I haven't thought about it since…" Her words trailed off and her eyes widened at his serious expression.

"Avianna, do you regret we stopped seeing each other?"

She swallowed. "It was the hardest and saddest day of my life."

He blew out a long breath. "I'm sorry. In ways you can never know. Would you ever reconsider?"

She felt like he had slugged her. "Reconsider what? Sawyer, you're preparing to marry another woman. Did you forget that?"

His lips thinned. "No, I haven't forgotten, believe me. Just indulge me here, Avianna. Be honest. If I were free, would you reconsider a relationship with me? A serious one?"

Her heartbeat stalled. Was this a cruel game? "Of course I would. Like the song goes, I will always love you. Is that what you wanted to hear? That watching you with someone else would rip me to pieces and I'm kind of glad I didn't get the job. I'll find the money for the roof with other, smaller jobs. It might take longer, but at least I won't have to see you in the arms of another woman." She finished, exhaled, and swiped at a tear.

Sawyer blinked, drawing back. "What makes you think you didn't get the catering job?"

"Isn't that what you came here to tell me? Why you went to such extremes to find me to deliver your mother's decision in person? She gave the job to another caterer." She knew her voice was rising but she didn't care. "I wasn't good enough back then to date you and I'm not good enough now to cater your party." She crossed her arms over her chest, ending with a sigh.

Sawyer held out his hands to her. "Wait a minute. Back up a second, Avianna."

"Why did you come here?" Never in her wildest dreams did she think she would ever ask such a question of him, like this, but her pride demanded it.

He lowered his hands. "To tell you that you're hired. You have the catering job."

She blinked. "I do?"

"Yes, you can get that roof for your aunt and uncle now."

"Your mother picked me to cater your event?"

He nodded. "With some heavy prompting from me. It's my celebration after all. I think the coffee cake was a strong convincer."

Avianna could only imagine how that conversation had gone between them. She had the job? "At my asking price?"

"Of course."

"So why didn't she just call me with her decision? Like she said she would?"

Sawyer leaned back, head tilted to one side. "Aren't you glad to see me? Or did the light dancing in your eyes when we met yesterday lie?"

Her eyes danced?

"Even now, upset with me as you are, your face tells me you still yearn for me. Does your face lie to me?"

"No, but what does it matter? How can you want me and still pledge yourself to another? It isn't fair to any of us."

He scrubbed his face and then pulled her to him. "Avianna, I need to know. Do you love me?"

"Yes, I do." The admission tumbled out before she could reconsider.

He exhaled a heavy sigh. "Good." He wrapped his hand behind her neck and drew her close, kissing her.

He tasted of fresh mint and cinnamon. He felt solid and warm. Her fingers reached out to explore, lifting his sweater and going under it to find the matured, toned muscles.

His fingers twined in her hair. Bolts of white heat rippled over her and a moan escaped her. Her eyes slid closed as his fingertips moved to slowly drag along her back.

Pulling breathlessly apart, she gasped for air. "Wow." She ran her tongue over her lips. He'd grown into a great kisser.

"You taste like chocolate."

She smiled. "Guilty pleasure." She was pleased he was just as winded as her. It felt just like when they had made out years ago.

Then that contemplative, serious look returned to his eyes, sobering her. "Do you trust me? Completely?"

She nodded, not trusting her voice. She always had and always would trust him. He traced his fingertip along her jawbone, lightly brushing her lips and then gently cupping her chin. He looked deep into her eyes for a moment before drawing a breath and speaking again.

"I'm going to ask you to please follow through with the catering, just like you explained it all to my mother. Leave everything else to me."

She stilled, his dark look chilling her. "Sawyer?"

"Just trust me, okay? Be there and do everything as you planned. I'll take care of everything else."

"I don't understand."

"I know you don't. That's why I'm asking you to trust me. Please?" Mute, she nodded.

He rose, taking her with him. "Before I go, can we have just one dance?"

"There's no music on."

He took her hands into his.

"I hear plenty of music between our two beating hearts."

The room seemed to grow dimmer as he swept her into his strong arms and his fingers landed at her waist.

She rested her head against his shoulder, arms wrapped around his neck, hearing the steady, reassuring rhythm of his heartbeat. Their steps matched perfectly as they slowly swayed to their joined tune.

"I'll always love you, Avianna."

Chapter Five

"What are you sulking over now, Sawyer?"

His mother's irritated tone reached through the thoughts churning inside his mind. He wasn't looking forward to the conversations he planned, but in his heart, he knew it was necessary. Now that he'd reviewed it, he wished he'd been more concise when he talked to Avianna. He knew she didn't understand yet because he hadn't made his thoughts clearer. He could blame it on the rush of excitement when her eyes danced and her face lit up, making it so hard for him to breathe. The old spark still burned as strong and hot as before.

"Sawyer!"

He pulled his gaze from the view outside the solarium at the pavilion and turned to his mother. She stood at the doorway, a folder of papers in her hand and disapproval lining her face.

"I'm not sulking, Mother. I'm thinking. There is a difference."

She sniffed. "It looks the same."

"Perhaps. However, I assure you they are different." He eyed her file. "Was there something you wanted?"

"Not particularly. I have not seen you in a while and came to see to how you are."

He nodded. "Very thoughtful. I'm fine." He patted a spot on the chair across from him. "If you're free, can you sit a moment? There's something I'd like to discuss."

She entered the room and settled herself, looking at him expectantly. He exhaled, already feeling his stomach muscles tighten. "This is not a new conversation, but I need you to really listen to me this time. It's important. Okay?"

At her slight nod, he made sure he had her attention and began. "It's about Avianna, the caterer. She's the woman I was dating for so long before Father died. Before you decreed your silly inheritance mandate."

She started to protest and he stopped her with a raised hand. "Allow me to finish, please. I walked away from her and have regretted it ever since. So you and I have a couple different options we can explore about my birthright, but I know what I want to do about getting married."

"Sawyer!" Her hand flew to her chest. "I don't know what to say."

"Then say nothing, Mother, and honor my decision."

~ * ~

Avianna, Paula, and their mother sat around the table, sharing coffee and cake and discussing her conversation with Sawyer. She tactfully glossed over their emotional dancing, and the powerful, soul shaking kisses that followed before he finally left. Nor did she tell them that by the time he walked out the door later, Avianna knew she had never stopped loving him, and apparently, his love for her had endured.

"What do you suppose he has in mind?" Paula asked.

Avianna blew out a breath. It could be anything, knowing Sawyer, though no possibilities came to mind. "I really don't know. I'm just glad Mrs. Steele gave me the job. That roof is as good as done now."

So why was he still marrying this other woman? Evidently it was a condition of his inheritance. Her opinion of Mrs. Steele wasn't helped much by knowing that.

Linda, Avianna's mother, thoughtfully sipped her coffee. "It seems to me this is a blessing in many ways. I'd always hoped you and Sawyer would stay together. Now, not only do we finally get that roof for Bonnie and Tony, this catering job also brings you and Sawyer back together."

"Mama, you're forgetting the reason for the job in the first place." Avianna said, dropping her elbows to the table. "So he can formally propose his well-known engagement to… her." She wasn't even able to say his fiancé's name. It made her sick to her stomach.

"How exactly do you expect Sawyer and me to be brought together while he's married?"

"There's always affairs," Paula suggested, wearing a wicked smile. "Lots of those wealthy people have them."

"Well, not with me. Honestly, Paula." She turned back to her mother.

"No, I think this is good for the roof, but I just don't see a future for Sawyer and me." That's what hurt the most when their hearts so obviously wanted one.

"Perhaps that's why he's asking you to trust him, my dear," Linda said.

Maybe, but she sure couldn't see any connections. Or any way to end this with a positive note. She'd do the job, get the roof, and walk away with her heart shattered in a basket. Just like she had originally planned.

~ * ~

Avianna opened the sliding door on Paula's minivan and turned to her assistants, Wendy, Maddie, and Jewel. "Ready, gang?"

Their echoing chorus of optimistic yeses helped push the dark clouds away. This was it—Operation Steele Celebration. This was why she had a team of assistants, to ensure each part of the catered event ran smoothly and professionally. They didn't need to know about her personal involvement.

Everyone reached for a cart or tote and started hauling. They had a lot to do before the appointed time. Avianna blew out a tight breath, rolled her shoulders, and grabbed a cooler.

Neither Sawyer nor Elizabeth put in an appearance. A servant met Avianna and her team and showed them first to the kitchen where they could set up supplies and then outside to the pavilion where several tables were already in place. Without any further instructions, the team got to work. The trailer behind the minivan held more tables and the tent. Soon the tables were set up and arranged perfectly. Dozens of starched table cloths were soon spread out. Tables were then decorated and food added.

Appetizers first, the sweet candied bacon lollipops. Sausage and kale soup, Greek salad, and braided breads sat arranged on another table. The main course of grilled flank steak with sides of risotto cakes and grilled vegetables were next. Another table held the hot and cold beverages and the dessert table held her glazed streusel coffee cake. She'd baked six of them and cut them all into bite sized squares. She then dipped each square in a pot of maple glaze.

Finally, it was done and she and the team stood back to study the effect. Multiple shades of reds, pinks, and white for the balloons and streamer decorations looked romantic and tender, without screaming a Valentine message. Perfect. The aromas rising from the food smelled heavenly. A mixture of smoky grilled meat, sautéed vegetables, hickory bacon, warm bread, and broth all blended together in a sweet and savory blend.

Avianna checked the time. Soon the guests would arrive. It was time for everyone to take their appointed stations. Wendy had kitchen duty, making sure food was kept hot or cold as required, and garnishes were topped off as each new dish was served. Jewel had clean up duty, ensuring dirty items were removed and clean replacements made available. Maddie had replenishment duty, guaranteeing there was plenty of everything for each guest. She was the runner who watched supply and went for more of whatever item was needed. Avianna was overseer, making sure it all ran smooth, taking up any slack to help the girls and circulate among the guests to assist if necessary.

She blew out another breath, straightened her uniform, glanced at the girls' white uniforms and smiled at each one in turn. They were going to do this.

"Rock on, ladies."

The guests arrived, helping themselves to the candied bacon. They mingled, some shaking Avianna's hand and congratulating her team on a splendid set up. Elizabeth arrived next, nodding approval at Avianna. Quiet pleasure shot through her, though she wanted to shout out and pump the air. Drifting around, she couldn't help but overhear Elizabeth's excited banter to the guests about the upcoming marriage and what changes it would bring for Steele Financial.

Avianna slipped away, desperate to avoid the excitement. Good for Joselyn, good for Sawyer, even good for Elizabeth. She just didn't want to be smothered in all their happiness and oozing excitement. Her stomach clenched from the constant flipping each time she heard another enthusiastic comment.

She'd hide out in the kitchen for a few minutes. Long enough to give Wendy a break and settle her nerves down.

"Ah, there you are. I thought you were hiding."

Sawyer's cheery voice broke through the wall she was building around her heart. Turning, she stared into his dancing eyes. He was dressed in fitted tan trousers and a green sweater that highlighted the small bits of green in his gray eyes. Not a hair out of place and his shoes shined. She felt like a common laborer compared to him.

He held his hand out to her, beckoning her. She shifted from foot to foot, resisting his touch and drawing in her bottom lip.

"Aren't you coming out to see the party? You have done a fantastic job."

She shook her head, tears welling in her eyes. "I can't."

He blinked, hands dropping to his side. "Why ever not?"

She shifted again and took a step back. "After everything that happened last time we were together, I can't."

"Avianna." He sighed deeply, his smile fading like sun going behind the clouds. He stepped closer, bridging the distance between them and cupped her chin, tilting her face up to him. "I asked you to please trust me," he reminded her softly. "Do you?"

She fretted under his touch. It both burned and cooled her. She wanted to throw her arms around him and kiss him madly. She wanted to spend all day just breathing in his clean, spicy cologne. She wanted to scream yes, she trusted him.

"I do," she whispered, a clog forming in her throat to match the tears in her eyes. "But I can't go out there and watch." Her lip quivered.

He grinned, dimples deepening. Her heart skipped. "I really think you ought to, Avianna."

"Sawyer, please."

He bent his lips to hers, touching gently at first, then deepening the kiss with hunger. His tongue pushed into her mouth while his hands moved to her waist, dipping lower to cup her rear end, holding her close.

She felt his heart beat through the sweater, matching her own racing pace. Her body heated as fire licked through her veins. Desire knifed through like lightning bolts. Breathless, she pulled away.

"Umm, I love how you kiss, Avianna. I love how you make me feel. Like I could conquer anything."

Yes, she rather felt like she could triumph over most anything. Except for one thing.

"Sawyer, please don't make me go out there now. I'll come out later." She would owe her assistants some sort of explanation for her unusual behavior, but that would all have to come afterward.

He gave a sad shake of his head and again reached for her hands, capturing them and holding tight. "Trust me. I won't hurt you. Promise."

She fidgeted. This was going to hurt. How could he not see? Staring into his eyes, deep and dark, a long sigh escaped her. She swore her shoulders sagged and her head suddenly ached. She gave a silent nod, forcing back the determined tears.

"Wonderful!"

He took her elbow and guided her out of the kitchen to the double doors leading outside, one hand resting on the small of her back. They crossed the lawn toward the milling group of guests. She looked for Joselyn but didn't see her. Had she just stepped inside through another doorway? Elizabeth stood at one of the tables, a dissatisfied frown on her face. Was something wrong with the food or service?

Guilt dropped on her as she scouted out her assistants and scanned the tables. All seemed well. Jewel, Maddie and Wendy appeared oblivious to whatever upset Elizabeth as they moved around the scene.

What was the matter? Where was Joselyn?

Sawyer led her to a podium that had been set up prior to their arrival. Gripping her hand tight, he picked up the microphone and shot her a bright smile. "Trust, sweetheart," he whispered before turning it on.

Her heart pounded, thudding like a kicking horse inside her chest. Sweeping the crowd, she turned to look at Sawyer, envying his bubbling joy. Cold sweat beaded her neck, dripping down her shoulders.

"Ladies and Gentleman, if I may have your attention for a moment. By now you've sampled some of the great food prepared for us today and enjoyed the lovely ambiance. I'd like to introduce the creative genius behind our celebration. Meet Avianna Goodman. She and her team have worked hard to provide us with this enchanted afternoon. Let's have a round of applause for all their efforts."

Hundreds of people, clapping together, created a thunderous show of appreciation. Avianna flushed, heat warming her, as she searched for her team. Spotting each one, she nodded and smiled to add her own praise for them. They really stepped up when she fell behind, despite whatever Elizabeth might think.

"Okay, folks, you came here for a celebration. We all know the story.

125

Today I inherit my birthright by pledging myself to the chosen lady who will pilot Steele Financial to greater success at my side."

Avianna's stomach turned over. Those conditions were unfair. Why were rich people so unjust in their way of treating others? His mother. The bankers who refused her aunt and uncle. Why did enormous wealth make a person mean?

"However, there's a bit of a change of plans," Sawyer continued, bringing Avianna's attention back by the smile in his voice. "A surprise if you will."

She stared at him and his bright smile. He turned from the crowd to her, his smile faltering, and her heart skipped. She wanted to whisper, but her throat turned dry as sandpaper. That look. At her.

He held both her hands in his, a soft query in his eyes. "Avianna, you are the lady I choose to always be at my side. To love and cherish forever. Avianna, I am so sorry I ever left you. Will you please become my wife? Marry me?"

Her knees weakened and she struggled to breathe around the startled gasp. Someone nearby in the crowd chuckled. Did she look so flabbergasted?

"Avianna?" Apprehension slid over Sawyer's face, coloring his voice. His hold on her hands tightened as he searched her eyes.

Unable to find her voice, she lunged into his arms, flinging her cheek against his chest and nodding vigorously. Cheers and applause erupted around them but she only was aware of Sawyer's quiet strength as he held her tight and gently, his own heartbeat racing next to her ear.

Chapter Six

"You had me so scared," Sawyer said, smoothing her hair as she lay, legs curled, snuggled against him on the loveseat in the solarium. "I was terrified you would turn me down."

"Never. You certainly have the element of surprise though."

He chuckled, hand rhythmically rubbing her hair, trailing down her neck and shoulders and back again. She closed her eyes, content in the moment, loving the tingling shivers his touch created. A lifetime of this? Bliss.

The celebration was a success. The guests eventually left full and satisfied. Her assistants handled the clean-up and followed the guests. She and Sawyer were finally alone to digest their experiences.

"So I was thinking, once we're married your aunt and uncle can move into your place. Temporarily of course."

"Why?"

"So they have somewhere to stay without dealing with the hassle of the construction. Not only are they getting that new roof, they are also getting new insulation, siding and some other improvements and upgrades."

"Upgrades?"

"Yes. Once I decided it was you I wanted in my life, I had some work to do. Part was to discuss the change of plans with my mother and Joselyn. I also went back to your parents to get their blessing. They agreed to stay away to avoid ruining the surprise. By the way, the whole thing was videotaped for them. They made me promise. I also looked your aunt and uncle's house over."

She pulled away from his chest. "Sawyer, I didn't make enough from today to cover all of that for their house."

Yes, they probably needed all that in time. However, the roof was just the biggest concern. She was touched he went to such measures for her, but her family had no money for all that.

"Sweetheart, you're not to worry. Consider it my wedding gift to you. Or at least one of them. We still need to pick out your rings. I was thinking thirty days should be enough time to plan a wedding. Do you prefer here or in a church?"

Avianna's head swam with all his news and his question. "Thirty days?"

"Yes, I want to get started right away on our own big family to fill up this place. By the way, do you know of any good caterers? Because, as my bride, you'll be too busy that day." He gave a wicked laugh. "You might have time to whip up some of those great coffee cakes, but I have plenty of other plans for you that day, and that night."

She leaned forward, close enough for his lips to capture hers.

THE END

About the Author

Ryan Jo Summers is an author who writes across the genres. She pens romance novels blending elements of Inspirational, suspense, mystery, paranormal and time travel in any combination. She covers non-fiction as well as fictional short stories and poetry.

In her spare time, she likes to hang out with her pets, go to the nearby forest and river or gather with friends. She collects wicker baskets, lighthouse figurines and houseplants. She also likes to cook, creating new recipes from old favorites. If she has any time left over, she paints ceramics and acrylics on canvas She makes her home in the beautiful mountains of Western North Carolina.

Author Contacts
Website: www.ryanjosummers.com
Blog: summersrye.wordpress.com
Facebook: facebook.com/pages/Ryan-Jo-Summers-author-page/312875648810797

Dear Readers,

Many years ago, I was an accomplished baker. My family used to adore this streusel coffee cake recipe. It was crazy simple to make, so while the kids were eating breakfast and getting ready for school, I'd whip up a batch and send it with hubby to take to work. Still warm from the oven, his co-workers loved the treat and adored me. He'd return the empty pan at night, always ready for more. Enjoy the recipe on the next page!

—Ryan

Streusel Coffee Cake

Preheat oven to 375 degrees.

Filling: Mix below items together with fork in small bowl before mixing cake:

- ½ C brown sugar
- 2 Tbls. Flour
- 2 tsp. cinnamon
- 2 Tbls. melted butter
- ½ C nuts (optional)

Batter:

- 1 ½ C sifted flour
- 1 ½ tsp. baking powder
- 1 tsp. salt
- ¾ C sugar
- ¼ C shortening
- ½ C milk
- 1 egg (Well beaten)

Directions:

Sift dry ingredients. Cut in shortening with pastry knife or fork. Blend in egg and milk.

Spread half of batter in greased, flat 8 X 8 or 6 X 10 inch pan.

Sprinkle with half of filling. Add rest of batter and sprinkle remaining filling on top.

Bake at 375 degrees for 25 minutes. Good served warm or room temp.

The Song of Hiawatha

Henry Wadsworth Longfellow

By the shores of Gitche Gumee,
By the shining Big-Sea-Water,
Stood the wigwam of Nokomis,
Daughter of the Moon, Nokomis.
Dark behind it rose the forest,
Rose the black and gloomy pine-
trees,
Rose the firs with cones upon them;
Bright before it beat the water,
Beat the clear and sunny water,
Beat the shining Big-Sea-Water.

Apple Pie Delight

Sonja Gunter

Cool morning breeze signaled the end of the Minnesota summer and the beginning of fall. Toril Swenson didn't feel the sting as she strolled around Lake Nokomis. The fallen dry leaves crunched beneath her Ecco walking shoes.

The area was unique with the lake and homes. Everyone who'd been raised in the neighborhood knew the lake had been renamed in 1910, from Lake Amelia to the current name, Lake Nokomis, after Hiawatha's grandmother.

The walking path along the parkway gave a glorious view of the rippling water and numerous old oak trees. The past week of cold weather turned the leaves to an array of green, orange, red, and brown. Their beautiful colors were a special treat today with the sunshine.

A sudden vibration in her pocket reminded her how times had changed. The phone lit up with her grandson Trygg's toothless grin and her daughter Erika's smiling face.

"Hello."

"Hey Grams, can I have an apple donut on Saturday?"

Toril's dislike of the new cell phone technology made her come to a stop since she couldn't manage to walk and talk at the same time.

"Do you mean when we go apple picking?"

"Uh huh, Grams."

"One for sure, but two if you can pick the biggest apple," Toril said.

"I will for sure."

Trygg's excitement touched her heart. Picking apples was a fall family tradition dating back to when she was a little girl.

"Give the phone to your mother."

"Okey-dokey. Love ya Grams," Trygg said.

There was a smooching kiss sound, scuffling noises, and then chatter. Toril kicked at the fallen oak leaves and admired the colorful trees while she waited for her daughter to pick up the phone. A bright, cherry red truck on the parkway clashed with the fall earthy tones. As it neared, she was reminded of her long ago high school boyfriend, Erik's, 1974 truck. He'd purchased his truck new a few months before all the trouble had started. They'd cruise Nokomis Parkway a minimum of ten times in succession before they'd stop at the Dairy Queen. She'd order a sprinkle dip cone and he'd get a suicide Mr. Misty drink.

Toril stared at the vintage Chevy as it moved closer. Her jaw dropped open and she gasped.

Oh, my gosh, it was Erik.

"Mom! Mom, are you okay."

Erika's voice was so loud Toril held the phone away from her ear.

"Oh sorry, I swallowed wrong."

Toril stood fixated. The truck continued along the parkway, around the curve and then vanished.

"You... the ABC Apple Orchard... Saturday... pie... you?"

"What? I can't make out what you're saying. I must have a bad signal. What good are these phones if I can't hear people?"

"I hear you fine, Mom. You have a date with Trygg on Saturday. Apple orchard... picking apples... the bake sale."

"You're breaking up. Yes, I'll pick him up around ten o'clock."

Toril turned in a circle and took a few steps in hopes of a better signal. It worked.

"…Ronnie and I will come a little later. You and I ought to talk about your reunion. Did any of your old flames show up?"

"Erika, I'm too old to hook up with anyone."

"You're not old, Mom. Dad would've wanted you to find someone to spend your golden years with… travel to places… make new memories."

"Golden years?"

Her daughter laughed in reply.

"Why don't you guys come over for dinner? I'll make your favorite Norwegian meatballs and potatoes."

"You're mean. Don't tempt me. I'm on a diet remember. I have to lose weight for Trisha's wedding in November. I'll call you later."

"Okay, bye."

Toril pressed 'end call' then changed direction and returned to her stone two-story house, a block from the parkway. She went to the backdoor and entered through the kitchen.

In a frantic motion, she turned on the coffee maker and hurried down the stairs to the basement. She grabbed a bin labeled high school stuff, popped the lid, removed her senior yearbook, and hugged it to her body.

At her fortieth class reunion, her fellow classmates mentioned Erik had returned to the area, but no one could confirm it. Some said Erik became a millionaire. Others thought he'd invented several things and made a fortune. She'd anxiously and nervously waited in anticipation for him, but he'd been a no-show.

She carried the book upstairs into the family room, sat on the couch, and slowly flipped to page one-hundred-fifty-seven.

Erik Sutton.

His easy smile, blue eyes, and blond hair were embedded in her memory. Even though the picture was in black and white, she didn't need the colors.

Why did his parents take him away? He was and remained her lost love.

Toril quickly glanced at the fireplace mantle to her deceased husband Thomas' picture. They'd shared thirty-years of marriage before he'd fallen ill and died of cancer. His black hair had stayed until almost the end.

133

Erika was right. Thomas told her to move on. But would it be okay if that person was Erik?

Knock. Knock.

She dropped the yearbook onto the sofa, still deep in thoughts of what ifs and Erik, as she dashed to the door. She opened it and through the screen door saw a man. He smiled, showing off his unforgettable dimple.

"Oh my, Erik?"

"Hello, Toril."

"Are you real?"

"That's a funny question to ask a man standing in the cold."

His baritone laughter brought her out of her speechless state. He appeared to be her Erik, but older. His blond hair was lighter, filled with gray, and laugh lines were etched around his still remarkable blue eyes.

"Erik, it's been a long time."

"Yes, it has. May I come in?" he asked.

"My goodness, yes. So sorry. You are the last person I expected to find at my door. Come on in, we can sit in the family room."

Toril held the door, moved aside, and motioned to the left.

"Thank you."

As Erik passed by, she got a whiff of his cologne, Polo. Memory after memory flooded through her. She stood riveted in the doorway not sure if she should laugh, cry, yell, or faint. She reached up and fluffed her hair, yanked up her velour sweatpants, and tugged down her hoodie.

She wasn't dressed to meet him. She hadn't even put on any makeup yet.

"Are you, okay, Toril?" Erik asked, poised to sit on the sofa.

"Yes. This is a surprise… uh… this is very unexpected. I heard at the reunion you were in town. What brings you back to this neck of the woods?" She banished all thoughts of what he must think she looked like.

"You."

For the second time in an hour her mouth opened, but no words came. Moistening her lips, she pressed them together in displeasure. The only sane thing she could do, she did—sit in her favorite lazy boy chair.

"I've come back for you. I know it's been long overdue, Toril. I finally found the courage to right the wrong I did… my family… did to you and our daughter."

~ * ~

Erik stared at the woman who'd been his first love. He knew with pulse-pounding certainty he still loved her.

She'd changed of course, just like he had, but her eyes had stayed the same beautiful brown. Her face sported some lines, which gave her a certain grace that could only have been earned.

How many of those creases had he given her? He should've been there to see each of them occur. Been a part of them.

"Do you want water or something?" Erik asked with concern.

"I'm fine. No, dammit I'm not."

Her voice rose an octave. She stood and then paced. When Toril lapped the dining room table four times, Erik walked to her and took a hold of her arm, so she faced him.

"Toril, listen to me—"

"No! I can't. You left me pregnant to face my parents and… and everyone else," she said and jerked her arm away.

He shifted backward as she brushed past him to the front door. Erik followed with heavy footsteps.

"I think you better leave," she said tersely.

Her words stung. The bitterness in them left him feeling apprehensive. His confidence faded.

"Please, listen to me, Toril. Let me explain," he implored.

"Your actions said it all years ago. Now leave."

Her face was etched with determination and showed no relenting. Toril jerked the door open and pointed for him to leave.

"I aim to make you love me like you did," Erik said and boldly met her eyes.

Before Toril could move away, Erik took her hands in his, leaned in and gently kissed her lips. He gave her fingers a squeeze before releasing them and stepping outside. When he turned, he saw tears in her eyes as the door shut.

No. He wasn't ignoring her happiness anymore. He'd prove to her how much he still loved her.

His family had circumvented all chances of him returning to her, but not this time. Nothing would stand in his way of reclaiming her love and trust.

~ * ~

Toril leaned against the door, brushed the tears off her cheeks, and slowly shifted her hand to her lips, letting her fingers feel his kiss.

"Breathe," she said aloud.

He kissed her. He'd been real. He had no right to be in her life.

Time stopped as the past, present, and future twisted possibilities in her mind.

The phone ringing broke her state-of-shock sulk. The room was the same, but somehow different. His presence and the Polo cologne scent lingered.

She went into the kitchen and picked up the landline.

"Hello?"

"Hello, Toril, it's me Erik. I would like you to meet me at Lord Fletcher's for dinner at six-thirty."

Toril sat down at the table. Hearing his voice over the phone brought more tears. The tenderness in how he said her name tore at her broken heart. She gripped the phone tightly.

She must be having a stroke or something.

"How did you... never mind. This isn't going to work. You can't just show up and expect me to fall all over you like old times. You had your chance. You walked away."

"Yes, I did, but I'm here now—"

"Now, won't fix or take away the guilt and the shame I had to endure alone," she said, her voice curt with anger. She held her breath to calm her racing pulse.

"I know. Meet me for dinner," Erik pleaded.

"No."

"Think about it, Toril. I'll be there waiting. Six-thirty. Bye."

"No—"

The phone went dead.

The nerve of him. Who did he think he was? Of all places. No way.

The distinctive old fashion ringtone of her cell phone caught her off guard. Toril replaced the landline phone in its cradle and then rushed into the hallway. She picked up her iPhone from the table.

The screen showed Erika's name.

Crap. Not now. She slid her finger over the answer line. "Hello, honey."

"Hi Mom. You're not going to believe what I just heard. Carol from Lidia's hair salon, who knows Rachel, who works at the DNB office, said Erik Sutton is in town."

"Oh really? And that affects us how?" Toril glanced out the window to ensure Erik was gone.

"Mom, he is my father. Has he contacted you?"

Toril didn't answer right away. Her inner self warned her to be careful. She sat on the couch and glanced at the yearbook at the other end.

"Erika, what makes you think he wants to see me... us?"

"Carol said, Rachel heard, he moved back here to find someone."

"This is crazy. Absolutely insane," Toril said, swallowed, and cleared her throat. "I did see him. I talked to him today."

"Mom. When? Where? Did he ask about me?"

Toril bowed her head in defeat. Erik's presence tormented her, and she experienced a rush of pain. Not from hurt, but from the senseless logic that she was still attracted to him. She'd have to hide her inner anxieties and be civil to Erik for her daughter's sake.

How did everything go out of control in such a short period of time?

"Let's say he stopped by, left, then called, and asked me to dinner," she said in a shallow tone.

"For real, Mom? You're going, right?"

"I hadn't planned on it. He left us. Why would I want... why would we want him in our lives now?"

"I'm coming over. See yeah in a little bit," Erika responded in excitement.

"No, Erika—"

It was no use, her daughter disconnected.

Life hadn't been very fair to her and now it was being even more cruel. She'd mentally prepared herself for this day, but all her preparation and planned words were gone. One view of Erik's face and time vanished. The euphoria of contentment, pleasure, and love returned in one brief moment.

~ * ~

Erik pressed the gas pedal and drove away from Toril's home. He'd just kissed the woman who'd been lost to him all these years. His expression hardened as anger clouded his features. His nostrils flared as anxiety gnawed at his confidence. He hit the steering wheel with a clenched fist.

Damn his mother and father. Why?

Thankfully a red light stopped him. He gritted his teeth, then shook his head and breathed. Erik reached over to the glove box and took a legal sized brown envelope. He emptied the items onto the seat. Several recently opened letters lay there detached from the sorrow, mistrust, and pain they'd caused. All fifty of them addressed to him from Toril. His sister found them unopened in their mother's dresser drawer six months ago, when they'd cleaned out their parents' home to put up for sale.

Somehow, he had to get her to understand he hadn't known.

His cell phone rang. Erik clicked the speaker button on his iPhone, since the vintage truck didn't have Bluetooth. "Hello, Sis."

"Hey Bro, how's it going?"

"Okay. I saw and talked to Toril," Erik said.

The light switched to green and he continued cruising around Lake Nokomis.

"Good for you, Bro. Have you seen my niece?"

"Not yet, I have to take things slowly. Remember, those were your words of advice. I saw a picture of a woman with blonde hair and blue eyes. It was her. I invited Toril out to dinner. Not sure she'll show up," Erik answered matter-of-factly.

"I'm betting she does. I have faith in you. Keep me informed. Anyways, Mom and Dad are settled in at the nursing home. Mom had a good day, but Dad not so good."

"We made the right choice. It was time. I'm on my way to meet with my new partners. Talk to you later, Anna," he replied.

"Okay, don't forget to call Mom and Dad."

They disconnected.

A new plan took on a life of its own. Holding down the button of his phone he spoke.

"Siri, find Lord Fletcher's restaurant."

"Did you mean Lowell's?"

"No, find Lord Fletcher's restaurant."

"One number found. Would you like to be connected?"

"Yes."

With dinner reservations set, he concentrated on his new business venture, the ABC Apple Orchard. He made his last loop of the lake and turned on Cedar Avenue, he watched for Interstate 494E sign. The road had changed in the past forty years. The two lanes were now three in some spots and confusing in other areas. He merged onto the lane to Hastings.

Several huge billboards marked the way to the orchard. When the red building with a ginormous apple on the roof came into view, Erik chuckled. Ignoring the Welcoming Center arrow, he followed the other signs leading to the main office.

He parked, proceeded to the building, and pushed open the door labeled, Office. The room was alive with activity, phones ringing, talking, laughing, and music. It didn't take long for the noise level to lower when the employees noticed him. A man who he recognized from the business closing as Mr. Worthington, Sr.'s grandson stood. Erik advanced toward him.

"Mr. Worthington, can we talk?"

"Yes, Mr. Sutton, but call me Tony. I didn't know you were coming today. We can use my office."

"No, let's talk outside. It's a beautiful fall day."

"Of course," Tony said.

Erik exited the building into the sunshine and waited. Everything was as he remembered it as a boy and a teenager, right down to the Radio Flyer wagons, the play area, and the petting farm. Loud squeals from kids and parents talking caught his attention.

"Is there a problem, Mr. Sutton?" Tony asked.

Even though the sun was shining, Tony zipped up his jacket. Erik didn't mind the chill and left his jacket open.

"No, no and you don't have to be so formal. I thought it best we discuss business out here. I want to thank you and your family for allowing me to become a silent partner," Erik replied with a warm and appreciative tone.

"Sure, it was a hard decision for my family to make," Tony replied.

"Be assured the apple orchard is as special to me as it is to your family."

They strolled a bit before Erik spoke again.

"The trees seem overly full. Did you know I worked here for two fall pickings?"

"My grandfather mentioned it yesterday. This is the opening weekend for our Annual Apple Fest. It brings in more than three-fourths of our yearly sales. Would you like to walk the path?"

"Wonderful choice. The October weather has turned in your... our favor. The two years I worked here were the best times I had while growing up in Minnesota. My parents would take me and my sister here to pick apples. It's those happy memories that made me agree to be your family's silent partner. I want other families to have those kinds of recollections."

The sidewalk ended and a path of mulch and wood chips began. Tree after tree lined both sides, their branches heavy with red apples. Erik breathed in the sweet smell. It was here among the apple trees he'd first kissed Toril. The apple aroma always reminded him of her.

They walked awhile in quiet, and Erik saw Tony's face was flushed with pride.

No one will take this away from them. As long as he was here to stop it.

"Mr. Sutton... sorry, Erik, I'm pleased... we're pleased your offer came along when it did. Otherwise, we were going to be procured by a builder who wanted to bulldoze the entire orchard."

"I heard. I'd say things happen for a reason. Your grandfather said you had some plans to bring in new business. I'd like to meet with you in the next week or two to go over your proposals."

The conversation was put on hold as a line of kids with teachers filed by. Erik smiled. The kids all held an apple. Some things never changed.

"Thank you," Tony said. "I'd love to discuss the possibilities of building the business. My grandfather and I don't always see eye to eye on many occasions. You know old school verses new school. Our newest variety apple is the Zestar, developed by the University of Minnesota. I'd like to advertise nationwide. It will increase the consumers' knowledge of this awesome apple and make our profits sky-rocket. How would next Tuesday work for you? It's a slow tour day,"

"Sounds great. I have an office set up at my house."

"Oh, sure. Would ten o'clock be too early?"

"No, it would be perfect. I have a special request," Erik said.

"Okay, I'm ready," Tony responded.

They came to the end of the path and the sidewalk started again. They now stood facing the ABC Apple Orchard restaurant and the Welcome Center.

"Does the restaurant still sell... make the Sugar Kissed Apple Pie?" Erik asked.

"It does. It's our all-time favorite and the best-selling item we have."

"Fantastic. I'm about to pick one up right now. It's for someone special."

Tony laughed and Erik grinned. A third group of kids and teachers passed, followed by a wagon filled with bushels of apples pulled by a worker.

"If you don't mind, I'll leave you here so I can make my purchase. I'll call you later with my address."

"Great and thanks, Erik, for joining our family. You don't know how much it means to us... my family. Talk to you later," Tony said and held out his hand.

Erik shook his hand and turned away. He followed the apple pie shaped signs to the restaurant door. As he walked, he took mental notes concerning items that required fixing or changing.

~ * ~

"Mom, you're beautiful."

Toril turned to glance at her daughter, whose voice cracked with excitement. Erika stood with hands on her cheeks and eyes wide.

"I can't do this, sweetie. I know you want me to see him, but I just can't."

Toril felt for the zipper on the back of the fitted dress and yanked it. She slipped the dress off her arms and then over her hips.

"Mom, stop. Just think of this as a free dinner. If you don't want to wear a dress, put on something more casual like a pair of jeans."

"Jeans? Okay, that... no. I'm not going," Toril said almost choking in an ominous tone.

"Mom, it's your chance—how can you not want, too?"

She ignored her daughter's frantic outburst and withdrew from the closet with a pair of jeans, a white blouse. and a brown, orange, and teal scarf. She dangled the clothes as if they were candy to a child. Her face alight with false eagerness.

"Fine, just this once. But it's for you, so I can make sure he meets you. Then we won't talk about this again. What you do on your own time, is up to you."

Erika squealed in delight, did a happy dance around the bedroom, and fell onto the bed.

"Which shoes do you want? If it was me, I'd wear those new high heel boots you got last summer on sale. Have you even worn them yet?"

"I have. Once to go grocery shopping."

"Ugh, Mom You really should get out more often. I brought a couple of pictures of me, Trygg, and last year's family Christmas card for you to put in your purse."

Toril watched her daughter move around the bedroom like a nervous kid. She could see how the possibility of finally seeing her biological father was affecting Erika. She'd known since her eighteenth birthday that Thomas wasn't her real father. However, it hadn't mattered. He'd been the only father she'd known till now.

She had to do this for her, too. She had to keep her anger to herself.

Toril brushed away a tear so Erika wouldn't see. Her bedroom looked like a tornado hit it. Clothes and shoes lay everywhere. All because she hadn't been able to decide what to wear.

"Mom, I want you to know I love you for always being there for me."

Toril heard the sadness in her daughter's voice and turned. Erika stood next to the door in tears.

"Oh honey, I wouldn't have changed anything. Thomas loved you as his own. I love you too," she said and engulfed Erika in a hug.

"We've never talked…but I know people pressured you to give me up—"

"Erika baby, don't make me cry too. It took me forever to do my eye makeup."

Erika's tears were replaced by gulps of laughter. She then tucked and straightened the scarf she insisted added style to the plain blouse.

"I think I'm ready for whatever happens tonight. I'll be on my best behavior for you."

"Thanks, Mom. You go ahead, I'll clean this mess and lock up."

"Are you sure?"

"Yeah, Ronnie's taking Trygg to Broadway Pizza for dinner. I'm too nervous to eat. Call me when you're on your way home. I want to know everything."

"I will."

Together they walked down the stairs. Erika handed her the pictures she'd referred to earlier, and gave her a hug. Toril glanced at the front door as she backed out of the driveway. Erika stood on the front step waving. She blew her a hand kiss and drove away.

Traffic across town to Lord Fletcher's was light. She hadn't driven this way since high school. The road weaved along the west side of Lake Minnetonka and then to Sunset Drive.

A *déjà vu* feeling made Toril hesitant as the brick building came into view. This was the restaurant Erik had taken her to for her sixteenth birthday, against both families' wishes. He'd worked and saved his money to treat her to a birthday she'd never forget. It had worked. They'd made love for the first time that night. It had been the pivotal point in her life. She'd gotten pregnant.

She merged over to the entrance of Lord Fletcher's Restaurant and contemplated turning around.

No turning back now. She was doing this for Erika, not for herself.

"Welcome to Lord Fletcher's," a girl valet said and handed her a ticket.

"Thank you."

Toril glanced around, but didn't see Erik. She pushed open the heavy wood doors and there he was. Standing tall and as handsome as ever. She hadn't taken the time earlier to really appraise how he'd changed, but did now. The fabric of his sport coat outlined his broad shoulders, not the youthful physique she'd known by heart, but a man's. He wore a white shirt, open at the neck just to tease the viewer with a trace of his chest. The beginning of a smile tipped the corners of his mouth.

How times had changed. She didn't know this person.

Toril gave him an unconscious smile. He moved forward, each step fluid and memorizing.

Stop. Damn it. She was over him. He didn't mean anything to her anymore.

"Toril, I'm glad you came."

"I'm only here because of our daughter," she said evenly.

"Yes, I talked to her."

"You talked to her?" Toril said, her voice a little shaky.

"A few minutes ago. I called your house to see if you had left. If you hadn't, I was planning on driving over to pick you up."

"Oh," she said.

Holy cow why was she nervous? She was a grown woman now. No, she was an old woman. She couldn't be having crazy sexual feelings.

"Our table is ready."

"Good, I need a drink."

He laughed and her pulse quickened as it had forty years ago. When the waitress arrived, she ordered a Sweet Salted Caramel Apple Martini and Erik ordered an ice-tea.

"I'm only here—"

"Let me start first," he said and then reached inside his sport coat. He laid a stack of envelopes on the table.

"What are these?" Toril's stomach took a nasty dip.

Pointedly, he flipped them over, and she saw they were all addressed to him with her old return address.

The waitress brought their drinks. "I'll give you a few moments to look over our menu. Unless you're ready to order."

"Please give us a minute," Erik said.

The waitress nodded and walked away.

Toril took the drink, needing the alcohol to numb her feeling.

"Your letters to me. My family moved away because... No, they found out you were pregnant."

"And you want to show these letters to me now? Why?"

"I just received them six months ago."

Toril lifted her martini and took a gulp. No. He'd known she been pregnant.

She set down the drink and avoided exploring his eyes.

"Right. I talked to your dad he said—"

"Toril, I never knew you were pregnant or knew we had a daughter. Anna found the letters in my mother's things. They were all unopened except the birth announcement," he said, reaching inside his coat again. This time he withdrew a small hospital picture of Erika.

Draining her drink, she slumped downward in the chair. He reached across the table and took hold of her hand, brushing his thumb across the inside of her palm.

Lord no. This couldn't be.

"I called and called your number until it was disconnected and then there was no forwarding information," Toril murmured in an unnatural tone.

"I guess we were played big time."

She lifted her eyes to study his face. The age lines around his brows and the corners of his eyes deepened with the seriousness of his statement. His somber expression tore at her. She raised her chin and boldly met his sad blue eyes.

"Played? Is that what you call leaving me pregnant and alone?"

"I'm telling you the truth. If I had known you were pregnant, I would've returned to your side. My parents told me I couldn't contact you after we moved. I did try to call you a couple of times. I spoke to your mom, and she said it would be best for me to move on and to never try to contact you again. She hinted you were dating someone else. It broke my heart. I loved you. Toril, you have to believe me. I've never, and I mean never, stopped loving you."

She tugged her hand away, rose, took her purse, and stomped away from the table.

She would not forgive him.

~ * ~

"Toril, please," Erik pleaded.

She didn't stop. He watched her walk away. He pushed his chair back to follow, but decided to wait and see if she returned. The envelopes in front of him brought a haunting realization.

He should've been stronger. Hell! Why hadn't he gone against his family's and her family's wishes? He'd been stupid all these years.

He glanced over his shoulder. Not seeing Toril, Erik sipped his iced-tea.

"Excuse me, would you like another drink before ordering dinner?"

Erik peered at the waitress, "Yes, bring me another and another martini for the lady."

The waitress nodded. Not knowing what to do as he waited, Erik flipped through the letters and removed the one dated a month after he'd moved away and read.

Erik,

I need you. I have to talk to you. I feel so alone. I miss our talks, your laughter and your beautiful smile.

Please, please call me ASAP! If you can't call, then write. It's important.

XXXXOO

Toril

He'd just refolded the letter when she returned. Her face appeared a little flushed and her jaw was tight with determination.

"I ordered you another Sweet Salted Carmel Apple Martini."

"Thank you. I'm sorry, Erik," Toril said. "I'm just so confused, hurt, and angry. My daughter… our daughter is always telling me things happen for a reason. She's very excited to meet you, but please remember she had a father for a long time. He was very good to her and loved her as his own." She wiped a tear from her face.

"Toril, there are no words I can say to change the past. I guess we'll never know why our parents did what they did to us—"

"Excuse me, are you ready to place your entrée order?" the waitress asked.

They each ordered steak and waited until the waitress had gone before continuing the conversation.

"I can't believe my parents and… or yours did this to us. Where have you been all these years?"

"Sounds fair. First, we moved to Cedar Rapids, Iowa. We stayed there for a year. Then we moved to Lexington, Kentucky where I went to college. After I graduated, I moved away from my family. As far away from them as I could, San Diego. That's where I've been till earlier this year."

"As you can see, I never moved away. Did you even try to find me after you graduated and were on your own for all those years?" Toril asked.

"I could lie and say yes but, no, I gave up and then too much time—"

"Time? Really? One month, six months, one year? Forty years is a long time?"

"Yes, it is. I said I gave up and moved on, but if I had known about the baby, our daughter, I would've been by your side. You have to believe me. I haven't changed that much," Erik said.

"We dated two years. It was a speck of time considering the years we've been apart."

Her vivid anguish showed on her face and in her words. He was failing. He'd been prepared for tears and anger, not her lack of respect for him.

"Do you remember this table?"

"Again really? Just because this is the spot we sat at forty-one years ago, doesn't mean it's the same table. Maybe that's the table over there or maybe the one in the corner or it's been broken and replaced."

He laughed. She'd acquired a unique sense of humor with a dryness he couldn't ignore. It was a side of her he definitely wanted to know better.

"That's a possibility. Tell me how to win your heart again?" Erik asked.

"No way Mr.—"

"Who had their steak medium?" The waitress interrupted their conversation again.

Erik and Toril glared at her with open mouths.

"I did," Erik said.

The waitress turned to Toril. "That means you ordered yours medium rare."

"Yes," Toril said.

"Can I get the two of you anything else?"

147

"Yes, I'll take another one of this thing. It's delicious." She held up the empty martini glass.

Erik's eyebrows rose.

Three drinks. Was she trying to get drunk? He should stop her.

"I'm calling a truce for tonight, Toril. Let's make this a date of sorts. You know, to get reacquainted," Erik suggested.

"Fine, but you better not kiss me again."

Oh, hell, maybe not now, but he would before the night ended.

"What was your husband like, things you've done, and places you've seen?"

A frown instantly appeared on her face. Erik reached across the table and squeezed her hand. After a few seconds, she removed her hand, but not before an old spark of desire pounded through him.

"You never met him. After I had the… our baby, I had to secure a job to support us. My parents wouldn't allow me to live with them. I became a teller at the Richfield Bank and Trust. Thomas was a customer. After two years, I finally agreed to go on a date. The rest is history. We were married for thirty years."

"I'm thankful you found someone to love and to take care of the daughter I abandoned."

"When you say the word abandoned it sounds so… so harsh. I know there was more to why you never came back for me, I won't get in your way of seeing Erika. That is… I mean if you want to try to have a relationship with her." Toril paused and sipped her drink. "But you better not hurt her. If you initiate a relationship with her, you have to promise to continue to be in her life. Not any of this on and off crap."

"I promise. I love her name. I told you I'm here to stay," Erik said.

This time he took a hold of both her hands and brought one up to his lips and kissed it.

"Are you ready for dessert?" the waitress asked.

Before Toril could say no, he said yes, and winked at the waitress.

"I don't think I could eat anything else," Toril said hesitantly.

"Well, if you can't, you can always take it home."

As if on cue, the waitress brought over the Sugar Kissed Apple pie. Toril's expression was priceless.

"Erik, they don't serve this here."

"I know, I stopped at the ABC Apple Orchard today and picked one up. It's my way of a peace offering. Do I get to kiss you now?"

"No! I'm here for Erika, not us."

He scanned her face and his smile broadened. A part of him reveled in the fact there was still a tangible bond between them. It was an intoxicating feeling long buried away, but was escaping.

By the time the waitress brought the bill. He noticed the third martini had taken over her senses. Toril's head started to roll, and she was having trouble keeping her eyes open.

"I don't think you should drive," he said with a tinge of authority.

"I suppose. This day has been exhausting. I hadn't eaten. How many did I have, ten? Oh my, I'll have to call Erika. She'll come get me."

"No need to call her. We can arrange to pick up your car tomorrow."

"I'm not—"

She didn't finish because when she tried to stand she wobbled. Erik immediately went to her side to escort her to the entrance. He requested both sets of car keys and explained to the valet that one car would be staying overnight.

Toril leaned against him as they waited for his truck. He helped her into the passenger side and buckled her seatbelt.

"Erik this isn't right."

"Don't worry, I'm here now. I'll take care of you."

He turned and found her eyes closed and asleep. Erik couldn't help but smile. He stopped before leaving the parking lot, reached over for her purse, and located her phone. Thankfully she didn't have it locked. He viewed the recently called numbers and tapped call on his daughter's name.

"Hello, Mom how did it go?"

"Erika?"

"Yesssss, who is this?"

"This is Erik. Your mother had a few too many drinks so I'm driving her home. I wasn't sure if you wanted to meet me at her house or not?"

"Oh my, she drank? She never drinks."

"She might have a headache tomorrow."

"She leaves the key—"

"Under the mat at the backdoor."

"How did you know?"

He laughed. "She would leave one there for me to sneak into her parents' house."

"That's too much information," Erika said and snickered. "You can take her home, I'll stop over mid-morning to check on her."

"Okay well... well, it has been good talking to you again. I hope you will call me sometime. I'll leave my number for you at your mom's."

"That would be so awesome. I'm very excited to meet you. Would you... I mean... would you like to go to the ABC Apple Orchard Saturday with us... maybe. If you're not busy, you could meet us there and I could introduce you to your grandson," Erika babbled.

"Thank you for the invitation. I would love to meet him. I'll be there."

They hung up and Erik drove out of the parking lot to Toril's house.

~ * ~

Erik gently stroked Toril's cheek. Her eyes fluttered open.

"Mmmmm, Erik," she whispered.

To his surprise, she tried to kiss him, but missed and wrapped her arms around his neck.

"I thought I'd lost you. I'm glad you found me," Toril mumbled.

"Come, let's get you inside."

"Shhhh, my parents will hear. Did you remember to turn off the lights?" Toril belched and gave him a lopsided grin.

"Yes, they won't know I'm here. We're going to walk to the door."

He unwrapped her arms, opened the driver's side door and went around the truck. When he opened the passenger's door, Toril literally fell into his arms. She clung to him and this time succeeded in kissing him on the lips. Her lips were soft and inviting. Gone was the present. They were teenagers, necking. Today was yesterday. She tasted as he remembered, sweet. Their tongues danced with each other's.

A motion detection light flicked on promptly. Leaves rustled as the wind blew, reminding him the past was just that, the past. Erik gave Toril's lips a quick kiss and drew away from her.

"Come, time to walk," Erik said and breathed deep to recapture control of his racing heart.

Toril hiccupped her reply. She gazed at him with unfocused eyes.

This is not the place or time to try and reclaim their lost love.

"Hold on, a few more steps," Erik said. "I'm going to get the key from under the mat?"

She hiccupped again. "No, Silly, in the flower pot."

"I don't see a flower pot."

Toril suddenly pushed free of his arms, and leaned against the door. "You're not supposed to be here. You have to leave."

"I can't leave you like this, Toril. You're a little tipsy. Is the key under the mat or not?"

"Nope. Can't tell you. It's a secret."

Erik leaned down and lifted the corner of the mat.

"So you found my extra key. I didn't need that one, I have one in my purse. I can let myself in." She reached to take it, but fell forward into his arms. "Oh my…"

He hauled Toril tight against him. He maneuvered around her, slipped the key into the lock, turned the handle, and pushed the door open.

"Okay, the door is open. Do you think you can make it inside?"

"Why do you have three eyes, two noses, and four heads?" she asked.

"You had too many martinis at dinner."

"Don't tell Erika. She'll laugh. I don't drink. I think I need help to my bedroom. I have stairs."

"I thought I'd have to work harder than this to receive an invite to your bed," Erik chuckled.

"You're not forgiven. You can't stay. I don't want to walk up the stairs by myself."

"I'll be your prince. Lean on me."

On their journey to the stairs, they bumped into the kitchen door frame, and nearly fell backward going up the stairs. When they made it to her bedroom, they were laughing so hard Toril hiccupped faster.

"Thank you, Prince Erik."

"You're welcome, Princess Toril."

"I haven't been called that since—"

"I left you, but I promised not to leave you again, remember?"

"When will you be leaving?" she asked.

"Tonight? Once I see you to bed."

Toril wandered to the side of the bed, lay down, and patted the spot next to her.

"Just for a few minutes, until you fall asleep like old times," he said.

"Like old times."

Erik joined her on the bed. They lay facing each other and holding hands.

"Talk to me. Tell me more."

Her brown eyes watched him and then slowly closed. The old feeling of melting in warm chocolate made him smile.

"Okay, I never married. I've traveled to Europe a couple times. Been to Sydney. What about you? Did you ever get to see England like you wanted?"

She didn't reply. He lifted her hand and it fell on its own with no resistance. Sound asleep. He moved to leave, but her hand tightened over his.

~ * ~

The growl and grind of a garbage truck woke Toril. Red numbers on the clock showed it was nine-fifteen. She stretched and rolled.

"Yaaaaa!" She screamed and sat upright when she touched a body next to hers.

"What? What's wrong?" Erik jerked upward onto his elbows.

They surveyed each other in surprise.

"Oh lord, you can't be... oh, my head." Toril groaned and sank back with her eyes closed. "What happened? Why are you in my bed?"

"You had three martinis," Erik answered with a grin.

"I did? Good lord, no way."

"Yes, you did. I drove you home. You asked me to stay, so I did."

Toril opened one eye. It was Erik. He hadn't been a dream.

"You can't stay. You have to leave."

She sat up for a second time, fought the alcoholic hangover, and noticed she was still wearing all her clothes.

"Nothing happened, Toril. I hadn't planned on staying the entire night, but I'm not saying I'm sorry. It was rather a pleasant feeling, holding your hand and falling asleep."

Unwilling to face him, she pondered her missing commonsense and manners. Strange and confusing thoughts raced through her fogged mind.

"I can't think..."

"Why don't I go and make us some coffee?" Erik suggested. "Do you drink coffee?"

Two souls who used to know everything about each other realized they didn't know each other at all anymore. Toril slowly stood and turned as her scrambled thoughts came full circle.

"Yes, I do. Plain black. I'll meet you downstairs in a few minutes."

"Okay, take your time. We still need to talk."

Her heart jolted in a way it hadn't in a long time. His charisma upset her. He unlocked feeling she had kept hidden for so many years. His footsteps echoed in the hallway.

Oh, my. This couldn't be happening. Why was she so easily able to forgive him?

~ * ~

Erik inhaled the fresh ground coffee smell. He located the coffee cups and put two of them on the table. Peeking into the pantry, a bag of bagels caught his attention. He sliced a couple and put them in the toaster. He could get used to this.

Just as the bagels popped up, Toril sat down at the table appearing better than earlier. Color had come back to her face. Gone were the wrinkled white blouse and jeans. To his surprise, she now wore a purple fluffy robe. He stared longingly at her. A delightful shiver of desire coursed through him.

Erik cleared his throat. "I found some bagels. Would you like butter?"

"Yes, please. This is strange. I haven't had a man in my kitchen since Thomas passed away."

He poured coffee into their cups, placed the toasted bagels in the center of the table, and took a seat across from her.

"I know it's too soon, but I'd like to take you out again. You can pick the restaurant."

"I don't think this is a good thing… me and you."

"Mom are you…"

In unison, they turned to the door as it opened. For the first time Erik saw his daughter, tall and beautiful with blue eyes and short brown hair that framed her face. He rose.

153

"Hello," Toril mumbled. She shook her head, folded her arms on the table, and bent her head.

"You must be Erika. I'm Erik."

"Is that your truck?" Erika said as she shut the door and joined them at the table. "It's awesome. Ronnie, my husband would die to have one like it."

"Would you like a cup of coffee?" Erik asked.

"Yeah, what the heck, the more the merrier," Toril murmured.

"Sure. This is kind of awkward. I didn't interrupt anything. Did I?"

Toril lifted her head and met Erik's surprised expression. "This one is all yours," she said.

"I ummm... we ummm... nothing happened," Erik said hurriedly.

"If you say so. Mom, are you okay? Erik said you had a couple of drinks last night."

"I did, three to be exact. Erik did the gentlemanly by driving me home and then escorting me inside to my bedroom."

"But that wasn't... nothing," Erik said. "I mean nothing happened. This is preposterous. We fell asleep talking. We just woke up a half hour ago. I better leave."

"See? You always take off when the going gets tough," Toril said.

Her hurtful words hit hard. He didn't have anything to say or do because being a father was new to him.

"It's nice to meet you, Erik. Don't forget the apple orchard tomorrow at noon. Oh yeah, no need to worry about mom's car, Ronnie's on his way over."

Erik pondered Toril's words, hesitated, and then shrugged his shoulders. He stood, stepped around the table, leaned down, kissed Toril's cheek and left.

~ * ~

"OMG, Mom. He's handsome. He doesn't look like me. I think Trygg looks like him. Did you guys have sex? Is that why you're wearing your robe?"

Toril sat up straighter, fussed with the collar of her robe, and sipped her coffee. Her head wasn't pounding quite as much.

"No, nothing happened."

"Sure it didn't. You never liked discussing this kind of stuff."

"When did you invite him to the apple orchard?"

"Ohh, when he called me last night," Erika said.

"He called you? How did he get your number?"

"He called from your phone. Did you give it to him?"

"No. I don't remember getting into his truck," Toril said. "Besides, what makes you think I would allow anything to happen? I haven't seen him in forty years."

"He still loves you. I saw it in his face, Mom, when he gazed at you. Tell me everything."

Toril poured more coffee into her cup then began to tell Erika about the letters and Erik saying he knew nothing about having a daughter till six months ago. They'd just finished the pot of coffee when Ronnie arrived.

Once the house was quiet, Toril went back to her bedroom. She pulled a small box from the depths of her dresser drawer. She flipped the lid. A Chevy logo keychain, a Dairy Queen red spoon, and a purple pet rock lay there. The only items she'd saved from her time with Erik.

~ * ~

The day was perfect for apple picking. Indian summer had come with one last spurt of warmth before fall would turn into winter. Toril and Trygg shared three apple cinnamon donuts and milk before heading over to the petting zoo.

"Grams, can I feed the goats?"

"Sure sweetie, hold your hands together so—"

"Let me help you, young man."

Toril froze at the sound of Erik's voice. She tilted her head and saw a mischievous look in his eyes as he held his hands under Trygg's, so no food pellets dropped.

She fought a private battle of restraint. The harder she ignored the truth, the more it pushed forward with clarity.

Her first love would be her last. Yet could she fully trust him this time?

She felt his strength as his body touched hers. Her cheeks warmed and she realized she was blushing.

"Thanks, mister. You wait here with my extras," Trygg said and ran through the gates.

"He's rambunctious. He looks like his mom. Where are Erika and Ronnie?"

Toril bit her lip. She couldn't give in this easily. He still had to prove himself.

"They should be arriving soon," Toril explained. "Trygg looks more and more like you every day. The orchard is my special time with him. I've taken him here since he could walk." Toril leaned against the fence.

"Have you given any thought to us having dinner?" Erik asked.

She had all night long, as she held the pillow he slept on to her face. She shifted from one foot to the other in a nervous gesture as Erik leaned on the fence too. When he placed his hand on hers, she gave him a side glance. They laughed at Trygg as he ran from goat to goat. Soon he came back for more food pellets and, to Trygg's delight, Erik purchased another handful.

"Hi, Erik. Hey Mom, you ready to pick apples?"

Toril moved away from Erik, embarrassed to have been found so close together. "Yes."

"Thanks for the invite, but I can see this is a family tradition. I don't want to intrude," Erik said.

"You won't, right Mom?"

Toril exhaled before nodding approval.

"I'll corral the little man," Ronnie said.

"Be right back with a wagon," Erik said.

When the two men were out of hearing Erika turned to her.

"Mom, were you holding hands?" Erika asked and snickered.

"That's none of your business. I'm here for you."

"Whatever you say, Mom," Erika replied. "We're going to go on ahead. See ya in a bit."

"Okay, don't go too far," Toril said.

She waved at the trio, smiling as they swung Trygg between them. By the time Erik returned with the wagon they'd faded into a row of apple trees.

"Thanks for including me."

"It was Erika's idea not mine."

They strolled in silence and entered the row of trees. She heard Trygg's giggles and Erika's laughter. Unexpectedly, Erik took hold of her hand and turned her toward him.

"I'm going to be blunt. Did you enjoy having me kiss you?"

Toril's eyes darted from his mouth to his eyes.

Time stopped. They were fifteen again, on their first date at the apple orchard, and surrounded by the trees. Erik gathered her into his arms, raised her chin, and claimed her lips. The kiss, like it had so many years ago, sent spirals of ecstasy through her. Toril surrendered and wrapped her arms around his neck, afraid he might let go. Their mouths separated for a moment.

"Toril, I still love you. I've never stopped. Will you marry me?" Erik kissed the tip of her nose.

"I've always loved you, too, even when I hated you. Yes. I will," Toril murmured breathlessly.

"Mommy, look at Grams. She's kissing that man."

THE END

About the Author

Born and raised in the cold and beautiful Minnesota, she escaped to Illinois for seventeen years to raise two boys, and now calls Florida home. She and her husband Andy, who's always her hero, have a new family to worry about; Cookie, an Assui-Po dog, Oreo, a black and white cat who thinks he is a dog, and Chip, a ragdoll cat, that their sons compare to Eeyore.

She loves to travel, read, and bowl. You can catch her writing her next novel at the lanes.

Sonja encourages you to check out her web site for more info and don't be surprised if she lets her Norwegian heritage come through in her stories. You betcha!

Website: www.sonjagunter.com

Sugar Crisp Apple Pie

Ingredients
Pastry
- 2 cups all-purpose flour
- 1 teaspoon salt
- 2/3 cup plus 2 tablespoons shortening
- 4 to 6 tablespoons cold water

- **Filling**
- ½ cup sugar
- ¼ cup all-purpose flour
- ¾ teaspoon ground cinnamon
- ¼ teaspoon ground nutmeg
- Dash salt
- 6 ½ cups thinly sliced peeled tart apples (6 medium)
- 2 to 3 tablespoons butter or margarine, if desired

Topping
- 1 tablespoon water
- 1 to 2 tablespoon sugar

Directions

Heat oven to 425°F. In medium bowl, mix 2 cups flour and 1 teaspoon salt. Cut in shortening, using pastry blender (or pulling 2 table knives through ingredients in opposite directions), until particles are size of small peas. Sprinkle with cold water, 1 tablespoon at a time, tossing with fork until all flour is moistened and pastry almost cleans side of bowl (1 to 2 teaspoons more water can be added if necessary).

Gather pastry into a ball. Divide pastry in half; shape each half into flattened round on lightly floured surface. Wrap flattened rounds of pastry in plastic wrap; refrigerate about 45 minutes or until firm and cold, yet pliable.

On lightly floured surface, roll 1 round of pastry into circle 2 inches larger than upside-down 9-inch glass pie plate, using floured rolling pin.

Fold pastry into fourths; place in pie plate. Unfold and ease into plate, pressing firmly against bottom and side.

In large bowl, mix 1/2 cup sugar, 1/4 cup flour, the cinnamon, nutmeg and dash of salt. Stir in apples. Spoon into pastry-lined pie plate. Cut (2 to 3 teaspoons) butter into small pieces; sprinkle over apples. Trim overhanging edge of bottom pastry 1/2 inch from rim of plate.

Roll other round of pastry. Fold pastry into fourths and cut slits so steam can escape; place over filling and unfold. Trim overhanging edge of top pastry 1 inch from rim of plate. Fold and roll top edge under lower edge, pressing on rim to seal; flute. Brush top crust with 1 tablespoon water; sprinkle with 1 to 2 tablespoon sugar.

Cover edge with 2- to 3-inch strip of foil to prevent excessive browning; remove foil during last 15 minutes of baking. Bake 40 to 50 minutes or until crust is golden brown and juice begins to bubble through slits in crust. Cool on cooling rack at least 2 hours.

Peanut Butter Kisses

Jody Vitek

In my downtown Minneapolis hotel room, I took one last look in the full-length mirror. My long dark hair was held up by a clip, exposing my neck and shoulders. The sleeveless black dress dipped between my breasts, but not to the point where I was uncomfortable. I slid my hands over my hips and thighs to smooth the fabric, no longer the lean, size ten girl at graduation ten years ago. By the fashion designer standards of the world I was a size fourteen. In my world, I was a healthy size twelve. With my shawl and small handbag, I left for the hotel ballroom.

My nerves heightened approaching the check-in table for my high school reunion. "Hi! Beth Franta Canton," I offered my name with a smile. I tried recalling the woman sitting on the other side of the table.

"You can locate your name badge on the table." The name badge on the chest of the twenty something blonde, read Tina Hill Brock.

"Tina, we sat beside each other in Spanish class. How are you?"

"Oh, yeah. Beth. Good to see you. Here's a booklet, listing all the classmates we could locate, and the parties inside. Have a great evening."

That was it? No, how have you been? Have I changed that much? I stuck the sticker with my name and terrible senior picture on my dress the best I could. The only logical place I could stick the badge was on one of the straps, otherwise it would be pasted to my boob. And I didn't care to draw more attention to the twins. I folded the sides of the tag to the underside of my dress strap. This hid the awful photo of the awkward girl

161

who looked like a boy, and I smiled. No reminders of then, only now.

I entered the ballroom of tables and streamers in blue and green, our school colors. Everyone mingled. Searching the room, I found my closest friends in high school, Brenda and Tammy, and acknowledged them with a quick wave.

In need of a drink to assist in calming my nerves, I went to the bar and ordered a vodka cranberry. While waiting, I searched the room for Hank McGrath but didn't spot him in the crowd. Either I was just missing him, or he wasn't here. I'd have to look him up in the booklet to see where he now lived. Maybe having to travel would keep him from coming tonight.

You'd think after being out of high school for ten years, my crush on the guy would've passed. You'd think that when I met and married another man, the feeling would've gone away. Nope, the guy was always in the back of mind. Hank popped up in a dream randomly throughout the years, setting my heart a flutter.

Hank had been my crush since fifth grade. As we got older, I kept my crush on him a secret. I wasn't his type. Oh, I tried. He was the popular jock. Me? I was the girl who participated in sports, but was never the star player and eventually gave up doing anything. I wasn't popular, but I wasn't a nerd either. I fell, well, in the middle. I knew everyone at school and befriended most of them.

"Beth! How ya doin'?"

I turned to a familiar face.

"Paul Martin."

"Oh, yeah, Paul. I'm doing well, and yourself?" I did remember Paul. He was one of Hank's good friends in the old neighborhood. I paid the bartender and took a sip of my alcoholic concoction.

"I'm doin' good. You look great!" His eyes drifted to my cleavage. Something I lacked until after graduation. "Where's your husband?"

"I'm divorced. What about you, are you married?"

"She's over there." He pointed to a table across the room. "We're celebrating our fifth wedding anniversary this weekend."

"She's lovely and congratulations." I lightly touched his arm. "I'm sorry, if you'll excuse me, there's someone I need to go see."

"Sure." He turned to the bartender and ordered his drinks as I walked away.

I joined Brenda and her husband Mark of three years, along with Tammy and her husband Jim of nine years. We had stayed in touch through the social world of the Internet. We sat and chatted while browsing through the booklet and talking about high school classmates and memories. It was hard to listen to my friends about how happily married they were and hearing about their kids. Sure, there were those who still weren't married, a few others divorced, and the unfortunate ones who passed away.

Eventually, the Italian dinner buffet was set up and available. I snagged a plate from the pile and browsed the buffet. It all looked wonderfully sinful.

If I was going to continue drinking, I'd better eat. I put some of what I believed to be Caesar salad near the edge of my plate. Grabbed two rolls and then scooped, what appeared to be manicotti onto my plate. Being a light weight, I felt I had enough food to have another drink.

I rejoined my friends at the table we commandeered an hour ago.

"We got you another drink, Beth." Brenda smiled.

"Food looks good," Mark said, rubbing his belly. "I think I'm going to go grab some before it gets picked over."

"Go ahead, dear."

"Thanks for the drink. I'll buy the next round." I took a bite of salad. It was heavy on the dressing, but not bad.

"I'll join you, Mark." Jim pushed back the chair and left the table.

"So, Beth, have you been on any dates?" Tammy asked eagerly.

I shook my head while I placed a large forkful of salad in my mouth.

"Are you interested in dating? Because I know some really hot guys I could set you up with."

Nearly choking as I swallowed, I politely replied, "Thanks, but I'm not interested."

Voices boomed from across the room.

I turned.

Hank stood in the entrance of the ballroom, surrounded by the still as ever popular crowd. My nerve endings tingled and my lips parted as my throat grew thick. How could he be more handsome than I remembered? I'd read in the booklet that he was in Florida involved in banking. The yummy young man had grown into a hot hunk. He was lightly toasted by

163

the Florida sun.

The crowd broke away, and he maneuvered to the bar with his former guy friends trailing in his wake. I turned back to my plate of food and friends. Staring would be rude and impolite. Not to mention creepy. But I could stare all day at him and not get bored. Once in a while, I checked social media to see what I could find out about him, but never clicked to follow or like his profiles. I was too embarrassed. This was my crush.

After finishing my meal, I excused myself. "I'm going to go socialize." And I did just that, while sucking on my second vodka cranberry drink for courage. Even though I recognized these people from classes we shared or passed in the halls, it was a bit awkward to make polite small talk with them when I once considered them friends. I didn't *really* know them anymore. Sure we were connected on social media, but that doesn't mean you know the person as a close friend. Time passed and the committee announced they were going to show a video from our senior year in five minutes.

I stood in line at the bar.

"What are you drinking?" a deep voice from behind asked.

Oh, I knew who the voice belonged to. I swallowed and turned. "Hank … How are you?" I looked up into his mossy green eyes.

"I'm good. What can I get you to drink?" His long, brown hair from the days in school was shaved up the back and trimmed over the sides.

"Oh, thanks but you don't have to." I faced the bartender who was still busy making a drink.

"I want to."

My heart fluttered like the wings of a humming bird. Hank was talking to me. He wanted to buy me a drink. I faced him. Oh, God, he was smiling. The dimples. "Um, I'm drinking vodka cranberry."

"Don't drink too much of that hard stuff," his broad smile and tone teased.

"Ha," I said with a laugh, cocking my eye-brow. "This is from the one who partied hard every Friday night."

"Yeah, and I'm telling this to the one who didn't." He matched my cocked brow with his own.

Ouch, that hurt. It wasn't because I didn't want to party, it was because I wasn't invited to the parties.

I looked back to the bartender.

"I'm sorry," Hank's breath fell on my ear.

I closed my eyes to remember this moment. The moment my ovaries somersaulted over the warmth of Hank's breath on my ear. A warmth spread across my lower back.

"Are you okay?"

I opened my eyes. His hand rested on my back. "Fine."

"What can I get you?" The bartender asked energetically.

"A beer and vodka cranberry." Like the other men tonight, he wore dress slacks but instead of a golf shirt, he had on a long-sleeved dress shirt.

"Thank you, Hank."

His eyes smiled. "My pleasure. Maybe we can catch up after the video."

"Ah, sure." This should be an interesting conversation. We have nothing in common.

"Here's your drink. You can buy the next round." The dark purple shirt was a good color for him.

I nodded my head. "Next round." Like that was going to happen.

Sitting at the table again with my core friends from school, we watched the video. We all laughed so hard at the photos that reminded us of the days when life was simple. Maybe not so simple to us back then, but compared to life now, it *was* simple.

The committee then thanked everyone for coming. The DJ put a song on, taking us back ten years. Groans and cheers were mixed amongst the room. As for me, I needed fresh air.

~ * ~

For late June, the Minnesota night air was cool, but the hotel had propane heaters burning on the patio to keep guests comfortable enough to enjoy the evening stars. I didn't need the heater, as the alcohol warmed my blood. As well as a certain man attending tonight's events. I walked past a couple snuggled at a corner table and stopped at the far edge where it was dark enough I could have a moment of privacy.

It wasn't as though I was the only single person attending tonight, but it was frustrating to be single at your ten year reunion. The divorced years came at the twenty, thirty and forty year reunions. A small part of me felt like a failure because I couldn't keep my marriage together.

I plopped in a chair and sat back, tipping my head back to stare up into the clear night sky. The stars were bright, but not bright enough to be seen brilliantly over the surrounding city lights. It was something to gaze at and forget about life at the moment.

I wrapped my shawl around my bare arms.

"I'd offer you my jacket, if I had one."

At the sound of Hank's baritone voice, I turned my head and jerked at the same time in the direction of his voice. "Oh." I immediately dropped my head into my hands while leaning forward. The sudden movement wasn't good for my head or neck, as pain radiated from my neck down through my shoulders.

"What is it? Can I get you something?" His tall athletic body squatted in front of me.

God, did he smell good.

It wasn't musky, but light. Easy on the senses.

I closed my eyes. My head swirled. A deep inhale and a slow exhale. I slowly opened my eyes and lifted my head. "Hank, are you stalking me? Won't your girlfriend or wife be wondering where you are?"

"No, to both of your questions. No girlfriend or wife. Can you answer my question?"

"What question is that?" I gradually tipped my head to the right to stretch my neck.

"Are you okay?" He rested a warm hand on my bare knee.

Glad I shaved, I thought looking at his hand, touching my knee. Another memory to engrain on the brain.

"You startled me, and I twisted my neck too quickly." I steadily bent to the left to stretch my neck, giving me an excuse to avoid eye contact.

"I'm glad it's not from too much alcohol." He stood and I turned to face him. "Would you like me to rub it for you?" His hand rested mid-air above my shoulder, but close enough the warmth could be felt against my skin.

Yes! "No, I'll be fine."

He pulled a chair over and sat beside me. "What about you? Where's your partner?"

"He left me for another woman."

"Were you married?"

"Dated for two, married for five. I was young and dumb."

"He was dumb."

I wasn't sure how to respond.

"Where are you living?" He broke the awkward silence.

"Here in the city. I work downtown. What about you? Where are you living?" I didn't want to blurt out what I knew, so I played dumb.

"I'm in the process of moving back here. Actually, I'm looking for a place downtown. Are you in an apartment, condo, or do you have a house?"

"I bought a condo. It's a newer development. They have units available if you're looking to buy." I shivered and rubbed my arms.

"We should go back inside. You're cold. And I am, too." Hank got out of his chair and held a hand out for me to take.

I accepted his hand, and he continued to hold it once I was upright. "Thank you." I went to remove my hand and he stopped me. The man towered above my short five-five height. In high school, he was over six feet and I wouldn't be able to tell you how much more above, but I had to look up to him even in my three inch heels.

"Beth, I was wondering, I know we just, I mean we've known each other for practically our entire lives, but would you like to have dinner or a drink sometime this week?"

Hank, Hank McGrath just asked *me* out. My insides jumped around as though in a child's bouncy house. If I didn't know any better, I'd think he was nervous. He had difficulty asking, but why? In school, he was the ladies' man—smooth and cool.

I stared into those eyes of his and heard my voice respond. "Yes, I'd like that."

He let go of my hand and fished out his cell phone. "Can I get your phone number? I'll call you, and we can make plans."

I rattled my number off and he tapped his screen before returning the phone into his pocket.

"Would you like my number?"

"I don't have my phone with me." I held up my tiny purse strapped over my shoulder. "I have cash and my ID."

"Let's go inside." He rested a hand against my lower back and gently urged me forward. "Let's stop at the bar. I'll write my number on a napkin."

I simply nodded and moved alongside him.

In front of the bar, I ordered a drink for myself and a beer for Hank. I owed him one.

He handed me the napkin. "Make sure to put this in your phone so you know it's me calling. I'll give you a call Monday."

"Okay." I stuffed the napkin in my purse.

"Hey, Beth," Jack, a buddy of Hank's, said acknowledging me while slapping a hand on Hank's shoulder. "We've been looking for you, Hank. Where'd you disappear to?"

"I've been here all along. Thanks for the beer, Beth." He raised his bottle and walked away with Jack.

And my excitement dropped. He wasn't going to call. He couldn't even tell Jack he was outside with me. Time for chocolate. I strolled to the dessert buffet and put a few items on a plate. One being peanut butter cookies with chocolate in the center. I had a weakness for chocolate and peanut butter, in any form.

I sat at the closest table that had been deserted, and ate the chocolate desserts while drinking my vodka cranberry. Having seen everyone and visited with those I wanted to talk with, I downed the remainder of my beverage. I took one long last look at Hank. I smiled and a calm settled over me. I got to see him again. Not in a dream, but in person. Then he was looking at me with a smile that melted my composure. It was those damned dimples. I bee-lined for the exit door.

~ * ~

As I smiled at Beth, the focus of the conversation I was having with the guys was lost. She looked beautiful tonight, no longer the awkward teenage girl me and my buddies teased on occasion. It surprised me that she acknowledged my existence after all the teasing. Her blonde hair, now dark, was held up exposing her neck.

I watched Paul ogle Beth, then looked to a table where his wife sat talking to other women, and then leave out the door behind Beth.

"McGrath? What are you looking at, dude?" Jack asked glancing at the ballroom exit doors.

"I'll be back." I moved quickly through the room and out to the hall. Catching the backside of Paul going around the corner to where the elevators were located, I hurried past him.

Beth faced the closed doors.

I wrapped my arms around her waist. Her floral scent stopped me for a moment forgetting why I was doing what I was doing.

She spun in my embrace and wavered. "What—?"

"Damn, Hank, you always take the good ones," Paul's words slurred as he reached them at the bank of doors. He turned around and left them alone.

Staring at each other, I didn't know what to say. Did she know what Paul was up to? Shit, I didn't *really* know what Paul was up to, other than I knew he wasn't faithful to his wife.

"Can I escort you home?" My question was lame, but the quickest thing to fly out of my mouth.

"Um, I'm staying at the hotel." She rubbed her nose and blinked slowly. The vodka was taking affect. "What was Paul talking about?"

Elevator doors opened down from where we stood.

"Come on." I escorted her in the elevator. "What floor are you on?"

She stepped to the rail. "Eight. So what did Paul mean, you take all the good ones?"

With my hand at her waist, I pushed the button and the doors closed. "Nothing. He's drunk. Why are you staying at the hotel when you live here, downtown?" I couldn't help but ask because most people would just go home. Usually those who came from out of town for the reunion, like me, stayed at the hotel.

"Because I can. Because I want to. Do I have to have a reason?" Her tone was feisty.

"No, I was wondering, that's all."

The doors opened. We stepped out, and she went to the left down the hall. I continued to keep my hand on her back. With the difference in height, it rested easily in that position. Comfortable. Natural.

She stopped and faced me. "Well, this is my room." Fishing inside her purse, she retrieved the key card and opened the door. "You got me safely back."

I tucked my hands in my pockets, and swallowed hard. "I did. Have a good night's sleep, Beth."

Her mouth curved into a slight frown as her head bobbed. "Thanks."

Was that disappointment? Was I reading her body language correctly?

As she turned to step into her room, I removed my hands from my pockets, and quickly rested them on her hips. Taking my chances, I leaned down and kissed her thin lips. She returned the gesture, but I stepped back before this could go any further. I didn't want to take advantage of her alcoholic state.

"Goodnight, Beth." I retreated to the elevator without glancing back. I licked my lips. There was a hint of peanut butter on my taste buds.

On the ride to the third floor, I pondered the kiss and whether I crossed the line. We weren't close friends, didn't keep in touch, we briefly talked tonight about making plans, and yeah, I had crossed the line and owed her an apology.

The elevator doors opened and Paul and his wife stood waiting at the doors.

"That was a quick one, McGrath. Don't have the stamina of a teenager anymore?" Paul's words road a roller coaster as he spoke.

"I'm sorry, Hank. I need to get him out of here and to bed," his wife said, helping him get in the elevator as I held the door.

"It's okay. Do you need help?" Offering was the polite thing to do.

"Nah, I've got him. Go back and have a good night. They were starting to set up karaoke."

"Good night."

The doors closed, and I strolled back to the party.

~ * ~

I rolled over with a pounding headache and remembered with the darkness that I'd gotten a room at the hotel for the night. With the memory of Hank's kiss, my eyes shot open. Hank kissed me. He, kissed, me! My fingers touched my lips as if I could feel the kiss, his lips, or even will the kiss to happen again.

But why? Why did he kiss me, Beth Franta? I had nothing to offer him. I was used goods. A divorcee. I wasn't good enough for Hank McGrath.

Looking at the clock, I was shocked to discover it was late morning and check out time was out in an hour. Groaning, I tossed the covers back, slowly sat and stretched.

Coffee. I needed my coffee.

Staggering to the dresser where the small machine was located, I snatched the pitcher and went to the bathroom to fill the pot. Returning to the maker and coffee ready to brew, I hit the on button. While the carafe filled, I located my overnight bag and acetaminophen, popping two, I swallowed them down with a five dollar bottle of water from the hotel fridge. Worth it in that moment.

I jumped in to take a quick shower and then drank my coffee while getting dressed and packing. There wasn't much. Just the clothes I wore to the hotel, last night's dress and my cosmetic overnight bag. Set to leave, I checked the room one last time and took the elevator to the lobby. As I paid for my night's stay, my cell phone rang. It was an unknown number, so I let it go. If it was important they'd leave a message.

After a short ride on the light rail and walk home, I entered my condo. "Hey, Bootsie." I swooped my grey shorthaired cat into my arms after dropping my bags and gave her some much needed love. "How's my baby kitty?"

Bootsie rubbed her head against my chin.

"Let's go unpack." I set the cat on the floor and reclaimed my bags to rest them on the bed.

As I emptied my items, Bootsie jumped into my main bag. I played peek-a-boo, kneeling on the floor and bobbing my head up and down. Teased her with my finger over the bags opening, which she'd attack. And finally, I picked the bag up by the handles, with her in it, and carried it to store away in the closet. When I set it on the floor inside, she made her escape and tore out of the room.

I laughed at the silly cat and grabbed my small purse I'd used last night off the bed. Opening it, I removed the napkin Hank had written his cell phone number. I sat on the edge of the bed and stared at it until the tweedling of my phone startled me. Tossing the napkin, I sprang from the bed and raced for the kitchen table.

It was my best friend Lori. Accepting the call, I answered.

"Well, how was it? Did you hook up with anyone?" She didn't let me get past the hello.

"It was nice and no."

"Seriously, Beth. You need to spill the details. I know it was more than nice."

I wouldn't tell her about Hank because there wasn't anything tell. "The committee did a great job on the venue and food. They had a smaller ballroom decorated in the school colors with a patio off the room that we could go out on. There was a bar and DJ. They put together a booklet of where people were and what they're up to. It was nice."

"Any of your ex-boyfriends show up?"

"I didn't go looking for them and vice versa. I had a great time catching up with old friends."

"Well, I'm glad you had a good time. Are you up to dinner and a movie?"

I was thankful she let the reunion thing go.

"I could do dinner but no movie. I've got a headache. Too much vodka last night." I went into my room and sat on the edge of the bed.

"There was a guy then." Lori knew I drank to calm my nerves, especially when around men.

Shit! I needed a cover up fast.

"There was no guy. I needed a few to ... relax me because ... I was uncomfortable about you know, the divorce and all." My hand came in contact with Hank's napkin, so I picked it up. There was no need to tell her about him, or that kiss. Nothing happened. Then why was my stomach a flutter?

"Beth, you didn't do anything wrong in that marriage. He's the one that had problems."

"I know you're right. It was hard being around all the happily married or engaged couples." Back to the reunion again. I glanced to the napkin, to Hank's writing. The numbers were clearly written, the name not so clear.

"There had to be others there that were divorced. You just didn't talk to them."

"You're probably right, but it didn't make it any less uncomfortable. Do you mind if we do an early dinner? Say four." I lay back on my bed and closed my eyes. Oh, did that feel good.

We ended our call after making plans and I held the napkin up. My phone was right there in my hand. All I had to do was open the address book and put in the new contact info. So why was I so hesitant? Because it's Hank. Hank McGrath. My secret crush. The boy who never paid attention to me. Or for that matter, knew I existed. He was just being nice, that's all. But if he *does* call and I don't have him in my contacts, then I won't answer because I won't know it's him. I rolled on my stomach and entered his info into my contacts.

~ * ~

Monday afternoon, while at work, my phone pinged. Bringing the screen to life, there was a message, from Hank. My heart raced. I tapped the screen to open it.

Wondering about grabbing that drink tonight? Are you available?

Was he serious? I thought he was joking Saturday night. Did I dare meet him? But then why pass up on something I wanted so badly in high school? My breathing joined my heart in the race of keeping up. After staring at the screen for what seemed like several minutes, I responded: *Sure, I'm available. When and where?*

I read the message after I sent it and cringed at what I'd said. Sure he asked if I was available, but it sounded weird to say it, like I was a hooker or something. I shook my head.

He responded back: *What do you have planned for dinner?*

My response was immediate: *Nothing.*

Would you like to have dinner with me?

How did we go from a drink to dinner? My pulse rushed. It was just dinner. Dinner with an old friend. It wasn't a date. Just dinner. *Sure. I work until five.*

You said you're living downtown, and I'm still at the hotel, mind if we eat some place in the city?

Due to eating out on a regular basis, I asked: *Not at all. Did you have a place in mind?*

Mind if we go to Grumpy's? It's been a while since I've eaten there.

It was a little more than two blocks from my place. Nice and convenient. *Not at all. Love their food. What time?*

173

If I said 5:45, does that give you enough time?
Plenty. I'll see you then.

Oh, my God, this is really happening. Hank McGrath actually called, okay texted, *me*, and we're going out to dinner.

I put my phone down and shook my hands, as if that'd magically release the anxiety. Taking slow and steady breaths, I worked to calm myself down. I wanted to yell out my excitement, but put the energy into smiling.

~ * ~

My apartment door slammed behind me as I rushed to my closet. Standing there, I stared at my wardrobe. *What should I wear?* I wanted to look nice, but didn't want to be over dressed. Yet, I didn't want to appear like a slob if I dressed casually. Bootsie rubbed at my shin and meowed, as I flicked hangers to glance at my options. I let out a frustrated scream. I was overthinking this.

I picked up my black furry cat and stroked her fur to relax and ease my stress.

"What do you think, huh? What should I wear?" I spoke to my cat often and sought her advice frequently, too.

People laugh because an animal can't respond. What they don't know is, by talking, you can work through what might be bothering you, or need an answer, or as a simple stress reducer.

Bootsie rubbed against my chin, leaving a trail of hair. I set her down, wiped my face to remove said fur, and continued to stare into the abyss of clothing.

With a few more items pushed out of my way, I grabbed a casual-dress tank top and a knit skirt. Setting the items on my bed, I went to freshen up in the bathroom before changing my clothing. I switched my work shoes for a pair of sandals. Then transferred items from my large purse to the smaller one that held the essential items I'd need for the night. My wallet and phone. I checked my time and had fifteen minutes. It would take me less than ten minutes to walk there. Although I had plenty of time, I headed out the door to meet Hank.

The closer I got to Grumpy's, my heart rate accelerated to a pace walking could never achieve at the notion of having dinner with Hank. I slowed my pace, as much as I could. Standing on the corner of Eleventh and South Washington waiting for the light, I slowly inhaled and exhaled.

Crossing the street, I made the short trek to Grumpy's and opened the door on my last calming exhale. I glanced around for Hank before approaching the hostess to ask if he might be seated already. She escorted me out to the patio, where Hank sat drinking a beer in cargo shorts and a tee shirt. The sky was over-cast which brought little relief to the warm air.

The man could wear anything and look good.

"I'm not late, am I?"

He showed those damned dimples with his smile, and my heart sighed. That's why I fell for him in the first place. Maybe I was only attracted to him for his smile and nice body?

"Nope," he replied, assisting me with the chair next to his. "I got here a little earlier than I thought. They were getting busy, so I got us a table."

"Thank you." I gazed into his green eyes. Yeah, those were captivating, too. Add them to my list of what I like about the man.

"Hi, can I get you a drink?" the waitress asked, stepping to the table.

"I'll have a Corona, please."

"Did you want to order an appetizer?" she asked with a flirtatious smile directed at Hank.

"We'll have an order of the onion rings, please." He spoke to the waitress when ordering, then turned back to me.

"I'll put this in and be back with your beer." Her tone was a little less enthusiastic, probably because Hank didn't express interest.

"I tried to call you Sunday."

"Around eleven?" I sat forward toward him, maybe a little too excited.

"Yeah. I wanted to take you to breakfast and apologize."

"For what?" My face scrunched in confusion. He'd done nothing to...oh, this was all a mistake.

"I shouldn't have kissed you. I overstepped what I hope can be a friendship."

My head bobbed.

"Here's your beer, ma'am." The waitress set the bottle in front of me. "And the rings should be coming up soon." She left as quickly as she appeared.

I squeezed my lime wedge down the neck of the beer bottle, took a long pull and swallowed. "No problem. To friends." I lifted my drink, ticked his glass in the form of a cheers, and tipped the bottle back.

"Beth, I'm glad we talked at the reunion, not just because you can help me with finding a place here, but because I'd like to get to know you better."

My heart palpitated with the way he spoke the last words softly and with meaning. But didn't he just apologize for kissing me the other night? Ugh! Forever the hopeful, Beth.

"I was kind of a jerk in middle and high school."

"You were anything but a jerk. Hank, you were one of the nicest guys I knew. Trust me, there were bigger jerks."

"Thanks." He took a sip of his beer. "So, how long have you been divorced?"

"An order of onion rings for you." A server set a platter of rings on the table.

My mouth salivated as I set a small plate in front of Hank and one for me.

With another big drink of beer, the magic elixir began working to calm my nerves. "A little over a year. What about you? You've never gotten married?"

"Nope. Never made it to the altar." He grabbed a ring, setting it on the plate, while I did the same. I couldn't believe it. Maybe he was a playboy type. Date more than one woman at a time, keeping them at a distance.

"Would you two like to order or do you need a few minutes?" our waitress asked.

"Give us a few minutes." Hank watched her walk away. "I guess we should look over the menu."

I smiled politely, took a pull from the bottle, and glanced over the menu. "I'm ready."

"What are you getting?"

"The Elvis," I said with a crooked smile.

I watched his eyes widen with surprise. "Really? Peanut butter and bacon?"

I nodded. "It's that good."

"O-kay," he said drawn out, and focused on the menu.

A few minutes and our waitress returned. "Are you ready?"

Hank nodded at me. With our order placed, we worked on the onion rings.

"So what brings you back home to Minnesota?" I wanted to learn more about him than what little I remembered from our school days.

"A job opportunity came available that I couldn't pass up." He took a bite of onion ring.

"Doing what?"

"Investment banking, but I don't want to bore you with the details on our first date."

I coughed. Date? Did he say date?

"Are you okay?" He rested his hand against my back.

I took a swig of beer and swallowed. "Fine." I'm on a *date* with Hank. Maybe onion rings weren't a good idea.

In that moment, the rain poured from the sky soaking everyone and everything exposed.

Beth grabbed her bottle and my glass, as we ran for coverage inside. "Wow, they're busy," I said leaning into her.

"We're drenched," she said bursting into laughter. "I'm cold now. Listen, Hank, why don't we get our food to go and go back to my place where we can dry off and you can see my condo."

"Okay. I'll be right back." I left her standing by the patio door to go take care of the bill and our food. "We're all set. They'll bring our order to the hostess stand. Ready?"

"Yeah, but what should I do with my bottle?"

"Let's leave it at the bar on our way up front." I gestured to go ahead and took the opportunity to rest my hand against her back.

With the drinks left behind at the bar, we picked up our dinner from the hostess. Still raining, I asked as I opened the door, "Did you drive?"

"No, did you?" With so much skin exposed her body shivered.

I shook my head. "How far to your place?"

"A little over two blocks. I'm up for the run if you are." Her hazel eyes sparkled with the question.

"Is that a challenge?" I chuckled. "I can run on these beat up knees.

177

You lead the way."

She took off down the sidewalk and I stayed with her until we reached her building. We laughed our way inside.

"So, this is the lobby." She shook the water off. "I'm up on the third floor. This way."

We entered her apartment, and the view was amazing at the end of the hall.

"Don't just stand there. Come in." She had walked several steps in front of me. "I'll get you a towel." She disappeared down a hall.

A grey cat with white feet sauntered to my calf and rubbed its face against my hair covered leg. As I bent to pet him, he darted behind me, and Beth came from around the corner.

"Here." She tossed the towel at me. "If you don't mind, I'm going to change."

With the shake of my head, she closed a pocket door to a room off the hall and then I saw another door slide closed. I set the food on her kitchen counter and went back to the entrance. I dragged the towel over my head, then my legs and arms before wrapping it around my torso. There was a room off to the side. I entered her laundry room, where the cat tore out from farther in. Deciding to utilize the dryer to get out of the wet, I removed my shorts and shirt, tossed them in and started the dryer.

"Hank?"

I popped my head into the hall. "I found your dryer. Hope you don't mind if I use it?"

"No." Her voice drew near. "I was going to offer it to you." She stopped in the doorway. "Um, can I offer you my robe?" She glanced down.

With the dryer started, I approached her with the towel covering me. "The towel works. You look comfy."

She wore sweatpants and a t-shirt, with her hair down. Simple, casual, and damned if I didn't find it sexy as hell.

"You don't mind, do you?" She averted her gaze from mine. I wondered if she was embarrassed by me in a towel or my comment of her casual dress.

"Not at all. That's how I spend most of days at home, actually. Why don't we eat before the food gets any colder?"

She looked up and averted her eyes from making contact with me. "I'll get some plates and napkins."

"Beth," I touched her hand when she stood beside me. "If I'm making you uncomfortable, I'll put my clothes back on."

"No." This time our eyes connected. "You can wait for your clothes to dry. I'm fine. Do you like wine? I don't have any beer."

"Wine's good. What's your cat's name?"

She poured two glasses of red wine. "His name is Bootsie because—"

"Because he looks like he's wearing boots. It's perfect. He's very friendly."

"He is. You're not allergic I hope." She dished the food on the plates, and we sat and ate.

"No allergies. I love cats. You grew up with dogs, if I remember correctly."

She smiled and a pink color came upon her cheeks. "You remember? Yes, we had several dogs. Do you have any pets?"

"I have a black lab named Shadow. He's staying with a friend, since I'm at the hotel. Hoping to change that soon with having my own place. Yours is a nice size. The view is amazing." I glanced out the window at the Mississippi River. "Do you have a car, since you work and live downtown?"

"I do because I still need to be able to go places." She took a bite of a fry before continuing. "My parents still live in the house I grew up in and I visit often. Plus, I have friends I do things with that live in the 'burbs." She cut her burger in half and peanut butter oozed like cheese from the middle.

"That looks disgusting," I said with a laugh.

"Well, don't knock it until you try it," she teased.

"Would you mind if I took a small bite?"

She handed me her plate. I took a bite and absorbed all the flavors on my tongue. A creamy, nutty flavor, with the salty of the bacon, finished by beef. "That, is good." I returned her plate.

"Do you like living downtown?"

A person couldn't help but notice her bedroom right off of the dining room. The apartment wasn't super spacious but for a single person it could

179

work. Not for me though. I needed more space.

"Sure. Now. After I first bought the place, after the divorce, I thought I made a mistake. It was after being in the condo for a month that I questioned what I had done, but knew I couldn't go back to the suburbs. Now, here I am and I love city living." Her mouth wrapped around the burger and she took a bite. Peanut butter squeezed out sticking to the corner of her lips. Her tongue dashed out to lick it into her mouth.

The woman was torturing me and didn't even know it.

My mind was going where it shouldn't go. Not yet. I cleared my throat. "Do you ever see yourself leaving the city?"

She finished chewing and took a sip of wine. "I hope someday another guy will come along, we'd get married and have kids, which would lead to moving out of the city. Not saying that I have anything against raising kids in the city, but being from the suburbs, I'd want to raise my family there. What about you?"

"Everything you said." Maybe the someday would come sooner rather than later.

~ * ~

We sat on my couch talking and drinking. I finished explaining my job to Hank at the ad firm, petting Bootsie who had plopped on my lap the moment we sat in the living room. As I grew anxious about wanting to clear the air with Hank, I must've petted the cat too firmly because she hissed and went to Hank.

"Traitor." I curled my legs underneath my butt and leaned against the leather seating. "Hank, I…I just have to come out and say this. We're both adults. I like you. I've liked you since the fifth grade. I don't want to…to play the game of is he interested or not. The kiss Saturday night, did you want to kiss me? Or was it honestly a big mistake?"

The entire time I talked he remained silent with enough of an up ticked smile that exposed his dimples.

"I wanted to kiss you, Beth. Which is why I did. But after I did it, I felt it wasn't right of me to act that way when we…we didn't know each other well enough for me to do that." His smile faded and his face turned serious. "We're not horny high school teenagers anymore. We're adults and that's why I walked away when I did. I didn't want to take advantage of you."

I reared back. "Advantage of me? What are you talking about?"

The cat hopped down from his lap. "You had been drinking and I didn't know how much that would affect your decision making."

"A man with a conscience." I couldn't help but laugh. My own ex-piece-of-shit-husband didn't have a conscience, which was why he was my ex. "I'm sorry, I'm not laughing at you, but the ex."

"Since the fifth grade, huh? How did I not know this? Why didn't you ever ask me out?" His eyebrows drew in, scrunching his forehead.

"You're Hank McGrath. You were popular. The jock. Handsome. You were above me. I fell in the middle with the hand-me-down clothes. I wasn't in your crowd. Plus, like you said at the reunion, you and your buddies teased me. So why would I even *think* of trying to approach *the* Hank McGrath?"

I watched as his inquisitive face softened and turned sad. A part of me felt bad for what I said, but a large part felt relief. Relief for getting it out after so many years. No more secrets. I finished the remaining wine in my glass and got up to get more. Silence hung in the room.

"I'm sorry about the past. I want to think about the now. I'd like to be more than friends, Beth."

I turned to the man right behind me.

His large, warm hands rested on my hips. "Will you be my girlfriend?"

Dipping my shaking head to my chest in disbelief, his finger lifted my chin. I smiled. "Yes, I'd like that."

He raised me off the floor, sat me on my kitchen counter, and kissed me. This was the kiss I'd always dreamed about. The one that makes your inside melt and want it to never end.

But it does.

"I should be going." Hank lifted me off my ledge and held my hand as he led us to my door. "I'm going to be busy this week but I'll call you. We'll make plans. Thank you for the towel and letting me use your dryer."

"Any time. I'm usually home by five-thirty, so call me any time after that. Otherwise text me during the day."

He slid an arm around my waist, bent down and delivered another melting kiss.

181

~ * ~

The week passed slowly with two messages from Hank that were short and simple, but showed he was thinking of me. Friday morning, he texted asking if I would come over for dinner to his new place. When I asked if I could bring anything, he responded, a toothbrush.

I left work early and with my toothbrush tucked away in my purse, I set off on foot on South Second Street for Fifth Avenue along the river. The weather was beautiful, warm and sunny. I arrived and buzzed to gain entry. Riding the elevator to the twelfth floor, I fixed the few strands of hair that had fallen loose from my clip.

His door was straight ahead to the left of the elevator. I took a calming breath to settle the nerves that hit when I stepped off the elevator. I knocked, another relaxing breath, and…A beautiful, slender, blonde woman answered the door.

"I'm sorry. I must have the wrong apartment." I returned as quickly as possible to the bank of elevators.

I had the right apartment, but the wrong guy. Why did I fall for him? He found someone better looking. All the negative thoughts I'd say to myself ping-ponged in my mind. A set of doors opened, and I hurried inside and pushed the first floor button. The doors closed and I closed my eyes fighting the burn of tears. My giddiness turned to sadness before turning into anger. I was angry at Hank, but more at myself. The irritation fueled every step as I headed home.

Letting my front door slam closed, I tossed my purse to the kitchen counter where it touched down and slid to fall into my sink. Perfect. Hungry, but too upset to eat, I went into the bathroom and turned the water on to fill the tub. A relaxing bath was what was needed.

I stripped my clothes off and stepped to the bathroom. An urgent heavy knocking landed on my door. What the? Covered with my robe, I peeked through the peep hole. How the?

Cracking the door open, Hank stood before me breathing heavily.

"Why did you leave?" He worked to catch his breath. "Can I come in…please?"

I remained silent, standing behind the door, and opened it enough for him to pass through.

He set a plastic container on my countertop before eying me in my robe. "Beth, talk to me."

As he reached for me, I stepped back. "The fact that you're asking...I have nothing to say."

"She's my sister, Megan. You didn't give her the chance to say anything." His breathing was slowing to normal. "Can I have some water, please? I ran all the way here."

"There's bottled water in the fridge. Help yourself." The words came softly. I felt like an idiot. An insecure jerk. A teenage drama queen. "I'm sorry."

"It's okay. I can understand." Hank stepped to me. "Considering the situation with your ex, but I'm not him."

"Why was your sister at your place when you invited me over? And where were you, Hank?" It wasn't that I didn't believe him, I needed clarification.

"She was helping me finalize things around the apartment. I thought she was leaving when I got into the shower, but obviously not." His arms wrapped around my waist.

"What's in the container?"

"The dessert I made."

"You made and brought dessert?" I asked in disbelief.

"Nothing fancy. Just cookies. My favorite peanut butter cup cookies."

"Can I try one?"

He let go of me and opened the lid. The smell of roasted peanuts wafted out.

"Is that a miniature peanut butter cup in the middle?"

He nodded while picking a cookie from the container before setting it down. Holding it in front of my mouth, I took a bite. My eyes closed with the melty goodness. I had died and gone to heaven. With a smile, I opened my eyes and looked up at Hank.

"Are we good then?"

I replied with a tender kiss.

"I like your peanut butter kisses, Ms. Franta."

THE END

About the Author

Jody is a multi-published author with Satin Romance, an imprint of Melange Books, LLC. She has been a member of Romance Writers of America (RWA) and Midwest Fiction Writers (MFW) since 2001 and is a Provisional PAN member of RWA.

Born and raised in Minnesota, Jody remains close to home living with her husband of twenty-five plus years, three children and a cat named Holly. Growing up, she enjoyed reading V.C. Andrews' the Dollanganger series, starting with *Flowers in the Attic,* S.E. Hinton, and Stephen King to name a few. Today her tastes run across the board in fiction and non-fiction, in all genres.

She has traveled throughout the United States, to the Bahamas and Cancun, Mexico. Between watching her youngest son playing soccer, maintaining one of the many scrapbook albums, gardening and being the COO of the Vitek household, she writes contemporary romances.

Author Contacts

Website: www.jodyvitek.com
Email: info@jodyvitek.com
Facebook: https://www.facebook.com/pages/Jody-Vitek-
Author/142820225824162
Twitter: @JodyVitek

Peanut Butter Cup Cookies

You will need mini-muffin pans to make these cookies.

- 40 mini peanut butter cup candies (about two bags)
- ½ C butter
- ½ C creamy peanut butter
- ½ C white sugar
- ½ C brown sugar

- 1 egg
- 1 tsp. vanilla
- ¾ tsp. baking soda
- ½ tsp salt
- 1 ¼ C flour
-

Mix all ½ C's together, add egg and rest of the dry ingredients.

Roll into walnut size balls, and bake in mini-muffin pan at 375 degrees for 8-10 minutes, or until lightly browned.

Press peanut butter cup into center of hot cookie. (*Don't* push through to bottom of cookie.)

Let cool before removing from pan.

The Chocolate Queen

April and Holly Marcom

The Beginning... 8ᵗʰ Grade

I took an anxious breath as Eric and I walked across the school's noisy, crowded courtyard during lunch. Eric and I had been best friends for as long as I could remember, but we'd grown extra close this year. Close enough that I'd developed a crush and hoped he might feel the same way. Talking to each other on the phone right before we fell asleep was kind of our ritual, and the night before he'd said he needed to talk to me about something important today.

This was the first time I'd ever been nervous about being alone with him.

We set our trays down on one of the few courtyard tables still available. Of all the middle schools in the city of Arclarium, ours was the biggest. I glanced at our crummy cafeteria food of mashed potatoes and fish sticks when my stomach growled.

"I don't know how to say this, Clarissa..." Eric looked down and rubbed the back of his neck under his beautiful dark curls of hair like he was terribly disappointed. Whatever he needed to talk about, it had nothing to do with a crush.

The sun shone bright and warm in the sky, but inside a chill and a shadow of fear at whatever he was about to tell me took hold. I fumbled absently with the black bow tied at the center of the neckline of my purple loose-fitting blouse. I'd painted my nails to match my shirt and purplish-blue eyes.

"What is it, Er—"

"My family's moving away at the end of the month." He looked up at me.

My heart broke. The world darkened. My appetite deserted me completely. Then, he placed his hand over mine on the table.

A bunch of nauseatingly peppy cheerleaders laughed obnoxiously at something one of them had said a few tables away. It seemed cruel after what Eric had just said.

"I hate that this is happening. We really could have been something great," he said with a wink.

"Yeah?" A mixture of happy fulfillment and broken heartedness swirled through my chest.

He nodded in response.

A long silence followed, except for the rapid beat of my heart. The whistling wind blew my straight, brown hair against his shoulder, making him smile.

He finally broke the silence, reaching to scratch the back of his head nervously. "I wish I could change things."

"Are you sure your parents won't change their mind?" It wasn't fair that he was moving away after I'd just discovered his true feelings.

"They've already put a down payment on a house and started packing."

I reached out to smooth the collar of his plaid shirt down on one side, rubbing my thumb softly against his neck. "Maybe you can still visit. Who else am I gonna sing horribly with to all our favorite songs?"

He reached for my hand and laced his fingers through mine. "We're moving to North Carolina. It's like twelve hours away from here."

An intimidating voice came from behind us, making us both flinch. "So, old Eric's moving away." Julian glared down at me.

He was as popular as guys came due to his muscles and star basketball player abilities, but his nose and chin were dreadfully pointed. He'd hated my guts ever since I embarrassed him in front of his freshman girlfriend Makenzie last year by exposing his big secret. He'd faked another girlfriend just to make Makenzie jealous when they split up. He'd bullied me hardcore for months afterward until Eric told him to back off.

Even Julian wasn't stupid enough to stand up to Eric. He was lean, but all muscle. He'd taken martial arts since the first grade and even won a few awards in national competitions. I hadn't missed a single local match to date, mostly because he was my best friend, but partly because it was after one of these matches that he was at his most gorgeous. His dark eyes reflected stunningly against his sweating forehead and his hair pulled back in a ponytail was always damp and shining like silky dark chocolate.

"Eric may have things in check, but it's checkmate for you," Julian said to me.

Kids were already staring. I could just barely make out someone whispering behind us about needing to call a hearse for me.

My stomach protested at Julian's wicked grin. He looked like some vengeful goblin. The panic I began to feel escalated quickly at the thought of how bad things were about to get.

Eric stood up and got right in Julian's face.

I leaped out of my seat when our table began to shudder violently. Tremors of fear continued to vibrate through my body.

Screaming came from every direction. Kids scattered all over the place as every table in the courtyard rose above our heads like clouds floating in the sky. They banged and smashed together as they clustered to hover directly above Julian, Eric, and me.

"Principal Hawkins…" Mrs. Van shouted as she raced into the school. Half the students followed her inside, bumping into and knocking each other out of the way.

One of the cheerleaders screamed when she tripped and was trampled by the last of the terrified kids. She scrambled to her feet and limped inside behind them.

"Eric," I whispered, placing a shaking hand on his elbow.

Julian shook visibly, his face white as a ghost. "W… what is this, man?"

"Lay one finger on Clarissa while I'm gone and you can bet I'll be back to destroy you," Eric said. He took my arm and pulled me out of the way a moment before the tables tilted and all the trays and food and milk dumped all over Julian's head.

In spite of how totally freaked out I was, I laughed when he ran into the school, hollering like a maniac. I grew quiet again as I watched the tables return to their original spots in awe.

"How did you do that?" I said to Eric.

Every kid still outside crowded around us, staring at Eric in amazement. The brainiacs, punk rockers, cheerleaders, norms, and even the athletes didn't dare speak above a nervous whisper.

Eric surveyed them before turning his attention to me. "That was a fancy magic trick I arranged to keep Julian off your back. I've been planning it for a while."

"But..." I leaned over the table and waved my arm back and forth. Nothing. "There's no way—all the tables out here. How?"

"That's a secret."

Just then the principal walked outside with Mrs. Van. Kids began slamming into each other, trying to get out of the way, when Eric took my hand and led me toward the gym to hit up the vending machines.

"What's going on out here?" Principal Hawkins shouted behind us. "Someone had better start talking, NOW!"

Judging by the silence that followed, no one was brave enough to rat out Eric.

My mind raced madly as we crossed the sidewalk. A magic trick? One so massive, there's no way he could have kept it from me? So, why keep it a secret? We'd never had secrets between us. How on earth had he snuck onto school grounds and set it all up ahead of time? There were security cameras everywhere. It made no sense.

We both stepped into the outer hall of the gymnasium when a pipsqueak sixth grader who was leaving held the door open for us. She let it go a little too soon. The heavy swinging door shot toward the back of my head. Eric held up a hand. The door froze mid-swing a moment before he pressed his hand against it to keep it from crashing into me.

A thought hit me hard enough that I jerked my hand out of his and put it over my mouth. "Why didn't you ever tell me you have superpowers?" I mumbled from behind it. That made so much more sense than a spectacular trick.

I could hardly believe my best friend was a phylogenic, a human born with at least one incredible superpower. There were so few in the world, and the ones with telekinesis were the rarest. I'd always wanted to meet one.

"I don't have superpowers." Eric laughed. "I told you; it was just a trick, a very non-super, ordinary trick. Now, what can I buy you?"

I stared at him not knowing what to say. The look in his sharp black eyes I'd known so well all my life told me he wasn't giving up any more information. So I shook my head, too upset about him leaving to care about the pain of him putting secrets between us for the first time in our lives.

~ * ~

Eric and I spent as much time together as we could in the two weeks we had before he left. It flew by way too quickly.

I didn't know what to believe. Eric had never lied to me before, but it was difficult to accept that the flying tables were nothing more than an impressive magic trick. It didn't help that he refused to tell me how he did it.

My first morning back to school after he was gone was awful. When I opened my locker, and found the note shoved inside, I really lost it.

Dear Clarissa,

Leaving you sucks. I would have done anything to be able to stay. I'm already missing you while I write this letter. Just remember that you'll always be my best friend. That can never change.

I leave you with this promise: Sooner or later I'll return to you and things will go back to what they've always been.

I promise you,

Eric

Kids walking by gave me either sympathetic or bizarre looks when I started crying even harder right there in the middle school hallway, even though his note was so sweet. All I could do now was hope that he would keep his promise.

Chapter One

Years Later…

The morning was a nice mixture of sunshine and clouds. With the seasons changing, the weather was warm with a chilly breeze, like it couldn't quite decide if it wanted to remain winter or become spring. The day was still so young, I was yet to see anyone else out and about.

I was walking on the city sidewalks of Arclarium, the same streets I've walked my entire life, on my way to talk fashion with a good friend of mine named Eloise. I was running late.

My adult love life was pretty anemic. Yeah, it would have been nice to have a loving man with warm, powerful arms to hold me close at the end of each day, but I didn't have time for the effort of finding one.

As I grew from teenager to adult, fashion had taken over my life. Superhero fashion, that is. I designed clothing with the most famous superheroes of our day as the theme. I'd done quite well for myself since business began.

My best seller at the moment was a silver go-go style dress similar to the Diamond Star's, with bright red gloves and skirt lining to represent her red hair. Her mask was printed on the right hip with her eyes closed and her insanely long lashes gracing her cheeks, along with her grinning red lips.

I'd received countless messages on my blog recently with rumors that the Deadly Dragon had moved to our city, along with a few very convincing pictures. Eloise and I were planning to design a line of jackets representing him. We hadn't decided much over the phone, except that his reptilian dragon scales would be a major part of the design.

The ideas swimming through my mind were all wiped away when a hand closed over my mouth and someone began pulling me into a nearby alleyway. Sweaty fingers muffled my broken screams. My long hair shook wildly with all the jerking back and forth. I was petrified. With no one nearby, I was completely at this creep's mercy.

I was thrown mercilessly into the hard concrete ground and my elbow stung with a fresh scrape. Ugly black stains smeared up the side of my silk, Victorian-style top. I thought only of escape.

Green dumpsters with grimy seepage leaking out whizzed through my vision as I rolled over to face my attacker. The masked giant reached back as if he was going to hit me when something came slicing through the air behind him. A swift kick to the head sent him sprawling on the ground beside me. He lay perfectly still.

The man standing looked surprisingly familiar. His dark curls were mostly hidden under a baseball cap. The green Arclarium Central High t-shirt and black soccer shorts he wore revealed how well he'd grown into his killer body.

"Eric? Eric Caesar? Is that you?" I was terribly shaken. In spite of our initial efforts to keep in touch, we'd lost contact with each other years ago.

He held out a hand to help me up. "The one and only. I wasn't expecting to find you on the other end of this mugger. You all right?"

"I… I think so." I gripped his arm with my free hand when I swayed from side to side.

"Whoa." Eric put both hands on my sides to help me keep my balance. "Maybe you should sit down."

"No, I'm fine, just shaken. It's so good to see you." I put my hands around his neck so I could hug him, full of relief and excitement at seeing him. "Thank you for rescuing me."

He laughed and gave me a good squeeze in return. "Looks like you've still got a bully problem. Good thing I showed up when I did."

I screamed and jumped behind Eric when one of the masked man's legs twitched. I relaxed when no movement followed. Even if he woke, I knew I was safe with Eric there.

It was impossible not to feel the old crush I had for him years ago returning. I sincerely hoped this wouldn't be our only reunion.

"What are you doing back in the city?"

"I just got my first job as the soccer coach at Arclarium High School.

I'm on my way over there right now. Did you graduate from there?"

"Yep. Arclarium's always been home to me. I'm the designer behind SUPERHERO 101 Fashions now."

"No way. So you write SUPERHERO 101?"

"That's my blog."

"That's awesome. You want to go get something to eat after I call the cops to come get this creep? I'll probably have to call in late, anyway."

"Yeah."

I felt more anticipation at the idea of spending time reminiscing with Eric than I had in a long time. I hadn't been invited out by a man for anything other than business in such a long time, and this one in particular would always hold a special place in my heart.

Ring, ring.

My cell went off inside my purse still lying on the ground. Eric took his phone from his pocket and dialed the police as I fished out mine. The caller ID told me it was Eloise.

"Oh no. I totally forgot Eloise," I said, putting the phone to my ear.

"What's the deal?" she said. "You were supposed to be here fifteen minutes ago."

"I know. I'm sorry. I just had a little run-in with a mugger, but I'll be there as soon as I can."

"Oh my gosh; are you okay?"

"Yeah, just a little skinned up. By some miracle, an old friend showed up to rescue me."

"Too bad it wasn't Apparition or Breech. Being rescued by either of our city's superheroes would have made a great up close and personal story for your blog."

"I don't know. I kind of prefer it this way." I smiled at Eric, catching his eyes as he disconnected from the police and then dialed the high school to let them know he'd be late.

"Well, I'll keep the pizza warm," Eloise said. "You just get here when you can."

"See yah."

"Bye."

I waited a minute for Eric to clear things up with the principal.

As soon as he finished, he reached out for my arm to get a look at the wound. "You're bleeding. I'd offer to get something to clean it up with if I wasn't afraid to leave you alone with this guy."

"It's just a little scrape; I'm fine." I rummaged through my purse until I found a Kleenex to wipe the blood away with. "Sorry, Eric, but I've got to be somewhere when I'm done here."

"No worries. Maybe I could buy you dinner tomorrow night?"

"No way. You just saved me from an attacker. Dinner's on me. Why don't you come by my place and I'll make us something to eat? Maybe around six thirty?"

"Sounds great. Just remember, I'm—"

"Allergic to nuts? I know."

"I'm impressed." He laughed. Already, talking with him was beginning to feel like old times.

"Hey, what happened here?" A pudgy man with a tiny head like a marble balancing on a watermelon stopped at the edge of the alleyway when he saw us. The ribbons of smoke drifting away from his cigarette danced through my nostrils.

"The police are coming to handle it," Eric said.

"You two are all right, then?"

"Yep."

The passerby nodded and continued on his way.

Eric and I didn't have to wait long for the police to arrive. I was grateful for Eric staying with me since I would have been helpless if the assailant awoke. An ambulance came for the mugger shortly after the police arrived. They got the footage from a surveillance camera across the street and filed a report.

I would have been happier to get away from it all if it didn't also mean leaving Eric.

A thought struck me like lightning after we'd gone our separate ways. The Deadly Dragon had allegedly just joined Arclarium, a known telekinetic. Eric just moved here, appearing out of thin air like magic… or like a phylogenic. I never really did decide whether I believed the table incident years ago had only been a trick or not. Suddenly I felt terribly inadequate to be going out with him.

Chill out, I told myself. He showed up without a mask, without throwing flames like the Deadly Dragon always does. There were no powers involved. I was getting worked up over nothing.

I chuckled to myself as I shook my head. Besides, it wasn't an official date or anything. It was just two friends getting together to catch up and remember old times.

Chapter Two

Finally, I heard the apartment buzzer alerting me that I had a guest. I put the book I was reading down on the coffee table and hurried to the door. Eric was already seventeen minutes late and I was beginning to think he was a no show.

I pushed the intercom button. "Eric, is that you?"

"Yeah. Sorry I'm late."

"Come on up."

I glanced in the oval mirror hanging to the left of my front door as I waited. My sleek, modern apartment decorated to look more retro reflected behind me. I much preferred bold, bright colors to the dull gray and shining white everyone seemed to be into these days.

"Ah," I gasped when I saw my mascara had smeared under my left eye. I rubbed at it until a knock sounded at the door.

Eric held out a dozen red roses when I opened it. He looked so handsome in his blue collared shirt. It seemed a bit strange in comparison to how messy his brown hair was, like he'd driven all the way here with the top down in a convertible.

"You look really beautiful tonight," he said.

"Thanks." I glanced down at the simple purple dress I'd designed and made myself. Purple was always my best color.

"Come on in. Dinner's already on the table."

"Good. I'm starving."

He followed me through the sunken living room into the kitchen, where I'd set a small glass-top, triangular table with steak and my own recipe for loaded potatoes. I got an orange vase from the cupboard for the roses before I sat across from him.

"Sorry it's not super fancy," I said. "Maybe I'm stereotyping, but I

197

figure men prefer meat and potatoes."

"Hey, I love steak."

I watched him pick up a fork and stab his hunk of meat like he was right at home. Eric obviously wasn't half as nervous as I was.

"Any new stories coming out on your blog?" he said as he cut through his steak.

"Now that you mention it, I've been getting a ton of messages about the Deadly Dragon being in the city and lots of requests for a post about him. If I could just get some hard evidence, I'd be set."

"This city?"

"Yeah. I wish I could get an interview with him or see him at least."

Eric laughed.

"What's so funny?"

He only shook his head and kept eating. "This is amazing. You could be a gourmet chef."

"Thanks. It's a hobby of mine to mess around in the kitchen."

"Mmmm." He'd just taken a bite of the potatoes. "These are almost better than the steak."

"Just wait till dessert."

He smiled and lifted an eyebrow. "You really went all out. Why don't we talk about our favorites for fun, compare our nows and thens?"

"Okay."

"Favorite drink?"

"Kool-Aid as a kid, Pepsi now."

"Me too, but I like Coke now. Favorite color?"

"Blue then, purple now. What about you?"

"Yellow then, green now..."

This went on for most of the meal and I was having a lot of fun. It was quickly feeling more like two best friends being reunited than a first date, assuming it was a date. Hopefully it was a date.

We talked a long time after dinner before I remembered to get dessert. "I hope you still like chocolate," I said, cutting us each a piece of cake.

"You know chocolate's my favorite. You used to buy me a king sized Hershey bar for my birthday and Christmas every year, remember?"

"Of course I do, but you never know if someone's on a diet or their tastes have changed."

Eric held his hands up. "Well, just so you know, it's a safe bet that I will always love chocolate."

I watched him as he took his first bite, since he seemed to appreciate my cooking so much. He chewed it slowly, his eyes opening a bit wider.

"Wow, that's really good. What's in it?"

"I mixed crushed Butterfingers into the cake batter and added miniature chocolate chips and crushed M&Ms to the frosting. The rest is just another of my secret recipes."

"I could eat your cooking every night and never get tired of it." He leaned forward over the plate so he could take a giant bite of cake. Bits of cake rolled over his chin onto the plate, and he acquired a slight frosting mustache. It reminded me so much of when we were kids and he'd shove nearly an entire candy bar into his mouth at once, filling me with nostalgia.

"Why don't you come over for dinner Wednesday night? Tomorrow I'll be busy working on my Deadly Dragon design with Eloise."

I blushed, realizing I'd just asked him out. I squeezed my knee under the table, suddenly feeling extremely nervous again. It would be worth it, though, to see him again.

"Really?" Eric smiled.

"Yeah. Um… this, this was a lot of fun and I like that you love my cooking. It's nice to have someone appreciate it."

"Okay. I'm looking forward to another meal as great as this one." He stood up when he was done eating. "I should probably head out. I've got to get up early for work tomorrow."

I stood to walk him across the living room.

"Thanks again for dinner," Eric said. "It's one of the best meals I've ever had, and that cake was insane."

We stopped at the door. "Thanks for keeping your promise," I said, thinking of the last note he'd written me.

"I'm surprised you remember that," he chuckled. "That's sweet."

"How could I forget? I even still have the note hidden in one of my dresser drawers."

"Nuh-uh."

"Yeah, I'll get it out to show you next time you come over for a date." I froze. Why did I keep blurting stuff like that out?

Eric laughed and leaned forward to kiss my cheek. "I can't wait."

With that he was gone, and I was left alone to squeal with excitement.

My hair flew behind me as I held up my arms and did several ballet-style leaps across the living area to my SUPERHERO 101 coffee table. Printouts of some of my most popular blog posts and fashions made up a colorful mod podge on the surface of the long stand.

After grabbing my cell, I went to climb out of the giant window in the back of the room opposite my front door. I sat on the fire escape outside for some stargazing. As I thought about my wonderful date, I found myself making heart-shaped constellations in the sky.

A flicker of strange light caught my eye from below. My apartment was on the third floor of the building, so I had a clear view of the empty sidewalks. I only saw a lone man walking by with a dark jacket that had a row of spikes running the length of his spine, like a dragon. When he looked in my direction, I saw the famous, scaly mask. The ball of fire he held in his bare hand left me with no doubt. It was the Deadly Dragon.

I grabbed my phone frantically, opened the camera, and...*CLICK*.

Chapter Three

Wednesday night came quickly. I was just taking my chicken pot pie out of the oven. The sweet meaty smells reminded me of Thanksgiving Day, putting a warm, happy feeling inside me. The zucchini and squash were already done, so I could stop worrying about dinner and start worrying about putting the finishing touches on my Deadly Dragon jacket design.

Wanting to encourage a bit of romance, I had chosen a gold silk lounge with floppy sleeves to wear. As I crossed the living room, I stopped by my stereo system to turn on some calming music. My nerves weren't much better than they were before our first date, in spite of how well it had gone. I focused on how funny Eric was and how comfortable it felt to be with him as I dialed in to some classical ballet.

Just when I started to feel completely at ease, a buzz came over the intercom. It jerked me from the peaceful atmosphere, especially because Eric still had five minutes and I'd kind of expected him to show up late again.

"Eric?" I said, pressing the button on the wall beside the door

"Yep."

I buzzed him in and waited expectantly inside my open doorway. A cold shot of rapturous adrenaline pulsed through my veins when he stepped out of the elevator into my hallway. He smiled brightly when he saw me. I noticed his hair was more in order this time.

"Well, you're early," I said, holding an arm out to welcome him inside. The loose fabric of my flowing golden sleeve swayed with my arm's movement. "What a nice surprise."

"I'd jump over a waterfall to get to your cooking," Eric said.

"Is that the only reason you're here?" I teased.

"Course not." He stepped inside, putting a hand on my back and pulling me closer, a devious grin spreading over his handsome face. It put a man's warmth into me I hadn't felt in a long time. "But there was something else…" He squinted as he turned his gaze upward, trying to remember. "What was it?"

"The note." I snapped my fingers. "I totally forgot. Just let me grab it and we can sit down to eat or we could just stand here and get cozy all evening."

My hands rested against his broad shoulders as I tried to decide if I was hungrier for dinner or for more of his delightful touch. A shiver raced along my spine at feeling his impressive muscles through his shirt.

"Decisions, decisions…" Both his hands slid over my back.

I laughed before I drew away, deciding it was better to take things slow. Eric wasn't just some guy who seriously attracted me. He was more than that.

I walked past my TV stand and stereo equipment to my room and began rummaging through my dresser. It startled me when I realized Eric was standing in the doorway, staring at the mannequin sporting my unfinished design.

"You've never met the Deadly Dragon before, have you?" Eric said.

"No, have you?"

"I've met him a time or two." He circled the mannequin. "The scales aren't dark enough. They're also not pointing the right way."

"So you're an expert on the Deadly Dragon?"

"Well, I said I've met him before."

"Not fair. I'd love to meet him, but… Here it is." I finally felt the note under my Tornado Man T-shirt. "As promised." I held it out to Eric.

My stomach fluttered as his eyes roamed over the old letter. Hopefully it didn't make me seem obsessed.

"I'm glad you kept your promise," I said.

"Me too." He smiled at me for a moment, then sniggered. "Yeah, sorry, that just got cheesy. Did Julian ever bother you again?"

I burst out laughing, remembering the terror in Julian's eyes every time they met mine. "Actually, he bolted every time he saw me after you left. He even had his mom make sure we never had any classes together. Thanks, by the way. You probably saved me from years of torture."

"Any time."

"We should probably eat before everything gets cold."

"Right. What's on the menu tonight?" Eric returned the note to me.

"Chicken pot pie with roasted squash and zucchini."

"Sounds good."

I decided to let the music continue playing as we sat down and served ourselves. The excitement of seeing Eric take his first bite of my pie far outweighed my anxiety.

He chewed slowly, leaning forward and closing his eyes for a moment. "Man, you must be the best cook in the world."

I giggled, ignoring the wailing sirens racing by outside. "What would your mother say if she heard you talking like that?"

"She'd probably ask if she could come along to dinner with me next time. She was always more of a microwave dinner kind of cook." Eric took a giant bite of pie, like he hadn't eaten since the last time he was over.

"Don't choke, for goodness sakes."

"I can't 'elp it; it's so good," he said through the mouthful.

I shook my head and started on my own plate of food. I remembered we never really ate dinner at his house growing up because Eric hadn't cared much for his mother's cooking.

He hardly got to his zucchini and squash before a loud beeping came over the radio.

"Sorry for the interruption, folks," the announcer began. "We have an important announcement for the citizens of Arclarium. An armed robbery has just occurred at The Downtown RDC Bank."

I stared at Eric, wide-eyed. "That's right down the street." I got up and went to the window. Lights from police cars and ambulances flashed wildly outside the bank. It was a tall red brick structure about five buildings away from mine.

"Two were shot and one killed," the radio announcer continued. "The robbers escaped with more than a quarter of a million dollars and are still at large. They're considered armed and extremely dangerous. Police are doing everything they can to find them, but for now they're advising everyone in Arclarium to stay inside and lock their doors.

"I hate to do this, but I've gotta go," Eric said, staring at his cell phone and rising.

"What, now? We haven't even had dessert yet."

"I'm really sorry, Clarissa."

"But... the police said to stay inside. There are dangerous men on the loose and you're just gonna leave me here all alone?" I couldn't believe this. What on earth could be so important that he had to leave right now?

Eric let out a sigh as he crossed the room to put his arms around me. "I've always protected you, haven't I?"

I'd never thought of it like that, but it was true. I was so stunned and angry at the moment, though, I couldn't bring myself to answer.

"Trust me when I say you'll be perfectly safe tonight." Then he leaned forward and kissed me.

My heart hammered. Every care melted away. All I could think of to do was put my arms around his neck and enjoy that kiss.

"Could we try this again tomorrow night?" he said softly, keeping his face next to mine.

I nodded, feeling blissful.

He kissed my cheek before he crossed the room and left.

Feelings of resentment began to return with his departure. Something inside me kept reminding me that he had always protected me, even when he wasn't there. No one was brave enough to be mean to me throughout my school years. It was hard to stay angry at his cryptic promise of safety.

The idea of Eric being the Deadly Dragon flitted in and out of my mind as I went to ensure all my windows were locked. There were so many signs pointing to it. Yet it seemed impossible that out of all the people in the world, and even in Arclarium, that the boy who'd been my best friend for years and who I was now dating could be this amazing phylogenic.

I'd hardly made it back to the kitchen to put leftovers away when a knock sounded at the door. A surge of excitement at the thought of Eric changing his mind shot through me as I raced across the room. However, when I opened the door, my next door neighbor stood there in a brown coat and pink house slippers. She was an old widow with crinkly, pale skin that rarely saw the light of day.

"Mrs. Hensley," I said, trying to hide the disappointment in my voice. "What brings you here?"

"I just saw the robbery on the news," she began. "I was looking out to make sure our hallway was clear when your gentlemen friend passed by. He suggested I come over here and we keep an eye on the news together until the criminals are caught."

"Aww." What a sweet thing for Eric to do. I really didn't want to be alone. I would have preferred that he stayed, but I appreciated him making sure I wasn't by myself. "I think that's a great idea. Would you like some chocolate cake?"

"Yes, please."

I was grateful for Eric looking out for me, even if it was in sort of a strange way.

Chapter Four

Thursday morning, I decided to take Eric a piece of my chocolate cake for lunch as a surprise. It was such a shame he didn't get to eat any the night before and, to be honest, I was dying for an excuse to see him.

It was a cheerful morning with a clear sky and a soft warm breeze. I smiled at a woman when she walked past me carrying a sleeping boy.

All that was ruined in a single moment. Just ahead of me, two shop windows shattered all over the sidewalk. The Deadly Dragon was thrown from the building to the street. He stood up and jumped out of the way onto a blue Volvo when a pair of lasers shot out of the damaged building toward him. People on the sidewalks ran away screaming. I stayed right where I was.

Apparition appeared running through the wall of my favorite shoe shop across the street. She wore a gray suit with smoky print rising all over it. She had the power to see through and pass through solid objects. The more established hero of our city raced to the Deadly Dragon's side.

"I got here as soon as I could. What—" Apparition did a backwards somersault out of the way when another laser was fired.

The Deadly Dragon held up a hand and shot a steady stream of fire into the opening from which he'd been thrown.

A man in all black stepped through the broken window—Arclarium's newest villain. His eyes glowed bright red. He advanced on the Deadly Dragon, seemingly unaffected by dragon flames.

The eyes behind the dragon mask met mine at that moment. "Get the woman to safety," he shouted to Apparition.

I suspected his deep voice was distorted by a small device hidden in his mask. Sparks flew from under the silver SUV behind the Deadly Dragon where the lasers had struck. A thunderous explosion and blinding light forced me to turn away.

"LOOK OUT," Apparition shouted.

The car sailed through the air right toward me. I screamed and fell over as I tried to run away. I stumbled, staggered, and scraped desperately at the ground, trying to escape. It surprised me when I wasn't crushed to oblivion. I looked up and saw the SUV hanging upside down not more than three feet above my head. The Deadly Dragon held his hand so it was facing the vehicle, keeping it midair.

I clutched my fallen purse as I scrambled out of the way and ran around the nearby corner where all sorts of bright, cartoony graffiti greeted me. The SUV fell behind me with a deafening CRUNCH. Its alarm began beeping wildly.

I pulled out my cell and used my video recorder to catch everything from a relatively safe distance. The picture trembled violently with my hand.

I leaned around the corner and only caught about two seconds of the action before Mr. Death Ray shot his deadly lasers right at me and Apparition slammed into his side. Sirens blared from the opposite direction.

When I didn't see any more red beams, I chanced another glance. The video was still rolling. Now the villain was lying on the pavement on his stomach. Apparition had her knee in his back and the Deadly Dragon held his head facing down so Mr. Death Ray could do no more damage.

Police car tires screeched as they slammed on their breaks in the middle of the street. The cops began swarming the heroes and the villain.

I kept recording as I approached the mass, knowing the playback would be awful. A lot of orders were being shouted back and forth.

The Deadly Dragon stood up when he saw me approaching, leaving the officers to drag away the new villain with a thick iron mask covering his face. I noticed a deep, curved cut on The Deadly Dragon's right forearm where his sleeve had been split open. It was bleeding pretty badly.

"I guess this is a bad time to ask for an interview for SUPERHERO 101," I said.

He nodded.

I turned the camera off and traded the phone in my purse for the piece of chocolate cake. "I was going to give this to my boyfriend, Eric," I began.

"Boyfriend?" His mask only covered the top half of his face, so I could see him smiling clearly.

"Yeah, he loves this stuff. I was taking it to surprise him at work, but after you just saved my life, maybe you should have it."

"Thank you," he said when I handed it to him.

"Thank you for saving me."

He nodded before running across the street and turning around a bend.

I withdrew my phone again to call Eloise and tell her everything that had just happened.

Chapter Five

"You showed up on time again," I said teasingly as I opened the door on Eric and mine's third date. Just like always, I was a little nervous.

"I came straight from practice."

He stepped inside and dropped his green duffle bag next to the door before he shut it behind him. Without warning, he pulled me close and kissed me. Really kissed me. Like, take my breath away kissed me.

"I've been looking forward to seeing you all day." He grinned, keeping his entire body pressed against mine.

"M... me too." I shook my hair to the sides away from my face. This was already going so much better than I'd expected. "I was going to surprise you for lunch, but I had a crazy run-in with this phylogenic who shot lasers out of his eyes. It left me shaken enough I came back home."

"Yeah? It looks like you survived. Did you see Apparition?" Eric took my hand and led me toward the table, where he pulled my chair out for me.

"Apparition did show up, but the Deadly Dragon's the reason I survived."

Eric grabbed a steaming smoked salmon to put on his plate, followed by a couple of rice balls. "So, it's official then? The Deadly Dragon's in Arclarium?"

"Yeah, I saw him a few nights ago, too, right after you left. I was hoping to get an interview with him today but he took off. His arm had a nasty cut he probably needed to get treated."

"So what happened exactly?"

I watched him take his first bite of salmon before I answered.

He gave me a little bow of the head. "This is incredible, of course."

"Thanks. I was going to bring you a piece of my chocolate cake, but

I opted to give it to the Deadly Dragon instead for saving my life. He smashed through a window right in front of me on my way to the high school…"

I took turns eating and telling Eric bits of the story. He listened without saying or reacting much, even when I said a car had nearly flattened me into a pancake, which seemed odd.

I wrapped it all up with the question that had been at the front of my mind all day. "So why'd you have to leave last night?"

"Family emergency."

I lifted an eyebrow. He left it at that. So I rose to get the fresh chocolate cake I'd made that afternoon, feeling slightly irritated with him.

Eric reached out for my hand once I'd set a piece in front of him. "Thanks, Clarissa. I really am sorry about last night."

I shrugged and sat down across from him.

"You know it's still pretty early," Eric said, glancing at the red lightning bolt-shaped clock hanging above my TV. "You wanna take a walk with me over to my place after this? It's not far from here."

"Sure." I cheered up at the idea of him letting me into that piece of his life. I didn't want to say anything so early in our relationship, but I was curious about his setup. "Do you have a roommate I should know about?"

"Nah, I prefer living on my own… You know, until the right woman comes along." The way he smiled at me made my heart beat faster.

"I know what you mean. I've always liked having my own space. What was the weather like when you got here?"

"It felt good to me, just a little breezy. But don't worry." He winked. "I'll keep you warm."

I had to smile back. It felt like everything was falling into place with Eric, like this was exactly the way it was meant to happen.

He stood up and held a hand out for me when we were finished. We chatted about my blog and the mid-sized town he lived in before moving back to Arclarium as we took the elevator down and left my apartment building behind.

The city lights mixed with Eric's warm hand holding tight to mine put a feeling of excitement into my heart. It was so much fun whenever I was with him. He only let go so he could put his arm around me when a chilly breeze swept over us.

We moved out of the way to let a woman ride her bicycle past us. Around the corner, a couple of street performers were breakdancing to a hip hop tune their little speaker and mp3 were playing. The sidewalks were interesting and busy, perfect for a nighttime walk with Eric.

I was surprised when he led me into the Crystal Falls apartment building only a few blocks away from mine. It was one of the most exclusive and expensive apartments in Arclarium. I couldn't imagine how someone on a teacher's salary could afford this place.

"Good evening, Mr. Caesar," the gentleman standing outside in a fine bellhop suit said as he opened the front door for us.

"Wow," I uttered softly, looking around at the white walls and floor that were so shiny you could see your own reflection. There was an opaque glass wall in the back with *Crystal Falls Spa* painted on a left side door and *Crystal Falls Patisserie* painted on the right side door, both in gold calligraphy. "I've only been here once before, to see Madame Lavendraess about selling some of my fashions in her boutique."

"Ah, Madame Lavendraess. She reminds me more of a batty, old witch than a designer."

I laughed as we entered a shiny silver elevator complete with a short elevator man who knew which button to push without asking. We were quiet on the short ride to the eighth floor. My mind was reeling with how Eric lived in a place I would have barely been able to afford. The hallway we entered was abnormally wide with fresh potted flowers on bronze tables and glittering chandeliers hanging from the ceiling.

"Eric, I don't want to be rude, but… how can you live here?"

He laughed as he walked me down the hall to the fifth door on our right. "A little family business I do on the sidelines."

"Right." They were always wealthy growing up, though I could never quite get it out of his parents what they did for a living. He didn't elaborate, but I figured I'd have to take one step at a time to dig deeper into his life.

We were greeted inside by three short beeps, followed by a robotic woman's voice. "Welcome home, Eric."

I entered a grand kitchen/living room. Top-end, touchscreen appliances filled the kitchen, and dark leather furniture and a ginormous TV hanging on the wall offered comfort in the living room.

"My place must seem like a shack to you," I mumbled.

"Don't say that." Eric stood in front of me and ran his fingers through my hair. "I love it at your place, almost as much as I love getting to see you. I would have invited you over sooner if I knew how to cook anything besides microwave meals." He kissed me gently on the lips. "Why don't we watch the news so we can see if they feature that new villain?"

"All right." I felt out of my element, even though I'd always considered myself and my apartment fairly upscale. It just seemed so miniscule in comparison to Eric's. Still, it felt good to sit close to him with his arm around me on his cushy leather couch.

We listened and talked through the weather report, through the recent drop in Arclarium's crime rate, and then finally news lady Lacy Dimly announced that a new phylogenic villain had surfaced in our city today. I couldn't help but yawn as she sent the story over to a pretty, young reporter who stood in front of the broken jewelry store under a dazzling streetlight:

"Local authorities were surprised to get a call today from the Jade Panache Jewelry Store saying they were being robbed by a man who could shoot rays from his eyes that are able to cut through ballistic glass. Apparition and The Deadly Dragon arrived on the scene prior to police and managed to apprehend the thief before anyone was harmed.

The man has been flown to a maximum security phylogenic prison where experts are still trying to discover his true identity.

A bystander sent us this video he caught with his cell phone."

The screen cut to a low-resolution video that began just as the vehicle exploded.

"There I am." I patted Eric's leg, stifling a yawn.

We watched the SUV coming right at me and freezing just above my head. The recording shifted sideways until it was focused on the Deadly Dragon. He had one hand facing the SUV and was using the other to pull out a long, piece of arched metal that had been lodged in his arm.

"That looks really bad," I muttered, staring at the long cut.

"Yeah, I bet he had to get stitches."

"I wonder if phylogenics go to regular doctors or if they have to see a specialist."

"Come on, they're not that different from us."

"Of course, of... of..." I couldn't avoid this yawn. "Of course they are," I said sleepily.

Eric pressed his lips together like he couldn't disagree more. "You look like you're about to fall asleep. Maybe I should walk you home."

"Sorry." I stood up and headed toward the door.

"That's okay. I've got work tomorrow, so I should probably get to bed too."

Chapter Six

We held hands again all the way through the walk to my apartment. If felt childlike and wistful and hopelessly romantic talking about our favorite memories of each other. I wasn't nearly as tired when we stopped in front of my apartment building to say goodnight.

"Ouch!" Eric jerked his arm back when I swung my purse a bit too carelessly over my shoulder and hit him with it.

"I'm sorry." My purse was so light though with only some cash, a mirror, and touchup makeup. I reached out for his arm and felt something poke me through his sleeve. He jerked it away again. "What happened, Eric?"

"Nothing, it's just a bruise I got in soccer practice."

That didn't sound right. I hated when someone lied to me. I thought of how he'd kept the side that arm was on opposite me all night and reached out to grab his hand so I could pull up his sleeve. It only went about halfway to his elbow, but it was enough to reveal the stitches holding part of a long, curved gash together... the same cut... on the same arm... as the Deadly Dragon.

Eric pulled his arm away again. "I said it's nothing, Clarissa."

"That's not a bruise," I said, furious.

"It's still not a big deal." He reached out to place a hand against my neck and stepped forward to kiss me.

At first I was too stunned to stop him. I was standing so still, it must have been like kissing a machine. It only took a moment for me to pull myself together and back away, not saying a word. Then I turned and ran into my apartment building.

My mind raced non-stop as I used my key to get to the elevators and took one up to my floor. This... was... horrible. Eric was the Deadly

Dragon. He had to be. The emergency last night. The telekinesis. The stitches in his arm.

I'd always had suspicions, but it seemed so unlikely I could be dating a superhero. We were best friends for years, and the only evidence I ever saw of it was at school that one day.

I clung to the slight chance that this was all a misunderstanding. There was no way I could be dating a hero. There was nothing super about me.

The light hanging overhead seemed to pulsate with my heart as I walked through the hallway on the third floor.

When I stepped into my apartment and saw the bag Eric had left inside the door, I knew I had to look inside it. Usually it wasn't like me to be so invasive, but this was more important than respecting Eric's privacy. This was potentially life altering. What if we got married and had kids someday? Would they be phylogenics too?!

I sat on the floor and pulled the zipper all the way open. At first, I only saw the things you would expect to find in the sports bag of a soccer coach—a soccer ball, dirty practice clothes, a whistle, a towel, a notebook, and several pens. Nothing out of the ordinary.

Digging deeper revealed the blue Gladware container I'd given the Deadly Dragon earlier that day. It was empty now with chocolate frosting smeared across the top.

"That's it then," I said to myself, shaking my head and feeling like I was trapped in a terrible dream. "Eric's the Deadly Dragon."

The door opened next to me, making me jump to my feet. "Mrs. Hensley buzzed me in," Eric said, coming inside. He saw his things pulled out of his bag and left on the floor.

Embarrassed, I had to explain. "I'm sorry. I had to know, Eric."

He shrugged indifferently. "I'm kind of surprised it took you this long to figure it out. You're the first person I've really let into my life since I moved away in middle school."

"Eric… I really want to be with you, but…"

"Yeah?" He reached out for my hand.

I dropped the box and pulled my free hand away from him. "I… I can't be with a phylogenic superhero. I'm just a blogger and a fashion designer. There's nothing extra-special or super about me. You should be with Apparition or Oceana or Tri—"

Eric grabbed me and kissed me, ending my pathetic speech. He kept it short so I wouldn't have time to get my bearings enough to run again.

"I don't want to be with them. I want you. You're the reason I'm here, Clarissa. How can you say there's nothing super about you? You're the greatest cook in the world. No other woman's superpower could compete with that."

I couldn't help laughing at him. "Thanks, but I don't deserve you."

"Being the Deadly Dragon is just a part of my life. It doesn't make me who I am." Eric reached out for both my hands and held them against his chest. "Once in a while I get a flash of foresight. I saw that mugger attacking you and leaving you in a coma. I would never let that happen, and it was the perfect excuse to come back here and be with you again. I also saw that things would work out between us, so I know this can't be the end."

"Really?" Foresight and telekinesis? He was becoming more spectacular by the minute.

Eric nodded.

"How far could you see into our future?"

"Far enough to know that you're the one."

My heart soared at that. The one. It was the sort of thing I dreamed of hearing from the perfect man, and Eric was just that. He had all my trust. He had always protected me. With his incredible powers, I knew he always would.

"I guess—I guess I could try to get used to being the Deadly Dragon's girlfriend."

He smiled and kissed me again. "So what should we call you: Lady Chef, the Stunning Sauteer, Kitchen Idol?"

I laughed and kissed him before I spoke. "How about the Chocolate Queen?"

"It's perfect."

We ended up staying awake half the night talking about all the adventures Eric's had as the Deadly Dragon. Somewhere in there it really hit me that he was right. He was simply Eric, my Eric. Superhero or not, he still felt like my best friend and the perfect man for me.

Maybe he was right. I may not have been phylogenic, but in his eyes, my baking abilities made me his own personal heroine. Maybe my passion and creativity in the kitchen was kind of super.

THE END

About the Authors

April's been Holly's biggest fan since the day she was born to her. Now, years later, they're best friends, so writing this story was a lot of fun for them! Holly's a super creative aspiring artist who loves everything Pokémon. She's also a straight A student.

April's a passionate romance author who works as a Pre-K assistant at her local school. A few of their favorites are chocolate, road trips, and cute puppies. They both live in the beautiful countryside of Oklahoma.

http://aprilmarcom.weebly.com/
https://www.facebook.com/authoraprilmarcom
chocolateswirlcupcake@yahoo.com

Clarissa's Chocolate Candy Cake

Cake Ingredients
- 1 ¾ cup self-rising flour
- 2 cup sugar
- ¾ cup cocoa
- 1 cup milk
- ½ cup oil
- 2 eggs
- 2 tsp. vanilla
- 1 cup boiling water
- 6 pack of regular-sized Butterfinger bars (If you're not a fan, choose a different favorite candy bar)

Instructions for cake:

Preheat oven to 350° F.

Use butter or non-stick cooking spray to line bottom and sides of two 9-inch cake pans. Dust bottom and sides with flour.

In large bowl, whisk together dry ingredients: flour, sugar, cocoa, and crushed Butterfinger pieces.

Beat moist ingredients into flour mixture on medium speed until well blended: milk, oil, eggs, and vanilla.

Reduce speed and add boiling water slowly.

Beat on high speed for about 1 minute to add air to the cake batter.

Pour batter equally into your two 9-inch cake pans.

Bake for 30-35 minutes, until a fork goes into the center of the cake and comes out clean.

Remove from oven.

Let sit for 10 minutes.

Turn cake pans upside down over cookie sheet so both cakes fall out in one piece.

Allow to cool completely before frosting.

Frosting

- 6 T. butter
- Cocoa: use 1/3 cup for light choc. flavor, use ½ cup for medium choc. flavor, use ¾ c. for dark choc. flavor
- ½ of 11.5 oz. bag mini chocolate chips
- ½ 10.5 oz. bag M&Ms
- 2 2/3 cups unsifted powdered sugar
- 1/4 cup milk
- 1 tsp. vanilla
- ½ 11.75 oz. jar hot fudge

Instructions for frosting:

Cream butter in mixing bowl.

Stir together cocoa, sugar, crushed M&Ms, and mini chocolate chips in a separate bowl.

Add dry ingredient mixture to creamed butter alternately with milk.

Beat to spreading consistency, adding milk a few drops at a time near the end, until it reaches your desired consistency.

Blend in the vanilla and room temperature hot fudge. Frosting will darken and appear silkier with these additions.

Spread over and in between cooled cakes.

Enjoy!